R

THE ALPHA ESCORT SERIES

SYBIL BARTEL

Books by Sybil Bartel

The Alpha Escort Series
THRUST
ROUGH
GRIND

The Uncompromising Series
TALON
NEIL
ANDRÉ
BENNETT
CALLAN

The Alpha Bodyguard Series
SCANDALOUS
MERCILESS
RECKLESS
RUTHLESS
FEARLESS
CALLOUS
RELENTLESS

The Alpha Antihero Series
HARD LIMIT
HARD JUSTICE
HARD SIN

Join Sybil Bartel's Mailing List to get the news first on her
upcoming releases, giveaways and exclusive excerpts!
You'll also get a FREE book for joining!

ROUGH

Jared

I'm not your boyfriend. I'm not the guy next door. I don't even play nice.

My hands twisting in your hair, my whispered demand in your ear—I'm the fantasy you wish you never had.

When I'm through with you, every inch of your body will know where I've been. You won't crave more, you'll beg for it, because I'm not just the cocky smile with military-hardened muscles you paid for—I'm the experience you'll never forget.

One night with me and you'll know exactly why women pay me to be rough.

DEDICATION

Mom, thank you for teaching me to follow my dreams…
and for not reading this book.

ONE

Jared

"D EEPER." MY HAND LANDED ON HER SEXY ASS with a loud slap.

Her tits spilled out of her bikini and she moaned.

My dick slid another inch into her mouth. "That's it, baby." I half-heartedly gripped a handful of her hair and pulled. "Suck harder."

Her tongue flattened against my shaft and her cheeks hollowed out, but she didn't listen to my instructions.

"Where's the goddess you promised?" I slapped her ass again. "That all you got?"

Bracing herself on my thighs, her knees on the lounger next to mine, she was hot, but she wasn't a client. I didn't even remember her name. She'd sat down next to me at the hotel pool bar, and two drinks later, she told me she sucked dick like a goddess.

Game fucking on.

I took her to the closest cabana and told her to prove it. She'd licked her lips and dropped to her knees.

But now she wasn't bringing it.

My phone buzzed and her gaze cut to the table where it sat. She sucked harder.

I smirked. "You motivated now?" I leaned close to her ear. "You worried I got somewhere to be?" I didn't have shit to do. I'd driven to a hotel near my condo to have breakfast because I was bored. Then she'd sat her ass down next to me. I didn't tell her women paid me to fuck them or that I'd had my dick sucked so many times, it all blurred together.

My phone buzzed again and she picked up the pace.

"Damn." I didn't give a fuck who was calling, but apparently it was spurring her on. "You like a little competition?" I was losing my touch. I should've pegged her as the competitive type the second she'd said she was a goddess.

She wrapped her lips over her teeth and applied pressure.

"Fuck, that'll work." My head fell back and I was no longer wondering how long to drag this out.

My cell buzzed again and she deep-throated.

Inspiration struck. I glanced at the caller ID on my phone, then stared at her as I answered. "What up, poser?"

"You booked tonight?" Alex asked.

"Is it Saturday?" What the fuck did he think? We were both escorts. Saturdays were always booked.

"Clear your clients. You're gonna make fifteen grand tonight."

"Bullshit," I grunted and the self-proclaimed goddess groaned.

"Jesus Christ," Alex scoffed. "Are you fucking a client right now?"

"No." Not technically. "Ahhh, *damn*. Hold on." I held the phone away and she moaned even louder. "That's it, baby, right there." I thrust once and she gagged. "Fuck." My balls drawing tight, I was almost there. Gripping her hair hard, I issued a command. "Take it deep."

She relaxed her throat and I sunk to the hilt.

"*Fuuuck.*" Shooting my load into her mouth, I almost dropped my phone.

She swallowed like a champ, then smiled up at me. "So?"

"Damn, that was good." I'd probably even remember it, at least until the next time I got sucked off.

She grinned and ran her hand down my abs. "Told you."

Releasing her hair, I pinched one of her nipples. "Thanks, goddess." I tipped my chin at my phone. "I gotta take this."

She adjusted the scraps of material over her tits. "Go ahead."

"Later." I tucked my shit back in my shorts, swung my legs off the lounger and turned away from her as I put the phone back up to my ear. "I'm back. Not a client." I only told him that to fuck with him, because Alex Vega didn't date, ever.

"You're still fucking for free?"

"Best kind of fucking." Or it used to be. I hardly remembered anymore. "What's going on tonight?" He'd never asked me to take his clients off his hands for an entire night. "I don't do bachelorette parties. Or any kind of party," I reminded him as I stood. Fuck that shit.

"No parties. I got three clients tonight."

I glanced behind me, but the goddess had taken a hint. She was already gone. "What's the matter?" I smirked as I walked past the pool to the parking lot. "Losing your stamina in your old age?" Vega was only one year older than me, but I never let him forget it.

"Fuck no. I got a scheduling conflict. You're taking all three and I get thirty percent."

The hell he was. "Ten." I unlocked my Mustang and slid behind the wheel.

"Twenty," he countered.

I didn't want to take his clients tonight, but he'd never asked me to help him out. I owed him more than I could ever repay him, except I had my limits. I sighed. "I'm not fucking your old-ass cougars for eighty percent."

"Define old."

I cranked the engine. "Fifties and shit."

"Stop being a pussy. You're off by a decade, and the second client tonight is young."

He said young like it was a warning. "She hot?"

"She pays five grand, what do you care?" he evaded.

I laughed without an ounce of humor. "I don't." I'd never had an unattractive client. It was a common misconception that women who sought out an escort were hard up, but mine were just rich and bored.

"That's what I thought. And don't be an aggressive dick with her, she's shy."

Jesus Christ. "Come on. You know I can't hang with that shit. I'm not a fucking pussy." My game was control and I liked it rough.

"Just take it easy and don't scare the shit out of her."

Was he fucking serious? "She should fuck a woman if she wants gentle." I wasn't going to fuck missionary, not even for five grand.

"Suck it up."

I chuckled without an ounce of humor. "Maybe I will."

"I'm texting you the details now. Stick to the script and don't be late. Let me know if you have any issues."

"I don't have issues."

He didn't call me on my bullshit. "Catch you tomorrow."

"Hey." I stopped him before he hung up. "What's the real deal? You haven't taken a night off in years."

"Business dinner."

"You branching out?" I'd be a fucking liar if I said I didn't think about getting out. I didn't need the money.

"Looking into a charity," he admitted.

I laughed. "What kind of charity does a hustler front? The boyfriend experience for needy chicks?"

"Fuck you. It's for veterans."

The muscles in my back tensed and my scars felt tight. "Since when do you give a shit about veterans?"

"I'm talking to you, asshole, aren't I?"

I snorted. "Fair enough. What chick got you involved in this?" There was no way he'd think of this shit on his own. He was all about making money. It drove him like the need to control drove me.

"I didn't say a woman was involved," he hedged.

"What restaurant?" I asked casually.

"Pietra's."

I laughed, hard. "You fucking dog, you're going on a date. Does she know how you pay the bills?" No chick would put up with that.

"Just take care of my clients tonight," he bit out.

"I do that and they won't want to come back to you," I taunted.

"Give it your best shot. I'll still collect my twenty percent."

"No way, one-time deal only. After that, I keep my earnings. Unlike you, I don't do charity. Later." I hung up and pulled into the underground parking of my condo as three texts came in from Vega. Each one was a name and number, but only one of the texts had two extra words. I stared at my cell.

Shy client.

What the fuck was I supposed to do with a shy client?

I pushed my car door open and bypassed the elevator for the stairs. Seventeen flights later, I'd graduated into obsessing about her. It wasn't that I couldn't think what the hell I'd do with her, it was that I could. A hundred fucking fantasies were working their way under my skin. I didn't make it five feet into my condo before I'd tapped the number in the text to call it.

I walked to my balcony and stared at the ocean as it started to ring.

TWO

Sienna

"WHERE ARE THOSE FILES?" COACH YELLED from his office.

"I'm sending them now." I re-sent them for the third time. My boss was useless with a computer, which was fine because it kept me in a job. "Check your e-mail."

The glass door to my office suite flew open.

Miami's six-foot-four quarterback stomped in and slammed his hand down on my desk. "Here."

I stiffened in my chair. "Mr. Ahlstrom."

"Cut the bullshit, Sie. This is yours." He lifted his hand to reveal the small turquoise blue box I'd mailed to him last week after he'd refused to take it back. "Don't send it to me in the damn mail. *Wear it.*"

I hated the nickname almost as much as I hated my ex. And the fact that he was coming into my office where he could expose us and cost me my job only made me angrier. I glanced over my shoulder, but my boss was thankfully on the phone with his back turned. I lowered my voice. "Not only will I not wear that, it's no longer mine." He could take his stupid ring and throw it out for all I cared.

"I *bought it* for you. That's what a man does for his girlfriend."

"I'm not your girlfriend. I never was." The cheating jerk.

"Who do you think you're talking to? Do I look like some stupid farmer?"

Blond hair, blue eyes, designer clothes, he didn't look like he was from Oklahoma. He looked like every other rich guy in Miami Beach. Except this rich guy was a quarterback prodigy on Miami's professional football team, and he was throwing a temper tantrum.

"Keep your voice down." I pretended to type something important on my laptop.

The anger in his tone bled into frustration, but he lowered his voice. "I picked that ring out for you." He shoved the box right in front of me.

I ignored it. If he'd known me at all, he wouldn't have picked an eight-carat monstrosity. It didn't matter that it was lilac tinted or in a rose gold setting, the ring looked silly on my small hand. Maybe some women liked that sort of thing, but I wasn't one of them.

I kept typing. "I'm sure you can take it back." I wasn't petty enough to tell him to give it to one of his cheerleader girlfriends.

"I don't want to take it back. That's the whole point." He scrubbed a hand over his head. "I want you."

Except he didn't say he wanted me like he really wanted me. He said it like the words were a strain to push out, and I was done having this conversation.

"Should I let coach know you're here?" I pretended to

check my boss's schedule. "I don't see you on his calendar, but he might have a few minutes." We both knew he had no reason to talk to the defensive coordinator.

"Sie—"

My cell phone rang quietly from my purse.

"Who's calling you?" he demanded.

Unfortunately, he knew as well as I did that someone calling when it wasn't him was rare. I kept to myself. Or I had until I made a stupid mistake four months ago and gone on a date with who I thought was a nice boy from Oklahoma.

"No one." I took my phone out of my purse to turn it off, but Dan snatched it out of my hand.

Swiping his finger across the display, he held it to his ear. "Hello?" he barked.

"*Dan*," I whisper hissed.

He smirked and tossed my phone on the desk. "Hang up."

I didn't get a chance to respond.

Coach stood in the doorway that separated his office from the small reception area where my desk was. "What do you want, Ahlstrom?"

My stomach bottomed out as I shoved the ring box into my purse.

Dan straightened with a smirk. "I had some plays I wanted to talk to you about, Coach."

Coach looked between us and my breath caught. We all knew a quarterback had no reason to talk to the defensive coordinator about plays.

Coach tipped his chin at Dan. "All right, you got five minutes. You can walk to the fields with me." He barely spared me a glance. "Go home, Montclair. It's Saturday." He closed his office door.

I didn't bother pointing out that he had me work seven days a week starting a month before the season and all the way through until the last game was played. Off season was a different story, but now, a few weeks before the season started? I was here every day of the week and half days on weekends. "See you tomorrow, sir."

He grunted a response and ushered Dan out as my phone lit up with a new text.

I glanced down.

Sienna?

The text was from a number I didn't recognize. I hesitated, but then I typed a response in case it was work related. All the defensive players had my number.

Who is this, please?

The three little dots that meant someone was typing a reply popped up, disappeared, then popped up again.

Jared Brandt. U had an appt with Alex tonight. Not anymore. I'm taking over.

My hands started to shake. I was barely able to type a response.

I'm sure I don't know what you're talking about.

I knew exactly what he was talking about. After my fiasco with Dan, in a moment of weakness, I'd hired a male escort. I didn't think it would lead to sex, but it did. Emotionless, no strings attached, no-demands sex. And when it was over, I didn't feel dirty or tawdry or even regretful. I felt empowered and my heart hurt a whole lot less from the betrayal of a certain quarterback.

The escort, Alex, said we should meet again. I'd said I was busy because I hadn't planned on meeting him again. He'd casually mentioned he was free in a couple weeks, kissed my cheek and walked out of the hotel room I'd booked and paid for. That'd been exactly two weeks ago.

The dots appeared again.

Seriously. U need a picture?

A photo popped up and I sucked in a shocked breath.

Oh. My God.

With incredible light brown eyes with streaks of gold, and chiseled features any modeling agency would die for, Jared Brandt didn't look a thing like the dark-haired, blue-eyed Alex Vega. He didn't even smile like him. In fact, Jared didn't smile at all. His dirty-blond hair was just messy enough to say he didn't care as his intense gaze dared you to question it. He wasn't merely handsome, he was striking.

Another text popped up.

We good?

He was so arresting, I'd venture to say he knew it. His texts bordering on bossy, I'd also bet he was controlling. I debated whether or not I should reply, but then I typed a response because I didn't want to be rude.

I'm sorry, there must have been some mistake.

I bit my lip and waited.

The dots appeared, then disappeared, then appeared again.

Answer

Two seconds later, my phone rang.

My hands shaking, I stupidly, foolishly answered. "Hello?"

"There's no mistake, sweetheart. I know you hired Vega. He's no longer available. I am. Seven o'clock tonight." Deep and captivating and so, so dominant, his voice filled my head and spread across every inch of my skin as if he were in the room with me.

"Mr. Brandt, I'm sorry to waste your time, but I—"

He interrupted. "We'll have dinner."

I closed my eyes. His voice wasn't smooth or calming. It was rough and demanding, and for some reason I couldn't explain, I wanted to listen to him speak for hours.

When I didn't respond, I could practically hear his impatience through the line. "You there?"

I swallowed. "Yes."

"Seven o'clock. I'll text you the address." He hung up.

THREE

Jared

I didn't get nervous. Agitated, irritated, pissed off, but not nervous. Nerves got you killed. The Marines trained me to assess and react. Be prepared, no excuses, no nerves.

Red hair, green eyes, she stood on my doorstep in a yellow dress and sandals. Her cheeks blushed. "Hello."

My heart pounded, my breath was fast and my hands broke out in a sweat as I stared at her. Vega didn't tell me she was fucking gorgeous.

"Jared?" Her voice was sweet, innocent.

Really fucking innocent.

"Yeah, come in." I didn't want to step back to let her in. I wanted to push her against the wall, shove my hand between her legs and watch those full lips part as she gasped. Because she'd gasp. She wouldn't know what the fuck to do with me.

My clients didn't show up in yellow, looking like a college chick going to the beach. They showed up half-dressed in fuck-me pumps, tits hanging out, ready to get down and dirty. But not this woman. She was innocent as hell, and that made me fucking nervous.

I stepped back. "Nice dress." Any other client and I wouldn't have been so polite.

"Thank you." She nervously walked past me.

The scent of fresh rain and honey hit me square in the chest, and I didn't bother stopping the muttered curse. *"Goddamn it."*

She turned. "I'm sorry, this was a bad idea. I shouldn't have come."

I wanted her gone. I wanted her sweet fucking innocence so goddamn far away from me that I couldn't fucking breathe. "Why did you?" It wasn't a question, it was an accusation. She was stunning. Young and pure and beautiful—I'd fuck her up in ways she'd never imagined.

Her hands twisted and she glanced at the door before dropping her green-eyed gaze to her feet. "I don't want a boyfriend." Her voice went even quieter. "Or a husband."

That last statement touched a nerve, but it shouldn't have. I told myself I didn't give two fucks why she was here, lying through her teeth about not wanting a husband. As long as she paid, that's all I should've cared about because that's what I did. Women paid me for sex, rough sex. But this chick? She looked like she was one step past a drunken frat party de-virgining.

I should've told her to turn and run while she still had a chance, but I selfishly didn't. "You don't need a husband to get off, Red."

She flinched, either at the nickname or the insinuation, but then she straightened her back and manners bled out of her. "I'm sorry, I should have clarified. I don't want any attachments."

"How old are you?" It was a rhetorical question.

"Twenty-four."

My nervous tension bled into anger. "You're too young to give up on white picket fences."

She stared at me. Direct, unblinking, her eyes the color of the poppy fields in Afghanistan, she took me in. "You're not much older than me."

In age, I wasn't. In experience, we were lifetimes apart. "Age is a number." I never should've agreed to meet her, let alone take her on as a client. The second Vega told me she was shy, I should've told him to go fuck himself. We had a system. Vega took the tame ones, I handled the kink, and overflow went to our Marine buddy Dane Marek, that crazy fuck. That's how it worked. That's what we'd done for three years. We all made bank, and we all stuck to the system. Until now.

The redhead inhaled. "Right, yes, of course." She glanced around my place. "You have a lovely home, but I should be going." She turned to leave.

Waves of thick hair swung across her back and I imagined wrapping those red locks around my fist. My dick had stirred the second I'd opened the door and seen her, but now it was pulsing for attention, and every muscle in my body went tight. "What do you drink?"

"Thank you, but I'll pass. Have a good night." She took a step.

Instincts kicked in and I moved to her side. My mouth inches from her ear, I lowered my voice. "Nervous?"

"No, yes, um…." Her hand shook as she reached for the door. "I think I should go now."

There was a fine line between seduction and coercion. My words a tool, I used my tone as a weapon. Controlled, quiet, I spoke, "You think or you know?"

"You're not what I expected," she blurted.

"How so?" I knew exactly what I was, and what I wasn't.

She turned and looked up at me with her big, innocent eyes. "You're... intense."

No fucking kidding. "You're shy."

"A little." The flush in her cheeks deepened.

Desire hit me in the chest like a blast wave, then shot south. "You shouldn't be here." She didn't look like she'd sounded on the phone.

"I'm sorry." Breathy, her voice wavered. "I thought you said—"

"I know what I said." I'd replayed every second of our conversation earlier. I'd fucking fixated on it because this woman wasn't like any other client I'd ever spoken to. She didn't flirt or make one suggestive remark. She was exactly how she was now. But a hundred times more innocent.

She drew in a breath through her sexy full lips, then straightened. "Okay, well, you said we should meet. We did. Thank you for your time." Slim fingers reached behind her and she fumbled with the handle of the front door.

I stared at her sweet mouth. "You know what I think?"

"I'm sure you have many thoughts, Mr. Brandt."

My name on her lips sounded too fucking polite. "Only two right now that matter." I stepped closer, wondering why the hell I'd told her my last name.

She pulled the handle, the door opened a few inches and she stumbled.

"Careful." I caught her arm and her hand landed on my stomach.

She sucked in a surprised breath. "I'm so sorry." She bit her bottom lip and pressed her legs together as she stared at her hand. "It was, um, the door." She flexed her fingers over my abs.

I leaned closer. "Do you know what separates fear from desire?"

Her chest rapidly rose and fell, but she didn't take her hand off me. "I believe those are two terms that should be mutually exclusive."

Hard and fast, I slapped my palm loudly against the door, slamming it shut. Perversely getting off on her startled reaction, I bit out two words, "That's fear." Calculated, slow, I dragged a finger a few inches up her bare thigh, then I cupped her face. She shivered and I dropped my voice. "But this?" I stroked her bottom lip as I stared at the thousand shades of fuck-my-life-up green in her eyes. "Biting your lip, pressing your thighs together—that's desire."

Her hand fisted, gripping a handful of my shirt, but she didn't say a word.

Still holding on to her, wishing like hell I wasn't about to let her go, I calmly shifted her to the side. Opening the door, I removed all threat from my tone. "Fear is triggered. Desire is provoked. Leave." I told myself not to say the next line. "Or stay and get what you came for." I stepped back and purposely put my hands in my pockets.

The flush crawled up her neck and heated her face to a color I imagined her ass turning from my palm. "You said we would just meet."

"No," I corrected. "I said dinner." My gaze all over her curves, fifty different ways to make her beg flew through my head like a fucking porno reel.

"Alex never took me—"

Anger flared, and I cut her off. "I'm not Vega." I didn't

buy four-thousand-dollar suits. I didn't drive a fucking McLaren, and I sure as hell didn't look like a pretty-boy model. My back was scarred to fuck, my attitude was bent, and my game was rough. There wasn't a fucking thing Vega and I had in common besides the Marines and screwing women for money. "You want him, call him."

To my shock, she didn't run. In fact, she did the opposite. As if she had every faith in the world that I wouldn't jump down her throat again, she looked up at me with the kind of trust that got a woman like her in trouble with an asshole like me. "My apologies, I didn't mean to offend. I was merely pointing out the difference in approach between you and him."

Approach? What the fuck had Vega done to her? Gotten his dick wet five seconds into meeting her? The thought pissed me the hell off. I didn't give a shit that I was guilty of doing the exact same thing with my clients, but this woman in front of me was no fucking client. She should've been out with a bunch of college chicks, or some asshole in a golf shirt who fucked her missionary style. "You want a different approach, find someone else."

Lightning lit up the sky and thunder shook the windows. Her gaze fixed on me, she didn't even blink. "I didn't say I wanted someone else."

Jesus fuck. I grabbed my keys and my work cell phone out of habit. "Then let's go." I held the door, but she hesitated. Her hands twisted and something kicked at my chest enough for me to drop my attitude. "Dinner isn't a commitment to fuck. It's food on a table and conversation." And enough alcohol to dull whatever the hell was happening to my attitude around her.

Her gaze went to my floor-to-ceiling windows. "There's a storm coming."

Tropical winds, storm, hurricane—the weather forecasters couldn't decide what the hell it was, and it didn't matter. The noise was going to fuck with me either way, and I needed to eat. "Then you'll be well-fed when it hits." This time I didn't wait for her. I went to the elevator and pushed the call button.

A moment later, she was standing next to me. "You're angry."

The doors slid open, and I let her go first to give myself a second to calm the fuck down because she was right. The moment I laid eyes on her, I was pissed as hell that she'd shown up at a stranger's house alone. It didn't matter that I was the stranger. The fact that she looked so damn innocent and pure mattered. She'd taken a dangerous risk coming here. I didn't want to think about the shit she could've gotten herself into if I was anyone else. "I'm not pissed," I lied.

Walking with the grace of proper upbringing, she ignored my lie. "I'm not sure if I've offended you or if this is your natural disposition."

"I don't have a natural disposition." The Marines beat it out of me and Afghanistan stripped the rest. Now I had two fucking moods, controlled and drunk. Neither was a goddamn picture, or what this girl needed in her life. But that didn't mean I wasn't about to test the fuck out of her. "Turn around."

"Excuse me?"

I pushed the button for the garage level. "You heard me."

She immediately faced the corner.

My nostrils flared, but my dick throbbed at her submission. I stepped up to her back, even though I should've walked away. Fisting a handful of thick, natural red hair, I exhaled. My breath landed where her shoulder met her neck, and she did exactly what I wanted her to do, she shivered.

I pushed my hips against her ass just enough for her to feel my cock. "I don't play nice. Or gentle." I tightened my fist and spoke against her hair. "And you've got vanilla written all over you, sweetheart."

The faintest of sounds escaped her lips. "I thought... I thought you needed me to turn around."

I didn't need a damn thing. Not from her or any other woman. "Want isn't need," I clarified. I should've taken my hands off her because she didn't know the fucking difference, but her soft hair was wrapped around my wrist, begging to be pulled, and I was shit for smart decisions. "Oxygen, food, water. Those, I need." Her desire mixed with her natural scent and she smelled like a fucking dream. "Your cunt wet, my dick down your throat and my mouth on your hard nipples—that—I want."

Her legs spread and she pushed against my cock like she was starving for it. "Oh."

The elevator doors slid open and I stepped back.

FOUR

Sienna

HIS CRUDE, DIRTY WORDS, HIS HUGE MUSCULAR arms, the dark, brooding intent in his eyes—he made every nerve in my body ache for him. But he was right. He wasn't anything like Alex Vega. Not even close. His hair was lighter, his muscles were harder and everything about him was sinister, including the barely contained civility in his amber-brown eyes.

He moved like a caged animal just waiting to be released. I should've run, not walked back to my car, but the second he'd touched me, I didn't have the good sense to even breathe.

"You coming?"

His voice was both sandpaper and liquid seduction. It melted my resolve as every hard edge of it spread across my skin like summer heat in the Everglades. I grasped for something to say that wouldn't give away my shameless thoughts, but I'd already shimmied on him like a bitch in heat.

I wasn't losing the battle to walk away from him, I'd already lost.

Itching to straighten my dress but refusing to do it in front of him, I belatedly noticed we were in the underground parking of his expensive condo building. "I'm parked at street level."

"I'm driving." His dress shirt stretching across his massive biceps, his trousers straining against his muscled thighs, he strode toward a sports car.

I practically shivered at the command in his voice, but it was the raw power in his muscles that had me sinking in my own pool of depravity. I didn't date or flirt or go on Tinder. I didn't even search match sites late at night with the lights off. I worked and pretended to be happy, until I made a huge mistake with a certain quarterback. Then thinking I could reset the balance in my life, I'd hired a male escort who gave me the least amount of personal interaction possible for one hour while promising nothing except no strings attached. I knew life wasn't perfect, but strings proved to be a painful lesson my daddy never preached to me about. So here I was, standing in a parking garage in my butter yellow sundress that said I was still a good girl on the outside.

Except the angry man with the tousled hair and face of a Greek god who opened the passenger door of a brand-new sports car told a whole other story. One with heavy breathing and slicked skin and more money flying out of my wallet than two mortgage payments, but I didn't care. I had a well-paying job, I was living life by my rules and the six feet three inches of pure alpha male in front of me was waiting for me to make the next move.

I let my gaze wander.

He wasn't smiling to break my heart or jockeying for my attention like a starved puppy. He was tall and strong, and my money was betting he'd be the best thing that ever happened to me between the sheets... if I let it go that far.

Two months ago, I'd been humiliated by Miami's favorite quarterback while he went clubbing with a cheerleader as I waited for him to come home. Remembering the pictures of Dan kissing the cheerleader that were on every local news channel had me thinking dinner with a male prostitute was a much better life choice.

I smiled.

FIVE

Jared

SHE SMILED.

It was fucking perfect. I hated her and I wanted her. I hated her *because* I wanted her. Women were disposable. They had to be. But that shy smile and red hair had me wishing they weren't, and that was a fucking recipe for disaster.

She got in my Mustang like she wasn't fazed by my attitude, and my hunger for her ramped up from insane to desperate as I slid behind the wheel. New leather mixed with soft rain and honey, and I refused to acknowledge she was the first woman to ever ride in my car.

I turned the engine over and the vibration of the 526 horsepower settled into my nerves. For a single moment, I was sane.

"I like your car," she said sweetly.

It wasn't a car, it was a Shelby GT350. "Mustang," I corrected as I pulled out of the parking garage.

"It suits you."

I didn't comment. I was watching palm trees bend with every gust of wind.

"Are you from Florida?" Her voice filled a space in my head I didn't want touched.

I didn't date. I fucked. I hadn't had to make small talk outside the bedroom since before I'd enlisted. And one thing you got used to really fucking quick being an escort—women didn't ask you personal shit. I debated not answering, but I couldn't come up with a reason not to.

"Homestead." Miami's western stepsister. Geographically close, but a fucking planet away from Miami Beach.

"That's a good place to be from."

No shit. I didn't comment.

After a moment, she turned in her seat to face me. "You asked me to dinner."

The text I never should've sent followed by a call I never should've made. I didn't fuck with shy women. I had two kinds of clients, rich, overconfident women, and bored housewives. Both of which wanted to fuck the second they saw me. "Is that a question or a statement?"

"I'm only pointing out that you asked me to dinner then you said it would be food on a table and conversation." She said *conversation* like she was talking to a four-year-old.

I threw it back on her. "You wanna tell me why you're single?" I was assuming. I didn't know who the fuck had answered her phone when I'd first called. I'd thought I'd dialed the wrong number, so I'd sent a text.

"You want to tell me why you're an escort?" she countered.

"Being single pay your bills?" Not that I needed the money I made escorting, but I wasn't going to tell her that.

She sat back in her seat with an indignant huff. "That is the most offensive thing I've heard all week, and trust me, at my job, that's hard to do."

I'd bite. "Where do you work?" Curiosity was a bitch.

"Downtown. You didn't answer my question."

If I had half a brain, I wouldn't have found her intriguing. "You didn't answer mine."

"I choose to be single."

"Were you a regular?" My teeth practically ground at the thought of her with Vega.

"Excuse me?"

"Of Vega's?" Why the fuck did I care?

"Oh. No." She didn't elaborate.

"Expensive hobby." I shouldn't have cared what the hell she did with her free time.

"Who? You?"

I tipped my chin because every time I opened my mouth, I sank myself further. I had no business going down this road with her.

"I can afford it, if that's what you're worried about."

I wasn't worried. I'd fuck her for free at this point just to see those gorgeous eyes when she came. But the second I thought it, I thought about that motherfucking asshole Vega taking her, and my nostrils flared.

"Did I say something wrong?"

I locked down my expression. "No."

She glanced out the window as I pulled up to the restaurant. "We're going to Pietra's?" Alarm sounded in her voice.

"That a problem?" Pietra's was the best restaurant in Miami Beach. A five-hundred-dollar dinner wasn't good enough for her?

"I'm not dressed appropriately." Her hands brushed down her thighs. "I'm in a sundress."

Bare shoulders, ivory skin, easy fucking access, I'd noticed the damn dress. "You're fine."

"Fine isn't appropriate."

I held a finger up to the valet before he opened her door, then I looked at her. Really fucking looked at her. "You hired a stranger to fuck you. I think we're past *appropriate*." Not that I ever gave a shit about doing what was right.

She inhaled, and for a second, she looked like she was going to slap me. "Pietra's is a black dress restaurant, not yellow, and for the record, I didn't hire you."

I scanned the dress that was a thousand times more provocative than any black dress and ignored the hire comment. "You color code your life?"

Her cheeks flamed. "No, but someone could—" She caught herself.

I finished her thought. "See you with me?" I didn't know if I should be pissed the hell off or laugh. Fuck it. Fuck her. I reached for my door. "Don't worry, Red. I'll be discreet." I was out of the car before she could respond.

The valet opened her door, and I waited for her because I wasn't a complete asshole, but when we turned to walk in, she took my arm.

Thrown, I moved away from the hostess stand and backed her into a corner. My chest crowding hers, I grasped her chin and lowered my voice. "You touch me when I say you touch me." Money didn't buy any woman the right to call the shots.

Her hand immediately dropped. "I'm sorry."

"You apologize one more time, I'm going to spank that habit right out of you."

She straightened. "You will *not* lay a hand on me."

"You pay me, I'll lay a lot more than a hand on you." She had no idea what she'd gotten herself into. "If you want

27

dinner, walk to the hostess." I dropped my hand. "Otherwise, go back to the valet and I'll drive you home."

She held my gaze for two seconds then she turned. Pride in her step, she walked to the hostess stand.

I stepped right up behind her and gave my name. "Brandt." The blonde hostess smiled. "Good evening, Mr. Brandt. Your table isn't quite ready, would like to have a seat in the bar?"

I nodded and put a hand on the small of Red's back. She sucked in a breath and my perverse self smiled. I leaned down to her ear. "You wanna walk on the wild side, this is how it's gonna work. I touch you when I want, where I want." I moved my hand to her full hip and squeezed. "You want to reciprocate, you ask permission." I settled her on a stool, but instead of taking the one next to her, I stood in her personal space and took her chin again. "Understood?"

Her knees pressed together, and I could practically smell her desire, but she drew her lips tight and her manners voice came out. "You are not the only one with some control here, Mr. Brandt. I will decide what, if anything, happens." She gave me her best throw down.

I laughed.

She didn't look amused. "I'm paying you."

"You're not paying shit. I'm taking you to dinner." I signaled for the bartender. "Knob Creek and a chardonnay." I leaned an arm on the bar, fixed my gaze and settled in to make her uncomfortable until the drinks arrived. She was so damn distracting, I'd almost forgotten the reason I'd brought her here.

Her eyes narrowed as she clasped her hands in her lap. "You ordered for me."

"I'm going to order your dinner too." I was so fucking

engrossed in Red, I didn't even glance around the place for Vega.

"No you're not," she challenged.

"Yes, I am." Her bottom lip fuller than her top one, I imagined sucking on it.

The bartender set our drinks in front of us.

Red waited until he'd walked away. "I didn't want wine."

My eyes never leaving hers, I lifted the tumbler to my mouth, took a swig, then set the glass down. I grasped the back of her neck and brought her mouth to mine. Touching the tip of my tongue to her lips, she didn't hesitate. She opened for me, and I let the whiskey flow into her mouth.

She swallowed and my dick throbbed. Any thought of retreat went up in flames. I drove my tongue into her whiskey heat and fucking devoured her. Dominant, aggressive, I kissed her.

And she fucking melted.

Her body bent toward mine, her throat vibrated with a moan and she followed every sweep of my tongue. One hand was in her hair and the other was shoving her knees apart when I remembered my promise in the car.

I drew back.

Panting, her big green eyes on me, she stared. But she no longer looked wary or suspicious or even pissed off. She looked hungry. Spread her out on the bar and bury my face between her legs, *hungry*.

And that's exactly what I wanted to do.

"Mr. Brandt?" The hostess appeared. "Your table is ready."

Fuck me.

SIX

Sienna

No.

No, no, no.

No one kissed like that.

My fingers went to my lips. They were on fire. They had to be.

My hands shaking, a pulsing pain throbbing between my legs, I wanted to cry for every kiss I'd ever endured before him. Then I wanted to beg him to touch me again.

No one kissed like that.

"Come on." His voice, husky and rough, crawled across my nerves like the sweetest lie life ever dealt. Then he took my hand and helped me off the stool like the gentleman he was not. "Let's get you fed."

The pressure from his hand as he'd pushed my knees apart to step between them imprinted in my memory. My legs barely holding me up, I pulled out of his grasp, but his hand only slipped under my hair and wrapped around the back of my neck. I didn't know if it was a gesture of his dominance or something more, and my heart didn't care. His possessive hold had my body bending toward him like a moving current.

I wasn't in trouble, I was drowning.

One kiss and I was ready to forget why I'd hired an escort in the first place. I couldn't sleep with him. I shouldn't even be at dinner with him. This wasn't an emotionless hour of fun. This wasn't even a public shaming in the making. Jared Brandt was complete emotional, sexual destruction. But I couldn't get myself to walk away, instead my traitorous body settled into the chair at our table.

All power and muscle, Jared lowered himself into a seat across from me.

Desperate words fell out of my mouth. "I'm not sleeping with you."

He paused only a fraction of a second as he took the menu from the hostess and tipped his chin at her. "Thank you." His eyes back on me, he set the menu down. "I'm not going to sleep with you."

Air whooshed out of my lungs in relief, but my stomach knotted in disappointment. "Good." I had to force the response past my tingling lips.

His gaze intent, he leaned forward. "I'm going to fuck you, Red. Then I'm going to fuck you again. When I'm through with you, your only coherent thought will be my name." He straightened and leaned back. "What do you eat?"

His phone rang and I was saved from muttering sloppy words of denial.

Reaching into his pocket, he silenced the ring. "Seafood?"

Inspiration fueled by desperation struck. "You should get that. It might be a client."

He eyed me, but he didn't reach for his phone.

I pushed ahead. "Maybe it's an appointment. You should take it because I have to go after dinner." I aimed for casual, but my voice shook. "I wouldn't want your entire evening to be a waste."

A waiter appeared with our abandoned drinks from the bar. "Good evening, Mr. Brandt, ma'am. Do you have any questions about the menu tonight?"

Without taking his eyes off me, Jared snapped a response at the waiter. "No."

"Excellent, then I'll give you some time to decide." The waiter slipped away.

Jared lowered his voice. "You running, Red?"

Coming from anyone else, I hated that nickname, but he made it sound sexy, like he wanted me. Except I wasn't a naïve preacher's daughter anymore, and I wasn't foolish enough to think this had anything to do with me. This was his job, and that kiss meant nothing. It had to.

"Busy day tomorrow, you know how it is. Make your call. And yes, seafood is fine." I folded my hands in my lap to hide the tremor that hadn't stopped since he'd gotten close enough for me to drown in his scent at his apartment. He didn't smell like expensive cologne and polished sophistication. Soap and musk and all man, he smelled like heartbreak.

Heartbreak that wouldn't take his eyes off me.

With a locked-down expression, he studied me. "Maybe I should have her join us."

A knife to my heart wouldn't have hurt as much. "Sure." I grabbed my wine and drank half.

He pulled his phone out of his pocket and placed it on the table.

The memory of his whiskey tongue mocked me with the

sour aftertaste of fermented grapes while his phone sat there like a giant test. I told myself he needed to call that client. "The table's big enough. We have plenty of room." I needed a reality check of who he was and who he wasn't, because Jared Brandt was not a man a woman fell for, not if she wanted to hold on to her sanity.

He picked up his tumbler and took a sip. "You want to know what I think?"

That I was a coward and a liar and I couldn't handle his kiss? "I have a feeling you're going to tell me anyway."

"You lied."

I wanted to taste the smoky whiskey on his lips. "About?"

He sat back in his chair, sipped his whiskey and took his sweet time. "A husband."

"No." I gripped my wine glass with both hands. "I definitely do not want a husband." Men cheated. "A woman doesn't need to be married to be happy."

"You do."

I wasn't sure what was more absurd—that I was out to dinner with a male escort or that I was having a conversation with him about marriage.

I tried to turn the tables. "You're not married. You look perfectly fine." But not happy. Happy and Jared Brandt didn't seem like two words that would ever be in the same sentence together. He'd laughed earlier, but there'd been no humor to it.

"I'm not you." He lifted his glass.

I stared at his lips as they touched the tumbler and sucked in a breath as his throat moved with a swallow. "On that, we can agree." I wanted to crawl across the table just to smell him again.

His large hand, a hand that'd gripped my knee, set the glass down and his eyes focused intently on mine. "Your back is straight, your legs are crossed and your manners are impeccable. You didn't have a hair out of place until I threaded my fingers through it."

I self-consciously ran a hand over my hair. "Is that supposed to be an insult?"

He leaned forward. "You don't want a husband, you're dying for one."

I pushed my chair back and stood.

"*Sit down.*"

His barked command was so abrupt and controlling, it took me off guard. Before I knew what I was doing, I was already sitting. "I am *not* a dog," I snapped.

One of his muscled arms shot out. He grabbed the arm of my chair and yanked. With one swift pull, he'd dragged me and my chair next to him.

His huge hand gripped the back of my neck and his voice turned one hundred percent alpha. "You want a man so bad, you're trembling for it. You want his hands on you, his commands in your ear, his scent on your skin and you want to be fucked, *royally.*"

Gooseflesh rose across my neck as I sucked in a breath. "You're wrong."

"I'm so fucking right, I can smell your sweet cunt from here. You were wet the second you turned around for me in the elevator." His hand landed on my bare knee.

I jumped. "What are you doing?"

"You don't want my cock pounding into you." His fingers ran up the inside of my thigh. "You want to be fucking claimed." He slipped under my panties and stroked through my heat.

My eyes fluttered shut but I didn't deny it.

His lips touched my temple. "You're so fucking wet."

I forced words out. "What are you doing?" *Oh my God.* Nothing, *nothing* had ever felt this good.

"Making you come in front of all these people."

My eyes popped open in alarm and I looked across the restaurant. "I am not—"

Rough, hard, he shoved two fingers inside me, and all the air left my lungs.

Thick fingers stretched my core as his hand tightened on my neck, forcing me to face him. "You look at me, *only me,* when you come."

His growled command made desire drip out of me. My hands searching for purchase, my legs locking, I bit my lip because I had no other anchor. My core pulsing, I wanted to climax more than I'd ever wanted to in my entire life.

"My name," he quietly barked.

"*Jared.*" Reverent, pleading, I wasn't saying his name, I was begging for release.

"Come," he demanded.

His thumb pressed down on my clit, and before he'd circled once, I was coming. My legs shook, my hands grabbed his forearm and my nails sunk into his skin. I wasn't in control of anything. My head locked in his hold, my core clenching and pulsing around his thrusting fingers, I fell apart. My body broke into a million pieces and my mind shut down.

I didn't think about where I was. I didn't think about my heart being broken. I didn't think about my job or my mortgage or my utter loneliness. I didn't think about a single thing, except intense brown eyes on a face so stoic and so hard yet utterly, devastatingly beautiful.

I whispered the one word that was my new reality. "Jared."

SEVEN

Jared

S HE DIDN'T SUBMIT. SHE HANDED ME HER ORGASM ON a silver fucking platter. Holding on to me with small hands and her gorgeous green-eyed stare, she let every muscle in her body go. She fell so damn hard, there wasn't a thing in her world except me.

I'd never seen a woman come like that. "You're fucking gorgeous, Red." Fuck my life up, *gorgeous*. My dick strained against my pants for a turn in that tight cunt. I wanted to lay her out on the table and fuck her till I broke something.

Her lips wet, her tight cunt still spasming around my fingers, she blushed at the compliment. "Thank you."

One last stroke, then I reluctantly slid my hand out. "Lose the manners around me." She opened her mouth to say something, but I put my fingers against her lips. "Suck."

The haze of lust left her expression and her lips clamped shut. The flush on her cheeks went from pink to bright red.

A smile tipped half my mouth. If she spoke, her lips would part and I would shove my fingers in. She knew it. I knew it. "What are you going to do, sweetheart?"

She tried to shove my arm away, but I was stronger. I rubbed my thumb the length of her neck. "One way or another, you're gonna get dirty with me." Indignation, shock, and a flurry of other emotions flashed across her face and my dick got harder. She opened her mouth a fraction and I shoved my fingers in. "Good girl."

She made one swipe with her tongue then pulled back.

I let her go. "Next time, use your teeth."

She grabbed her napkin and dabbed at her mouth. "There won't be a next time."

I almost laughed. "Don't make promises you can't keep."

"I will not—" She abruptly stopped talking as the waiter walked up.

"May I tell you about our specials tonight?"

We listened then I rattled off an order for food and more alcohol. The waiter left and Red looked at me like she wanted to string me up.

I swallowed the last of my whiskey. "Problem?" I wanted to fuck her. Hard.

"I didn't say you could do that."

"You didn't say I couldn't." Not once had she said no. The elevator, the garage, the ride over, when I'd dragged her chair toward mine.

"I didn't think I had to tell you not to... *in a restaurant.*" She glanced around and her cheeks flushed again.

I held the back of her neck and leaned to her ear. "What did you think would happen when you agreed to pay me to fuck you?"

She shivered and whispered, "You said dinner."

I stroked the side of her perfect neck. "You don't like it when I make you come?"

37

She tugged on the hem of her dress. "That was more than conversation."

Any other woman, the virtuous act would've had me walking the fuck out. Instead, I was fighting a smile and rocking a raging hard-on. "Don't worry, I won't charge you for that orgasm."

Her blush was fucking priceless. "If you're going to bait me all night, I'm going home."

The high of making her come tanked. "You already said that." I pushed her wine glass toward her. "Drink."

She was too polite to cross her arms, but her hands remained clasped in her lap. "No thank you."

I wanted to break her. I wanted her hair wild, body thrashing, nails digging into my flesh as she yelled my name and soaked my dick. I wanted to watch those fucking manners disappear as she begged me to spank her ass. "You know what your problem is?"

"I'm sure you'll tell me." She looked everywhere but at me.

I waited.

It took three seconds. She turned and gave me those gorgeous green eyes. "What?"

"Do you want me to fuck you?"

"No."

"Kiss you?"

"No."

Goddamn, she was a sexy little liar. "Make you come?"

"No. Is this conversation going somewhere? I think you have your answer."

"You wanna fuck a woman?"

"*No.*"

I liked her indignation too damn much. "You're problem

38

is that you lie to yourself. The reason you told me to call another woman is the same reason why you lied about wanting a husband." I had a fucking mountain of limitations, but reading people wasn't one of them. "You going to tell me why you're really here?"

She inhaled like she was fighting for patience, but the look in her eyes and her hesitation said she was reaching for confidence. "You are a very sexual man, Mr. Brandt, as you should be in your line of work. But it may surprise you to know that not only do I not want a husband, but I am not looking for commitment or attachments."

I ignored her dig about my occupation. "Did I ask you to marry me?"

She ducked her head and her voice went quiet. "No, you didn't."

I tipped her chin. "You didn't answer my question, Red."

Her gaze averted, she exhaled. "You're going to be with another client tonight anyway. What's the difference?"

There it was. I knew every word out of her mouth had been a lie. She talked a good game, but she was exactly as I pegged her. She didn't want to be some asshole's pound toy because she was horny. She was paying for dick because hurt was at the root of this for her.

And I wanted to know who the fuck had broken her. "Who was it?"

"Excuse me?"

"Who fucking broke your heart?" Because I wanted to kill him.

"There's no—"

"That's why you're doing this." She was fucking scared.

"What I do is none of your concern."

She was right, but from the second I laid eyes on her, I wanted to fucking protect her. But if I took money from her only to stick my dick balls deep, I was no better than the asshole that'd driven her to hire an escort in the first place. The only difference was, when I left her after I fucked her, I'd be five grand richer.

I vowed then and there, I was never taking this girl's money. She deserved better, but it was all I had. "When you're with me, everything you do is my concern." I nodded at her wine. "Drink."

She stood with the kind of grace that should've been backed by confidence. "Call your next client. I'm not going to be with you for long. Excuse me." She strode toward the restrooms.

The waiter came back and fate decided to fuck me in the ass. My phone vibrated with a new text as he set a double whiskey in front of me.

"Your drink, sir."

"Thanks." I read the text from another one of Vega's clients four times before I understood it.

What time are we meeting tonight, sexy?

I glanced up to see Red as she disappeared around the corner, and the past three years mocked me.

Alcohol and women.

That was my life. There wasn't a plan B, not if I wanted to stay fucking sane, but goddamn it I was tired.

I downed half my drink then my thumbs fumbled across the screen, because I hadn't made a single smart decision since I'd told Red to meet me for dinner.

Now. Pietra's. You don't want to share, don't come.

I sent the text and threw back the rest of the whiskey before signaling for another.

EIGHT

Sienna

I DIDN'T KNOW IF HE WOULD DO IT. I ALMOST PRAYED HE wouldn't. The part of my heart not completely broken foolishly thought he wouldn't even consider calling another client while he was out with me. But that only made me an even bigger fool. This was his job, and I meant nothing more to him than a paycheck and I needed to keep reminding myself of that. That was why I'd told him to call another client.

But my jaw wasn't clenched and my nostrils weren't flared because I was angry. I was fighting tears like David fought Goliath.

I wasn't special to him. It didn't mean a thing when he'd kissed me like he'd needed me to breathe. That's what he did. He took women to restaurants and did dirty things to their bodies then counted on them falling for his broken hero angst and ruggedly handsome features.

My traitorous body ached for his wicked hands, and I shivered at the fresh memory of them inside me, but I wasn't going down this road. Not again. Not ever. So I straightened my hair and my dress. I couldn't do a thing about the color

41

of my cheeks or the ache between my legs, except hold my head high, and that's what I did. I walked back out to that table intent on finishing what I'd started, because that's what my daddy taught me to do. It wasn't what you did, it was how you did it.

My bravado held to the very second I allowed myself to make eye contact with him. Then deep brown eyes took me in, stole my breath and held me captive. My body drawn to his, my lungs begging for oxygen, I walked to the table in a trance. Knowing I would never see a chair in a restaurant the same way again, I sat.

At a loss for words, I said nothing.

"I'm not taking you on as a client." Deep, quiet, his voice soaked into my skin before his words registered.

The sting was worse than an insult. "Then dinner...." Oh my God. And what he'd done to me in the chair? Humiliation heated my cheeks and I needed to leave. But as I picked up my purse, the waiter appeared and set plates in front of us with a flourish.

The scent of shellfish and herbs assaulted my senses and I wanted to vomit.

Huge fingers closed around my wrist. "Put your bag down." His lips touched my temple, and he issued a command like a tender request from a lover. "Stay. Eat your food." He pulled back and his next words were so soft, I couldn't be sure I heard them correctly. "You'll get what you want."

"Bon appétit." The waiter set my napkin in my lap then retreated.

I stared at my plate and the food blurred. What I wanted? Or what I needed? Because I needed to not *like* him. I needed to not have had the best orgasm of my life in a restaurant in South Beach. I needed to not hate every single thing in my life the second I'd laid eyes on him.

"Look at me," he demanded.

Like a moth drawn to the flame, I looked up.

His tousled dirty-blond hair in direct contrast to his measured stare, he looked at me like he saw right through me. "Red." He wasn't saying the color of my hair. He was using his name for me and he was drawing it out in warning.

The wine and the smell of food churned my stomach and I didn't care what he wanted. "I have to go."

He set his drink down and his gaze strayed to my neck then back to my eyes. "Take a breath. Right now."

My breath short, my heart pounding, I panicked. "I can get a cab." I'd heard what he'd said. I knew what he meant. I was getting my wish and his next client was coming. God help me, I needed to get out of here before that happened.

"You're not going to take a cab." His tone turned one hundred percent authoritative. "Take a breath and I'll drive you home."

"Your dinner." I knew how expensive Pietra's was. "Stay." I pushed to my feet.

He was up and at my side before I was standing. He took my chin and forced me to look up at him. "What's going on?"

"Nothing."

"You're panicking."

"I'm not," I lied. "I just need to leave. The wine made me dizzy." I sucked in a breath and grasped for the old me, the person I was before I'd knocked on his door. "Thank you for your time. Thank you for meeting me, but it just didn't work out."

"It worked too well. That's why you're running."

"No, no." I forced a fake smile. "I'm not running any-where. Enjoy your next client." I choked on the word *enjoy*.

"That was your idea."

"Right, of course." My façade was cracking. "I'll find my own way out. Stay." She could eat my dinner. She could sit in my chair. She could…. I shook the thought away and told myself Jared wasn't a keeper. I could do this. It was just like Alex, no attachment, no feelings. But nothing that was happening now had ever happened with Alex. Compared to the way my heart was trying to beat its way out of my chest every time I even looked at Jared, my hour with Alex had felt like nothing more than a turn in the road.

Jared threw some bills on the table and took my upper arm. "Come on." He was leading me out of the restaurant through the bar before I could protest.

My eyes on the exit, I didn't see her.

"*Jared,*" a voice purred.

Older than me, thinner than me, her makeup perfect, and hair styled by the best Miami had to offer, she was dressed in a black dress. Dripping money and confidence, she scanned the length of Jared's body then barely glanced at me.

"Hey." The rough voice he used on me, he used on her.

Thick jealousy crawled up my throat like bile.

She smiled like a movie star. "This is going to be fun."

My heart lodged in my throat. Had he? Did she think…? *Oh my God.* "I was just leaving. You two… have fun." Oh my God, his fingers still…. *No.* This wasn't happening. I tried to move away, but a strong hand wrapped around my neck.

"*We* were just leaving," Jared corrected.

"Oh no, it's okay, stay." My stomach crushed in on itself.

I had to do this. I knew I did. I didn't get to care who he slept with. *He was an escort.*

The brunette looked between us, but then her gaze landed on me. "I think someone needs a drink."

I held a hand up and fake laughed at the bitch. "Oh no, already had enough. But please, have a great night, you two." I pivoted and fled.

In my haste, I didn't consider where I was going. Five paces and I was back in the restaurant. Then a familiar face landed in my line of sight and I froze.

Alex Vega. My first and only full male escort experience sat with a stunning brunette because God hated me. I turned to flee and Jared's arm wrapped around my shoulders as he and his other client stepped up beside me.

"Hey, Sarge," Jared's voice rumbled out of his chest.

Alex looked up and anger contorted his features. "Jared," he bit out. His hand possessively on the beautiful brunette, he tipped his chin, but he didn't look at me or Jared's other client. "What are you doing here?"

Jared smiled, but it was off. "A little dinner." He checked out Alex's date. "A little fun."

My brain made the connection to Jared's nickname for Alex, and I blurted out a stupid question. "You were in the military?" I should have guessed. Both he and Jared were dominant, controlling, and alpha to the core. They screamed military.

Jared's arm stiffened and his smile dropped. "Staff Sergeant Alexander Vega, Second Light Armored Reconnaissance Battalion, United States Marine Corp. You're looking at a real live hero, ladies. He saved my life." He practically spat the words out.

Jared's other client leered at Alex. "Oh, he's a hero all right."

She licked her lips. "Too bad he's not working tonight." She rubbed a hand down Jared's chest. "He's missing all the fun."

Oh my God.

I was going to be sick. Did they just switch clients at will?

Alex's date seemed to figure it out at the exact same time as I did. Her face went white and she pushed away from Alex. "Excuse me." She got up and fled.

Alex growled words at Jared as he threw money on the table.

My mind reeling, my stomach rolling, I registered none of it. They switched clients. They *shared*. Jared wasn't taking over for Alex. I hadn't been passed off. I'd been shuffled. Like an inconvenience you had to handle when something better came along. We were just a paycheck to them. I knew this. I'd hired them. I'd known what I was getting myself into. But until this very second, the dirty truth of it hadn't sunk in.

I was worse than pathetic.

Jared said something to Alex, but I didn't hear a word of it. I was staring after the brunette, wondering which one of us was the bigger fool, when Jared kissed me on the cheek.

He kissed me on the cheek. Like I was important. I wasn't important, not to him, not to Alex, not to any man.

An anger I'd never felt brewed into a storm, and my life became crystal clear. Every screwed-up piece of it. My hand was in my purse, closing over my envelope of shame before I could think it through.

I slammed my foil-embossed monogrammed envelope against Jared's chest. "Here. I already got what I wanted." I glared at the brunette. "Your turn. But you might want to make sure he cleans up first."

My dignity in the toilet, I walked out.

NINE

Jared

INHALING, I RUBBED A HAND OVER MY FACE.

"Oh good," a female voice purred. "You're up." A warm body brushed against my ribs as a small hand cupped my junk.

"Shit." My back sore as fuck, I grabbed the wrist and pulled the ballsy brunette's hand away. "Why are you still here?" I sat up from the goddamn couch where I'd passed out last night. Fucking alcohol.

The brunette giggled. "You're hard."

I was hard because I needed to take a piss. I grabbed a fistful of her hair and gave her two seconds of my attention. "I told you I'm not fucking you." Five drinks in to a mind-numbing survival plan last night, I'd watched Red walk out on me. The storm raging, my head fucked, I drank until I couldn't feel my fucking legs. Then the brunette drove me and my car home. My last coherent memory was shutting the hurricane shutters, wondering if the wind would toss me off the fucking balcony.

The brunette licked her lips. "That was last night."

"Nothing's changed." I pushed her away, swung my legs to the floor and stood.

"Why?" She pouted.

If it weren't for Red and the fucking hurricane-force winds barreling down last night, I never would've gotten drunk with her. She had clinger written all over her, but I'd needed the distraction from the raging storm, both inside my head and the one pounding the coast.

"I'm getting in the shower. You'll be gone before I get out." I didn't leave any room for negotiation in my tone.

"My car's at the restaurant."

"If you can afford Vega, you can afford a fucking cab."

She got up in a huff in only her underwear and grabbed her purse. "You're an asshole."

I didn't even blink. Women either hated me or worshipped me. I didn't give a shit which—until a redhead walked out on me last night. Now Red was the only damn thing I could think about and this brunette was pissing me the fuck off. "You want to see how much of an asshole, keep standing there." My dick, conditioned for this exact kind of challenge, pulsed, but I crossed my arms.

Her gaze swung south and she licked her lips.

Fuck no. "Out. *Now.*"

She smirked, but she grabbed clothes off the floor. "Maybe I'll come by later when you're in a better mood." She pulled her dress over her head.

I was on her so fast, she didn't see it coming. My thumb and index finger grabbed her jaw, my fingers put pressure on her neck and I did what they taught me to never do in the Marines. I showed mercy. "You step foot near my place again, you'll fucking regret it."

Her eyes went wide as fuck but her voice was all bravado. "Are you threatening me?"

"No." I hated women like her. They thought their money bought them any privilege they wanted. I wasn't her fuck toy. "I'm making you a promise." I released her. "Get out."

She couldn't move fast enough. Thirty seconds later, I was locking my front door after her ass ran to the elevator. Lucky for her and her five-inch heels, the power was on and she didn't have to walk down seventeen flights.

I threw on shorts, grabbed my personal cell phone and started opening the hurricane shutters as I called the asshole that'd gotten me neck-deep in this business. Not that I was complaining, my fucking condo and car were paid off.

Vega picked up on the second ring. "Hold up." I heard the rustle of covers then a door shutting. "You fucking asshole, you did that on purpose."

He was right. I'd called the hostess and sweet-talked my way into a reservation after he'd told me where he was going. Curiosity was a bitch. I didn't know what the fuck my excuse was for taking Red. Maybe I had shit to prove. "You're right. I had to see what woman you were giving it up for."

"I'm not giving up shit," he bit out.

I smirked. I'd seen the woman he was with. Classy, gorgeous and young. She was a forever girl. I probably would've fucked her if I'd seen her first. But that's all I would've done with her. "So you're taking clients again?"

"No, you are." He didn't hesitate.

I smirked again as I opened the last shutter and surveyed the damage from the storm. Debris was everywhere on the beach, but all the high-rises looked like mine, intact. "I'm taking the day off, bro." Maybe I'd take every fucking day off. But

I wasn't about to tell him that, so I threw out a lie. "After last night, I'm gonna need Astroglide for a week." I walked back inside my condo to start coffee, but my eyes landed on my keys and the envelope.

"Learn to pace yourself," Vega lectured.

I went back out on the balcony without any coffee because I knew what the fuck was in that envelope. "I did pace myself, for eight hours straight through a damn hurricane." I drank for hours after we'd gotten back to my condo. The fucking noise was like goddamn Afghanistan all over again, but that wasn't even close to the worst of it. Red was fucking with my head.

He didn't comment. "I'm sending you my schedule and contact list. Don't wait to make contact with all of the clients. Confirm the dates and let them know you're—"

Oh hell fucking no. I didn't let him even finish that sentence. "Whoa, whoa, whoa, bro. I got my own clients." He'd already fucked me with Red. I didn't need any more bullshit, and I especially didn't need to be fucking fixating on a woman who'd walked out on me last night but still fucking paid.

"Now you have twenty more. They all pay bank, so weed your shit out."

If I were smart, I would've been fucking ecstatic, but I wasn't. I was staring at my paid-for view, watching the ocean churn from the outer bands of the storm and my gut twisted at the memory of Red's face as she threw money at me last night. I didn't want to fuck for money forever. I didn't even give a shit about the money. Or this goddamn view. I wanted peace of mind, but that was about as rare as the innocence on Red's face last night. I knew that. Vega fucking knew that.

"Jared?"

"Are you fucking serious?" I shook my head like he could fucking see me. "You're throwing your shit away for what? *Love?*" Like some goddamn fairy tale? I didn't wait for him to answer. "You think that shit's gonna last? Two weeks, tops, and the honeymoon's over." What the hell did he think was going to happen? That a woman like his arm candy last night or like Red was going to fall in love with a male prostitute?

"You don't know what you're talking about. Shut the fuck up."

"I know exactly what I'm talking about." He may have fucking blinders on, but I didn't. "If you pulled your head out of your ass, you would too. Take a week, fuck, take two, ride the fucking wave, but don't drown in it."

His anger took direct aim. "I'm not you. Two weeks is nothing."

Bitter and pissed the fuck off, I snorted. He knew damn well why I didn't do relationships. "Doesn't mean the piece of ass in your bed gives a fuck about you long-term." I hung up, then dialed the other person Vega had dragged into the business.

Dane Marek picked up on the first ring, but he didn't say shit. He never said shit unless you spoke to him first. "Where are you?"

His deep voice made him sound like a serial killer. "Babysitting."

What the fuck? "You got kids?"

"No." He didn't elaborate.

"Then who?" I'd served with Vega and Marek, they were both my brothers, but unlike Vega, I only knew two things about Dane. He was unhinged, and even though we'd walked away from the Marines, he'd never put his riffle down.

Silence.

I sighed. "This isn't fucking twenty questions and I'm not interrogating you, asshole. Make fucking conversation or hang the fuck up." We had an unspoken understanding. I didn't question him about his side jobs, and he pretended like I didn't know what the fuck he was doing.

"You called me."

Jesus Christ. "Keep your fucking secrets."

"Client."

I half laughed, half snorted. "It's daytime." Just like Vega, he didn't entertain clients in the daylight hours.

"I know."

"You sound pissed." Not that he sounded any different, you had to gage context with Dane, but this was fucking priceless. "Why'd you let her stay?" His place was his sanctuary.

"I didn't. She was here when I got home last night."

"You let some chick into your house when you weren't there?" Now I was curious as hell. "What, does she fuck like a porn star?"

"Don't know."

I busted out laughing. "You haven't even fucked her and she's staying in your house? You're a bigger pussy than Vega."

"She was his client," he admitted.

I sobered. "Damn. You too? He fucking saddled me with his castoffs, the whipped motherfucker." Red's smile flashed in my mind, and I rubbed a hand over my eyes.

"I have to go."

I dropped into one of the chairs on my balcony and put my feet up on the railing. "Why? She hot?"

"Russian" was all he said.

This was fucking funnier by the second. "That means one

of two things. Rich, old and body by vodka, or a model. Fess up." God, I hoped it was the first one.

"The latter."

"Then why the hell are you talking to me? Hang up and go fuck her."

"Not happening."

"You have principals now? You too good for sloppy seconds?" As soon as I said it, Red's innocent reaction to my kiss popped into my head and I wondered if Vega had ever kissed her. He'd lectured me about his rules, number one being never kiss a client. Fucker better have stuck to his rules.

"No." Dane hung up.

I scrolled through my history to the texts I didn't delete yesterday. Every second I'd gotten to spend with Red and her yellow dress was haunting me. I wanted to see her. The money as my excuse, it took me four tries to type out a fucking text.

How did u get home?

When I saw the three dots appear, it was like a punch in the gut. The memory of our kiss hit me and my dick got hard.

Who is this?

She fucking knew it was me.

You know who this is. Where are u?

The dots appeared then disappeared but she didn't reply. I struggled through another text.

U left last night before we could talk

Christ, I sounded like a pussy. She replied almost instantly.

I paid.

I got the fucking money. Money I didn't earn. I fucked up two responses before saying the words out loud as I typed.

Yeah, we're gonna talk about that. And other shit. Where are u?

That kiss, the look on her face when she'd come, they were both burned in my memory. And no matter how hard I tried to ignore them, they were eating at me.

I have to go.

Shit. I couldn't type anymore.

Pick up

I sent the text then called her. Two rings and her sweet voice filled my head like a fucking cure for every hangover, ever.

"You shouldn't be calling me."

"Why the fuck not?"

"This isn't appropriate. I'm at work and Alex never called—"

I cut her off right there. "Do I sound like Alex?" Anger burned in my veins like I was a jealous fucking lover being hung out to dry. "Did I touch you like Alex? Did you for one second mistake me for him?" I didn't know what the fuck just happened, but I was hair's breadth away from going fucking postal, and that should've been my cue to hang up. "Because I'm not him, and you're done thinking about Alex fucking Vega."

Silence.

I sucked in a breath and forced my voice to a marginally more civil tone. "You hear me?"

She cleared her throat. "Not that it's any of your business, but I was only with him once."

Vivid and so fucking consuming that there was no mistaking it this time, jealousy warped my brain. "You're done with him, Red." Guttural and unforgiving, I bit the words out.

Her voice went quiet. "I have a name."

I knew her name. It'd been on a loop for eight fucking

hours as a hurricane pounded my condo while I pounded alcohol. I knew her name like she'd crawled in my head and decided to haunt the fuck out of me. I knew her name like she was the one woman who could make my house of cards come crashing down. I knew it and I'd never said it. Because when I first saw her twelve hours ago, I knew she was fucking trouble.

The kind of trouble I never should've touched. The kind of trouble that made me call for backup the second she'd tried to take control of our train wreck. The kind of trouble no other woman could touch.

Sienna Montclair.

In a sea of fucking palm trees and sand, she was the forest.

And I was about to get lost.

"I know your name, Sienna."

TEN

Sienna

R AW AND DIRTY, MY NAME ROLLED OFF HIS TONGUE like the sweetest kind of temptation I never wanted to hear.

I shouldn't have answered his text, and I definitely shouldn't have picked up the phone or said what I said next. "I hope you and your client survived the hurricane." I was being jealous and petty, but worse, I was hurt. *By an escort.*

The snort was as deep and rough as his voice. "That was all you, Red."

His words were an insult, but the touch of sinister in his tone made gooseflesh race across my skin. I didn't even know why I was talking to him, except that I hadn't slept a wink all night. I hated what I'd done last night, but I hated the fact that I was jealous even more. I shook my head and reached for my work voice because I was done letting men get the best of me.

"Thank you for your time, Mr. Brandt. I won't be needing your services anymore." I started to hang up.

"You never had my services because I wasn't going to give them to you." He bit off the word "services" and delivered the rest of the sentence with an angry tone.

I should've hung up, but just like last night, I couldn't get myself to ignore him. I'd known the second I'd laid eyes on him, he was more than I could handle. "Let's keep it that way." I'd had to practice polite curtness so often for work, it was almost second nature.

"Tell you what. Answer one question for me, and if your answer is no, then I'll lose your number."

I bit my lip. The lip he'd dragged between his teeth last night right after he'd given me the best kiss of my life.

"Red?"

My eyebrows drew together. "I don't like being called that." I couldn't help my red hair any more than I could the swell of my hips or upturn of my nose.

"*Sienna.*" He didn't speak my name, he let loose with a low growl that made my toes curl. "Any man ever kiss you like I did last night?"

I sucked in a breath. His voice was so rough and consuming, my core still ached for him. No one had ever kissed me like that. And no one had ever made me orgasm like that. But I was nothing more than a client to him.

"I heard that."

My fingers went to my lips. "I didn't say anything."

"You didn't have to. I heard your intake of breath, and I bet you're touching yourself right now."

I dropped my hand. "I am not."

"*Right.*"

I hated his overinflated confidence. "Do you think every woman just wants to touch herself when you speak to them?" I couldn't believe I was talking to him like this, let alone doing it from work.

"One, you're not every woman."

"Not that that sort of thing matters to you," I interrupted.

"You trying to say something, princess?"

I stiffened at the nickname my father used to call me. "I'm not a princess." I sounded like a twelve-year-old.

"You're acting like one. You want to insult me? Take your best shot. But remember this. You walked out last night, not me."

I lost my composure. "You called another client!"

"You told me to!" he roared back. "I may have texted her, but you made that call. You set that in motion."

"And if I hadn't?" Who was he kidding? "You would've just called someone else later anyway."

"There wouldn't have been a later, and we wouldn't be having this conversation because you'd still be in my bed."

"For how long? Until my money ran out?" It was petty and mean because he'd told me he wasn't taking my money, but I said it anyway.

"You're pissing me off, Red."

"The feeling is mutual."

"There wouldn't have been another client," he ground out.

"I'm not stupid enough to believe that." Was I? And if so, for how long? He'd never answered that.

"Who's calling who?" he challenged.

He was infuriating, and all at once everything and nothing like all the players I dealt with at work. I told myself I could handle this. I straightened my shoulders and stood proud in my pink suit. "Just because I paid for services in the bedroom does not give you or anyone else the right to judge me or treat me without respect." There, I'd said it.

"You're right."

Surprised, I paused, but I didn't let myself fall for it. I had to get off the phone before I convinced myself I needed to see him again. "Why, exactly, are you calling?"

"Because we have unfinished business."

"No, we don't." But every second I listened to his sexy voice and pushy dominance, I fell a little deeper. I wanted us to have unfinished business, which was only asking for trouble, but so help me, he was all I could think about. I'd made myself sick last night with regret over telling him to call that client. Every bone in my body wanted to take that back. But I couldn't. And even if I didn't run out of the restaurant and hop in a cab, I had no guarantee that anything would have turned out differently.

"Meet me at Allero's on the patio in fifteen minutes." It wasn't a request, it was a command.

My equilibrium shot, I struggled for a response. "I'm not meeting you at a restaurant."

He didn't even hesitate. "Yes you are."

"And what makes you think I would do that?" I sounded exactly like I looked. Prim and proper and nothing like a woman who'd paid a male escort five thousand dollars for a kiss and an orgasm.

"Because, gorgeous, I'm fucking hungry and I want to see you." He hung up.

I stared at my phone.

Then I did the one thing I shouldn't. I picked up my purse.

My office door swung open. "Where you going, Miss Sienna?"

I glanced up at Terence Joyner, aka TJ. His muscles bulged out of every article of clothing like he couldn't be contained. His dark eyes stared me down, but I knew underneath all that intimidating bulk he was a teddy bear. "I have to run an errand."

The six-foot-five defensive end dropped into one of my guest chairs. "But you said you would talk to DeMarco. He didn't get no call, Red."

With everything that'd happened in the last twenty-four hours, I'd forgotten about Terence's little escapade a few days ago. Sitting down on the edge of my seat, I put my hands on my lap and schooled my features. "Terence, you can't keep doing this. You need to stop before you get suspended, or worse, in real trouble."

He threw his massive hands up. "I wasn't even drinking."

I couldn't help it, my judgy face popped out. "You do know the pictures are all over the Internet? You can't have sex with one of the cheerleaders while driving with the top down."

He dropped his hands. "She wasn't taking no for an answer, Red. You know how those girls get."

My jaw clenched because I knew exactly how they got. "She was naked, Terence, and you pulled over on the Seven Mile Bridge and stopped traffic in the middle of the day. What did you think you would happen?"

He hung his head like a child. "I didn't want to wreck my ride, Red. It's the nicest car I've ever had." He looked at me without lifting his head. "Come on, girl, just talk to Coach. He listens to you."

Despite Coach being my uncle, he didn't listen to me any more than he listened to TJ. I didn't even call him uncle, because he didn't want anyone at work to know I was his niece. I'd never even shared a meal outside of work with him. He ate, slept and breathed football. I'd asked him over to dinner a few times but gave up years ago when he'd declined every invitation. Now I kept it strictly professional between us. I handled his scheduling and paperwork and ran interference when the players got out of line, and Coach did what he did best, he trained the defensive players.

I sighed and stood. "Fine, I'll say something to Coach when I see him." I walked around my desk.

TJ jumped up with the speed and agility he was known for on the field. "Where you going? I can drive you."

My cheeks heated at the thought of Jared. "No, you can't."

TJ stepped into my path. "Aw, come on, Red. When you gonna let me take you out?"

Seriously? After his latest sexual exploit was plastered all over the news? My expression must've given me away.

He spread his hands out wide. "You know I won't need none of them girls if I got you." The back of his giant fingers brushed against my arm. "You're classy, Red. You could keep me honest." His brilliant smile sparkled like it did for the cameras.

This was the exact reason I'd hired an escort. I didn't want to keep someone honest. And I definitely didn't need to play house with a defensive linebacker while he cheated on me with every pretty girl who smiled at him.

I straightened my shoulders. "You know the rules, Terence. No fraternization." Not that I'd paid any attention to the rules when Dan had asked me out.

He winked. "Then quit."

"And who would run interference for you with Coach? Besides, I need my job, thank you very much."

"You don't need no money if you're with me, Red. I make *all* the money."

For a few more years or until he got injured, then his seven-figure salary would be gone as fast as his fans. I pointed a finger at his chest and gave him the best advice he'd ever get. "Save your money, Terence Joyner." Not that he'd listen. I'd seen it too many times. "Now, let me by. I have somewhere to be, and you need to hit the weights."

His hand moved to his chest as if I'd wounded him, but he grinned. "Always turning me down, Miss Sienna."

"Yes, I am."

"One day, you'll need me. I'll wait," he said it confidently as he held my office door open for me.

I was shaking my head at TJ when I stepped into the hallway. It was how I almost plowed right into him.

"Sie." Dan grabbed my arms to steady me.

Damn it. "Mr. Ahlstrom," I said curtly.

He lowered his voice to a sinister tone. "What were you doing at a condo on Collins Avenue last night?"

Anger straightened my spine and I spoke only loud enough for him to hear. "You *followed* me?"

"I came to your house to talk but you were leaving." He didn't even act sorry, he just looked pointedly at my left hand and frowned. "You're still not wearing it." He knew I wouldn't cause a scene in front of any other players, and he was using that to his advantage.

I glanced nervously at TJ as he looked curiously between us, then I looked back up at Dan and whisper hissed, "We're done. You're done. Don't you ever follow me again." I pulled my arms out of his grasp and looked over Dan's shoulder at his friend, the huge linebacker, Elliot "Sunshine" Washington. "Mr. Washington."

Sunshine tipped his chin once.

Dan took in my purse and his eyes narrowed. "Where are you going?"

62

I put on a fake smile and deflected. "Do you have an appointment with Coach?" Following me, coming to my office two days in a row, he was crossing the line. "I didn't see you on his schedule today."

"Team business." He glanced at my left hand again and his eyebrows drew even tighter together as he lowered his voice. "We need to talk. It's important."

I had no intention of talking to him. Ever. "I'll let Coach know you stopped by."

Dan moved slightly so his back was to TJ and Sunshine. "I'm serious, Sie. This is important."

I raised my voice just enough for TJ and Sunshine to hear. "Coach isn't here."

Dan took the hint, sort of. "Then I'll wait for him." He angrily pushed into my office suite and Sunshine followed.

TJ chuckled as the glass door shut. "You told him."

I purposely didn't look to see what Dan was doing. "What team business does he have with Coach?"

TJ shrugged. "Dunno, but I heard a rumor that old man Burrows is laid up."

"The owner of the team is sick?" I hadn't heard that.

"That's what I hear. Couldn't tell it from seeing him last week though. He was yelling at defense, same as usual."

There was nothing friendly about the owner of the team. He hadn't said more than two words to me in five years. He just angry stared. "Well, I hope he gets better." I didn't care one way or another as long as it didn't affect my job.

TJ glanced past me through the glass wall into my and Coach's offices. "Strom does too apparently."

"See you later." I forced half a smile and rushed to my car.

ELEVEN

Jared

I WATCHED THE NEW MERCEDES SLK CONVERTIBLE PULL up to the valet. Her red hair visible from a block away, she drove like she was mission intent.

Barely acknowledging the valet, she took the ticket as she scanned the outdoor seating area. I couldn't see her eyes behind her sunglasses, but I knew the second her gaze landed on me because she stiffened.

I didn't smile. Or get up. I stared.

In heels I never would've guessed she could manage, she and her pink suit swept toward me like a fucking hurricane.

"Mr. Brandt, I have a job. I don't have time to come running out for some clandestine meeting because you decided we have unfinished business. Say what you need to say and I'll be on my way."

I didn't like it. Not one fucking inch of it. The suit, the heels, the squared shoulders and perfectly pinned-up hair. I wanted to rip her jacket off, take her hair down and thread my fingers through the thick locks. "What do you do?"

Her back went even straighter. "I'm an assistant. Now if you'll—"

64

"You married?" Assistants couldn't afford new Mercedes. Looking offended, she frowned. "No."

"Divorced?"

"If I planned on getting divorced, I wouldn't get married in the first place," she huffed.

"Sit down," I commanded.

She stared at me.

Not sure if she was gonna stay or go, I didn't budge.

Two breaths later, she pulled a chair out and lowered herself to the very edge.

I studied her a moment then glanced at the valet as he drove off in her car. "Your daddy buy you that car?"

"I make my own money, Mr. Brandt."

For now, I was letting the mister bullshit slide. I nodded slowly, my eyes never leaving her gorgeous face. "What'd you come from?"

She held her posture like a detainee in an interrogation. "Not that it's any of your business, but my father was a preacher."

A preacher's daughter? *Jesus Christ*, I couldn't even make up that kind of irony. Every second in her presence, I was more intrigued by her, which only fucked with my head. I'd come here to give her the money back and make a fucking point, not act like a pussy with my tail between my legs, begging her for attention. I grabbed the menu and handed it to her. "Pick something."

Her hands remained in her lap. "I'm not hungry. I need to get back to work."

I wondered what kind of an admin worked on a Sunday, but I didn't ask. "You don't get a lunch break?"

"Not one I'm going to spend on you."

I got the double meaning behind the "spend" statement, but I didn't give a fuck. She was here and I felt like I could finally fucking breathe. I wasn't an idiot, I knew I had an uphill battle, but to what I didn't know. I just wanted to erase everything between us that'd happened last night after I'd texted the client.

I slid the envelope across the table. "Put that in your purse."

She stared at the money. "No."

"Non-negotiable." I wasn't going to let money come between me and this woman. She was too damn good for that.

"I don't take orders from you."

The waitress showed up. Overenthusiastic, young and irritating, she smiled at Red. "Your boyfriend is so sweet. He wouldn't even order a water until you showed up. What can I get you?"

I grabbed the envelope and slapped it on her tray to get her attention. "Here's a tip. Don't make assumptions. Now get us each something off the menu."

Her smile dropped and her mouth made an O. "I'm so sorry, of course, right away. We have a great special today...."

I glared at her.

"I'll just bring it." She scrambled away.

Red looked livid. "That was five thousand dollars." Her teeth clenched, she hissed at me like an angry cat.

A sexy, angry cat. "Now it's gone."

"What are you trying to prove? That you're irresponsible and impulsive?"

It was a rhetorical question, but I answered it anyway. "Money isn't going to come between us."

"There is no us." She leaned forward and dropped her

voice to a furious whisper. "You're an escort. You perform ser-vices. You *performed* a service. I paid you. End of story. We are *done*."

I forced half my mouth to tip up when all I wanted to do was drag her ass across the table and spank the anger right the fuck out of her. Then I wanted to sink my dick inside that tight cunt and pound her into submission until she didn't know a damn thing except my name. "You think I'm insulted by that? Try harder, Red."

Her cheeks flushed. "I don't care what you think. I'm only stating fact."

I moved. I ripped off her sunglasses, grabbed the back of her neck and brought my face within an inch of hers. "You want fact?" I dropped my voice. "You're here because you want to be here. You're here because you're squirming on the edge of that seat remembering how good I made you feel. You're here because you know you made a mistake last night." I paused, then I did something I never do. I admitted I was wrong. "And so did I."

Her chest rose and fell. "I don't want your apology."

"You're getting it anyway." I brushed my lips against hers and gave her more than I had to give. "I'm sorry, Sienna."

Her eyes welled.

Any doubt I had about what I wanted from this woman disappeared. "We're gonna move past last night." Seeing her, holding her, I didn't give a damn about giving up my clients. I just fucking wanted her.

"There's nothing to move to." She tried to pull back. "You're... who you are."

Panic flooded my veins with what I was about to do, but I tightened my grip and ignored the warning my brain was yelling. "Now I'm just a regular guy who's gonna take you to lunch."

She scoffed. "It doesn't work like that."

"It does now." I could have told her that I didn't fuck that client last night, but I didn't. Trust was gonna have to go both ways. I knew it was a dick move not to tell her immediately, but for once, I wanted a woman to want me for who the hell I was.

"So what? You just quit? You were working last night."

I laid it on the line. "I'm not escorting anymore."

"Right." Disbelief bled out of her tone. "Just like that, you're done? For how long? Until you need money again?"

I kept my voice even, patient. "I don't need money."

"I don't trust you. I don't even know you, and I'm not looking for a boyfriend."

"Good."

She looked startled.

"Because you're not getting a boyfriend. You've already got me, and I'm taking you to lunch." I kissed her forehead then sat back because I saw the waitress approach out of the corner of my eye. "What do you want to drink?"

"I'm so sorry," the waitress interrupted, nervously putting the envelope on the table. "But I think you made a mistake. I can't take that, sir. That's like, that's… whoa."

I glanced at Red.

She sighed. Then she picked up the envelope and put it on the waitress's tray. "It wasn't a mistake."

I smiled. "What are you drinking, Red?"

"Sweet tea, please," she said politely.

I winked then I glanced at the waitress. "I'll have a Corona."

The waitress burst into tears. "I really, *really* need this money. My son, he's autistic. Oh my God, you probably don't understand, but *ohmigod.*" She brushed at her tears. "I'm just… I'm crying!" She laughed. "But I want to say thank you, so *thank you!*" She leaned over and hugged Red. "Thank you so much!"

Red shed a tear.

Christ. I was shaking my head, but I was smiling at the fucking irony of it all. It's why I didn't notice them walk up.

"Who the hell is he?" an angry voice roared.

I looked up. Surprise didn't begin to cover it. Fifty fucking scenarios flew through my mind, each one worse than the last. "Who the fuck are you?" I knew exactly who he was. Dan fucking Ahlstrom. The quarterback for Miami's beloved professional football team. And he was looking at me like he wanted to rip me limb from limb.

"Sienna's boyfriend," he growled.

TWELVE

Sienna

THE WAITRESS SQUEAKED IN FEAR.

This was not happening. "*Dan—*"

Jared interrupted me. One arm spread across his chair, looking calm as ever, he glanced at the waitress. "Go grab us those drinks, sweetheart."

Dan glared at Jared as the waitress practically ran away. "I asked you a question."

Oozing control, Jared didn't even flinch. "And I asked you one."

TJ and Sunshine stepped up behind Dan. The three of them made a seven-hundred-pound wall of professional football player intimidation and I'd had enough.

"Terence," I snapped. "Did you follow me?"

The stiff set to his shoulders immediately slumped. "Ah, come on, Miss Sienna. Don't ask me that in front of Strom."

Dan's glare trained on me. "Leave TJ out of this," he barked. "What the hell are you doing? Who is this?" He jabbed a finger at Jared's shoulder so hard, it pushed him and his chair back.

It happened so fast, it was like a movie.

Jared grabbed Dan's wrist, kicked his chair back and was on his feet. He twisted Dan's arm and wrenched it behind his back. Dan dropped to his knees and Jared slammed his head into the table. Holding him down with both hands, his boot digging in to the back of Dan's calf, he bent and spoke in a murderously quiet voice. "You speak to her like that again, I will end you."

"Fuck you," Dan ground out. "TJ, Sunshine!"

Still in shock at the sight of what Jared had just done, the defensive end and the linebacker snapped their mouths shut and moved.

Jared was quicker. Still holding on to Dan, he kicked Dan's feet, and spun them both to face TJ and Sunshine. Lethal, threatening, he spoke. "Do you know what they teach you in the Marines?"

Curious and like an impressed child, TJ's eyes widened. "Special Forces?"

Sunshine slapped him on the back of the head then narrowed his eyes at Jared. "You break his arm, the team's gonna sue you."

"He speaks to my woman like that again, a broken arm will be the least of his worries."

My heart jumped from my stomach to my throat and gooseflesh chased across my skin. *His woman?*

TJ held his hands up. "All right, man, we're cool. Let's all walk it off. No one wants the lady upset." He smiled at me. "Looking real good today, Miss Sienna."

Both Dan and Jared growled.

TJ took a step back. "It's chill. I'm chill. Just keeping it real, giving the woman an innocent compliment."

"Cut it out, Terence," I warned.

Sunshine crossed his arms. "Let Strom go."

Jared released Dan only to kick him in the back. Dan fell forward, catching himself on his left arm before his face hit the patio. His nostrils flaring with each breath, he did a one-handed push-up and got up real slow.

Sunshine offered him a hand, but Dan slapped him away.

TJ eyed Jared. "Do the Marines really teach you a hundred different ways to kill barehanded?"

Jared didn't get a chance to answer.

Dan lunged. Head down, shoulder first, he went in for a tackle.

As if he was expecting it, without even blinking, Jared brought his arm out, elbow first. He made solid contact with Dan's nose as his knee simultaneously landed a crushing blow below Dan's belt.

Dan let out an inhuman roar and crumpled to the ground. His nose gushing blood, his hands on his crotch, he curled into a fetal position.

Sunshine dove at Jared.

Jared spun.

Halfway through the spin, his leg came up and his knee made contact with Sunshine's shoulder a fraction of a second before his booted foot slammed into the side of his head. Jared's martial arts strike took the force out of Sunshine's attack, but it didn't stop the linebacker. It only slowed his second pass, but Jared was two steps ahead. His hands on Sunshine's ears, he brought his head down and slammed his knee up. Sunshine didn't get his hands up in time. Stunned, he dropped to his knees as blood gushed from his mouth and nose.

Chest heaving, red splatters on his T-shirt and jeans, his face an impenetrable mask, Jared turned to me. "You okay?"

Speechless, I stared.

"Damn." TJ took in Jared's carnage and shook his head. "I shoulda joined the Marines."

I didn't know when I'd gotten to my feet, but I was standing. Then I was shaking. And once I started, I couldn't stop.

"Sienna." My name wasn't a concern on Jared's lips, it rumbled out of him. Low and drawn out, it was a warning like thunder in the distance, but I didn't register any of it.

I shook harder. He could've killed them. Two football players who were trained to tackle three-hundred-pound men, and Jared took them down like it was child's play. He didn't even break a sweat.

Jared reached for me.

"No!" My hands out, my breath gone, I backed up.

"TJ," Jared barked.

"Way ahead of you." TJ's arm wrapped around my shoulders. "Come on, girl. Let's hit it."

Three police cruisers pulled up to the curb. Doors opened, boots hit the pavement and chairs scraped. My world was spinning out of control, and in the middle of it all was a man with tousled blond hair and a brown-eyed gaze that didn't waver.

"Her purse." Jared pointed.

"Got it, boss."

A giant six-foot-six defensive end picked up my hot-pink Coach purse as a lethal, ex-marine, male escort stepped up and kissed my forehead.

"It's gonna be okay. Go with TJ." He put something rectangular in my hand. "Call Neil. Tell him what happened. The lock code is my address." He backed up and tipped his chin at TJ. "Get her out of here, *now*."

"Police! On the ground! *On the ground!*"

TJ tucked me under his arm and rushed me across the patio as Jared dropped to his knees and put his hands behind his head. Every restaurant patron had their phone out and pointed at either me and TJ or Jared and Dan and Sunshine as they all lay on the ground. So intent on getting us all on video, they barely moved out of our way as TJ plowed through the crowd and skirted the side of the restaurant.

By the time he led me around the corner to the back of the building, we had people following us and filming. As if it were an everyday occurrence, TJ kept his eyes ahead and didn't say a word. His car was parked in a small employee-only parking lot, and he took me to the passenger side, opened the door then tucked me in, normal as you please. Seconds later he folded his giant frame behind the wheel and turned the key.

Jared's phone heavy in my hands, TJ weaving us in and out of traffic on Collins Avenue, I realized my life wasn't falling apart—it'd gone up in flames. I'd get fired once Coach saw those video clips, Jared was getting arrested, the team would sue him, and I was supposed to scroll through his client contacts to call someone named Neil.

Miserable, I glanced at TJ.

He wasn't just smiling, he was grinning.

Oh God. "What?"

"Damn, girl, I don't know what's funnier. Strom gettin' schooled by your badass marine boyfriend or that you're gonna be the one pissing Coach off this week."

I wanted to cry. I knew how the video clips would look. "You didn't have to put your arm around me."

TJ laughed. "You think I was gonna miss out on the opportunity to piss off Strom? He had that coming." His face sobered. "So, you and him?"

"No." Resolutely, absolutely *no*. "There's nothing between us." The only thing I'd done right when I'd crawled between Dan Ahlstrom's sheets was not telling a soul about it.

"Not to mess with a brother's woman, but that wasn't nothing. He lost his shit when he saw you with your man."

"I'm not dating him, Terence. I don't date the players." Dan and I had never gone out, not technically. We'd never gotten past his bedroom or mine.

TJ's hand went to his chest. "Damn, girl. Right where it hurts."

"You're not hurt by that, and for the record, Jared isn't my boyfriend either." A few miles between me and him was enough for me to come to my senses. I'd worried a football player was a dangerous choice for a boyfriend, but I'd never met a pissed-off marine. I told myself I didn't care that he was only defending me. I knew Dan was being a jerk, but Jared could've ignored him. I glanced at the phone in my hands.

"Come on, who ya talking to?" TJ shook his head.

"Obviously, I'm talking to you because no one else is in the car." How many women would be in his contacts? Why did I even care?

He chuckled. "You know what I'm sayin'. That brother was straight-up marking his territory."

I hated how the very idea made my skin tingle and my stomach flutter. "I assure you he was not." It didn't matter what Jared had said. We'd had one encounter, and I wasn't Cinderella. He wasn't going to give up his life for me. I didn't even know anything about him. You didn't base a relationship on a kiss and an orgasm from a male escort. *Did you?*

TJ shrugged. "Can't blame him. We all know what you are."

Oh my God, I was losing my mind. I shouldn't have been thinking about Jared as anything other than what he was. "What's that supposed to mean?"

"You ain't no bottom bitch, girl."

"Terence Joyner!" Heat flamed my cheeks at the thought of what I really was.

He held his hands up. "You're way too good for us, Miss Sienna. That's all I'm saying."

He meant it as a compliment, but none of it felt good. I turned toward the window.

TJ nudged my shoulder. "You gonna make that call for your badass marine?"

I looked down at the phone in my hand. I didn't want to scroll through his contacts. "Do I have to?" I didn't realize I'd spoken out loud until TJ burst out laughing.

"Shit, girl." He laughed harder.

"Don't laugh at me," I snapped.

"Aw, come on. You know I'm just playin'." He sobered. "But a word of advice from a brother who's been there? Make that call. Ain't no one wants to sit in lockup."

"Fine," I huffed, feigning attitude to cover my apprehension.

Inhaling, I pressed the four digit number that was Jared's address into the lock screen but the phone didn't unlock. Frowning, I pulled my phone out of my purse to check the address, wondering if I'd gotten it wrong. I hadn't, but his condo number was also a four-digit number. I pressed that number into the screen. The phone unlocked and a picture from his balcony of a sunrise popped up.

Impulsively, I touched the photo album icon.

The sunrise and the profile picture he'd texted me were the only two photos in his phone. A loneliness I knew deep in my soul bled from those two pictures, and it made me sad, incredibly sad.

I hastily closed the photo album and brought up his contacts. Intending to only look at the *N*'s, his entire contact list came up. Jared only had six numbers programmed. Alex, André, Con, Dane, Neil and Talon. That was it. No women. Unable to stop myself, I went to the call log. My number was the only number listed. Exhaling, not sure how I was feeling, I dialed the number for Neil Christensen.

One ring and the call was answered.

"*Ja?*"

The accent was thick but not nearly as surprising as the deep timbre of the voice. "Mr. Christensen?"

"Who is this?"

"Um." Should I give him my name? Shoot. I figured attorneys had to be confidential, so I told him. "My name is Sienna Montclair."

"Where is Brandt?"

"There's been an incident, and he asked me to—"

"Are you safe?"

It was such an unexpected question, it took me off guard. "Y-yes," I stammered.

"Continue." His deep voice had zero intonation.

Intimidated by his briskness, I cut to the chase. "Jared was arrested at Allero's."

"Explain," Neil demanded.

"There was an altercation between him and the quarterback for Miami's football team and a linebacker named Sunshine Washington."

"Are you injured?"

"No. Neither is Jared, but I think he may have broken the other men's noses." Or arms, or both.

Silence.

"Mr. Christensen?"

"Where are you?"

TJ pulled into the training complex. "At work."

"Address?"

"I'm sorry, but with all due respect, I'm not sure that's any of your business, Mr. Christensen."

"I am picking you up then I am taking you to the police station."

Alarm spiked my pulse and stiffened my back. "Jared asked me to call you. My involvement beyond that is not necessary."

"Did you witness the incident?"

Shoot. "Yes, but—"

"The police will need to question you. I will take you. Address?"

My car. *Shoot.* "I can arrange my own ride to the station." I glanced at TJ and he nodded.

"With who?"

"Excuse me?"

"You were involved in an incident with two high-profile football players. If you have the means to handle the legal and media attention you will receive, then do not waste my time. Otherwise, give me the address of your location."

My stomach bottomed out, and I rattled off the address.

Pause. Then, "That is the training complex."

"I know. I'm the assistant to the defensive coordinator."

Silence.

"Hello?"

"Thirteen minutes." He hung up.

THIRTEEN

Jared

SHE *FUCKED* THE QUARTERBACK OF THE MIAMI
Dolphins?

Adrenaline still pumping, I paced the fucking
holding cell.

She didn't just fuck him. I saw the look on her face when
he showed up. I didn't know dick about relationships, but I
knew women. And her look had been one hundred percent
telling. Motherfucking fuck. *What the fuck am I doing?*

I wasn't a fucking football wonder from Kansas or
Oklahoma or wherever the fuck he was from, making seven
figures. What the hell did I think I was going to do? Offer her
my ass on a platter? Vanilla fuck her into a white picket fence
life with two kids and a damn minivan? She drove a fucking
Mercedes and fucked football players.

Goddamn it.

"Brandt!" The same cop that'd brought me in unlocked
the cell. "Let's go." He didn't bother re-cuffing me. We were
both vets.

"Thanks."

He tipped his chin. "Strom and Sunshine will probably press charges."

I knew they would. "Not surprised."

He handed me my keys and wallet and had me sign for them. "So." He smiled. "The redhead?"

I frowned. "She's here?" What the fuck was Neil doing?

"Oh yeah. Her Viking-sized bodyguard brought her in to give a statement."

Damn it. I didn't want her involved. But I should've thought of that before I decided to wipe the table with her boyfriend's face. "Thanks for the heads-up."

He walked me through the station and held the door open to the lobby. "They're waiting for you."

"Thanks." One step and I saw her. My heart jumped and the adrenaline already pounding through my veins amped up to mach one. No longer giving a shit about a damn thing except the rigid set to her posture and the look on her face, I walked right up to her. Taking her face in my hands, I bent my knees. "You okay?"

She inhaled. "Fine."

But she didn't say *fine*. No attitude, no posturing, she whispered it, and I wasn't buying it, not for one second. "Let's go." I'd get her talking after I got her out of here. I glanced around. "Where's Neil?"

She looked over her shoulder. "He stepped outside to take a call."

"Come on." I put my arm around her shoulders and started to take a step, but she stiffened. "What's wrong?"

"Nothing."

I stopped and looked at her, and that's when I saw it. Her purse clutched to her chest, her eyes too wide, her hands trembling slightly. She had fear written all over her. "I would never hurt you, Sienna."

She sucked in a breath. "You… you just—"

I dropped my arm and schooled my features. "I know what I did." And I'd do it again. Without hesitation.

"You were *arrested*."

"Detained," I corrected.

Neil walked into the station. "There is media waiting."

Six foot six and built like a fucking Viking, Neil was ex-Danish Special Forces. I'd met him in Afghanistan after our Humvee was hit. I'd be dead if it weren't for Vega and him. "How many?"

"Enough."

Goddamn it. I didn't want my name or my military record splashed all over the fucking news. Something I should've thought of before I kicked the quarterback's ass. "Take her and get her home. I'll call Vega to pick me up."

Red reached in her purse and handed me my cell. "It's all over the Internet. They've already seen me with you."

I shoved my phone in my pocket and glanced at Neil. Expression impenetrable, he waited for me to make a decision. "All right, take us back to my car, and I'll drive her home."

Neil nodded once, and we flanked Sienna as we walked out of the station.

Three paces and the media was on us. I took Red's arm. "Keep your head down."

The questions started the second the cameras began flashing.

"Miss Montclair, are you dating Miami's most eligible bachelor, Dan Ahlstrom?"

"Was Strom arrested for fighting with your boyfriend?"

"Mr. Brandt, are you the same Jared Brandt that received the Purple Heart for being wounded in Afghanistan?"

"Miss Montclair, is Jared Brandt your boyfriend?"

They fired questions the entire way to Neil's truck. I helped Sienna in then got in the front passenger seat.

I waited till Neil was behind the wheel. "My car's at Allero's."

"So is mine," Sienna spoke from the back seat.

I didn't bother telling her that I wasn't going to let her drive herself home. We were all silent, and a few minutes later, Neil pulled up to Allero's. "Drop me at the valet. You got a little more time?"

Scanning the street in front of the restaurant, Neil tipped his chin.

I turned to face Sienna. "I'm going to have Neil take your car home. I don't want you driving alone until this settles down. Wait here until they pull my car up." I didn't wait for an answer. I got out of the truck.

The valet's eyes widened when he saw me and my bloodied shirt.

"The Mustang and the black Mercedes the redhead was driving. Bring them both." I handed him my valet ticket.

"I'm sorry, sir." His voice cracked. "I'm not allowed to give you another person's car."

I nodded at Neil's SUV. "She's waiting in the SUV because I'm not letting her get out until you bring the cars around."

He looked relieved to have an excuse to get the cars. "Okay." He grabbed the keys from his lockbox and took off at a run.

I glanced at the patio. The furniture was all put back in place, but there weren't any customers out front. The valet brought the Mercedes then the Mustang. When he pulled up with my ride, Neil got out of his SUV and gave his keys to the valet.

"You know her address?" I asked.

"*Ja.*"

"I'll take my time getting there. Let me know what you find."

Neil leveled me with a stare. "She should not be one of your clients."

Guilt at last night hit hard. "She's not."

He didn't say jack shit. He got in the Mercedes and took off.

I opened the passenger door of the SUV and held a hand out.

Without making eye contact, she took my hand. "I could have driven myself." Her tone sharp, her attitude back, she dropped my hand the second her feet were on the ground and strode to my ride.

The valet opened the door for her, and I shook my head. Even with her hair pinned up and throwing attitude, she was sexy as fuck.

I slid behind the wheel. "Where we going?"

She rattled off an address in Coral Gables.

My eyebrows rose at the expensive zip code. "You gonna tell me what you do?"

Her phone buzzed in her purse, but she didn't reach for it. She turned toward the window. "What does it matter?"

"You gonna answer that?"

"No." She didn't elaborate.

"The boyfriend?"

"I don't have a boyfriend, you included." The phone stopped vibrating.

"I'll never be your boyfriend, Red." I wasn't fucking twelve years old. The second I claimed her, I'd be a hell of a lot more than her *boyfriend*.

Incredulous, she turned to me. "So everything you said in the restaurant was a lie?" She scoffed. "I should have known."

"None of it was a lie."

She called me on my bullshit. "You're talking out of both sides of your mouth." Her phone started buzzing again.

"Answer your phone." I wanted her taking that prick's call in front of me.

She yanked her purse open, grabbed the phone and started to turn it off. "I'm *not* answering it."

I snatched the phone out of her hand and answered. "Talk," I demanded.

"Who the hell is this?" an angry male voice barked.

"You first." Asshole.

"Ken DeMarco. Put Sienna on the phone, *now*."

The Ken DeMarco? The fucking coach of Miami's football team? "Tell me what this is about, then I'll decide if you can speak with her."

"Jared!" Sienna reached for the phone, but I switched it to my other hand.

"Jared, huh? Listen, you little shit, you put my assistant on the goddamn phone right now and I won't fucking crucify you in the press."

His assistant? I glanced at Red. Jesus. "Give it your best shot." I didn't give two fucks what the press said about me, but Jesus Christ, she worked with that asshole quarterback?

He played his hand. "You want that coming back on her, you asshole?"

Fuck. "What do you want?"

85

"You the one from the restaurant who busted up my players?"

"You should train them better." Fucking pussies.

"This isn't the Marines. They're not soldiers. They're highly paid, highly protected assets of the league."

"The Army has soldiers," I corrected.

"Do you know who the fuck you're talking to, son?" he snapped.

Did I fucking care was a better question. "Again, what do you want?"

"Give me the phone," Sienna hissed.

"You bring her to my office in the next fifteen minutes, and I won't fire her." He hung up.

I held her phone out.

She snatched it back. "What do you think you're doing?"

"Taking you to your boss."

FOURTEEN

Sienna

J ARED WALKED ME INTO WORK LIKE HE OWNED THE place. At least he'd changed his shirt in the car. But the workout shirt he'd grabbed from his back seat was almost worse than his bloodied T-shirt. Formfitting and stretching across his huge biceps, the moisture-wicking material showed every muscle in his washboard abs, not to mention the tribal tattoo on his right arm.

Everyone stared as we passed front reception. Jared either didn't care or didn't notice. His hand on the small of back, he led me through the lobby as if he'd been here a thousand times before. I used my badge to get us past a second security checkpoint, then we were alone in the corridor.

"You okay?" His hand moved to the back of my neck.

I hated how much I wanted him here with me, but at the same time, I didn't need him witnessing my humiliation. I'd heard what Coach had said to him. "You don't need to come with me." I could get fired all on my own. "I'll get a ride home from someone."

Grabbing my waist, he stopped walking and pushed me

to the wall. His hands landed on either side of my head and he lowered his voice. "Do you know what happened the second I laid eyes on you?"

My heart skipped, my stomach fluttered, and despite seeing how easily he could have killed two men, I remembered every second of his hands and lips on me. "This isn't the time for this."

"Do you love him?"

I didn't have to ask who he meant. I didn't hesitate. "No."

"Then this is exactly the time. I'm not here because I have to be. I'm not here because some asshole coach told me to bring you. I'm here because five and a half feet of fire walked into my life, and I want to know every damn thing about her." The backs of his fingers glanced across my cheek. "I want to taste her desire and her tears. I want to know why she's so fucking polite. I want to know what she looks like when she wakes up in the morning, and I want to know why the fuck she's running from any kind of attachment. Because she's running...." His thumb brushed across my lips, then he whispered, "You're running. But I'm gonna catch you, Red."

Soft and so incredibly sweet it made me want to cry, he kissed me. No tongue, no aggression, his lips brushed against mine, and for two heartbeats, he held it.

Then he pulled back and kissed my forehead once like I meant the world to him. "I'm taking you in, and I'm taking you out. You get nervous, you need me to take over, just give me a single look. Understand?"

I couldn't reply. My heart in my throat, I fought tears so hard, I thought I would break.

"Sienna?"

"I'm mad at you for sleeping with that woman last night," I blurted.

He inhaled and looked like he was going to say something, but then he didn't.

I pushed ahead. "I have no right to be."

"I have no right to be pissed as hell that you fucked the quarterback, but I am."

"That wasn't last night."

He nodded once, but he didn't say anything.

"Would you have slept with her if I didn't tell you to?"

He searched my face, then he answered truthfully. "I'm not a fucking prince, Red."

I pulled away, wishing I'd never asked.

His large fingers wrapped around my upper arm, halting me. "But not for the reasons you think."

I wasn't thinking about reasons. I was feeling like my heart had just been broken, and I didn't understand why. "I don't trust you."

"You shouldn't."

He was right, but I wanted to trust him. I stupidly wanted it all—the knight in shining armor, the castle, the whole ridiculous, irrational, mockery of every single real relationship out there—I wanted it. I wanted the fairy tale. And I wanted him to be it. But I knew better than to trust a man, let alone a man like him. "My boss is waiting."

"You shouldn't trust me, not because of last night, but because I haven't earned it."

Honesty. Like a blinking neon sign, the word popped in my head, and I grasped at it. Every sentence he'd ever spoken to me ran through my mind, and I realized there was one commonality underlying all of it. Honesty.

My mind reeled. "Do you have a Purple Heart?"

"Yes."

"You don't look injured." It was the single most inappropriate sentence to ever cross my lips.

He didn't take offense like he should have. "You haven't seen me naked."

I couldn't help it, my eyes dropped to his pants.

He chuckled. "I'm not injured there, sugar."

"Why do you sleep with women for money?"

As if he knew this was a test, he didn't hesitant in his honesty. "Because it's not only my body that's scarred."

My chest hurt, my heart broke and I wanted to reach for him so badly, it physically hurt to hold back. "I'm sorry."

"I'm not. I'm alive."

He was humble and human and honest. I nodded because that's all I had. A nod for the man who'd just destroyed everything I'd ever believed about men.

"You ready?" He took my hand.

I wasn't but I nodded anyway and my feet moved automatically toward an office I could find blindfolded. Leading us down the corridor and through the glass door to my office suite, I took us to my boss's closed door and knocked.

"Come in, dammit!"

I glanced nervously at Jared. "Please don't hit him if he swears at me." I was only half kidding.

"You're asking a lot, Red."

"Jared—"

He squeezed my hand then broke our connection to open the door for me. "I hear you."

Taking a deep breath, I walked into my boss's office.

Coach took one look at me and he practically growled. "I don't have time for this shit, Montclair."

Internally, I shrunk a foot. "Yes, sir." But when I saw who

was seated in one of the chairs on the other side of Coach's desk, I winced.

Dan's nose was taped up, bloodied cotton was stuffed up his nostrils and his eyes were already black and blue. He took one look at Jared and jumped to his feet. "What the hell is he doing here?"

"Shut up, Ahlstrom." Coach pointed at me. "Do you know how much headache you've caused this team?"

It was always about the team. Everything was *the team*. "Yes, sir."

"She didn't cause anything. You can blame your quarterback for that." Jared glared at Dan.

Dan snorted, as much as he could with his nose broken. "You admitting you know who I am now?"

"Enough!" Coach bellowed. "*Sit down.*"

Dan fell back into his chair.

"I prefer to stand, sir." I wasn't going to get fired while sitting in a chair like a coward.

Jared stood next to me. One hand over his wrist, the other hand in a fist, his stance widened slightly and his shoulders went straight. He looked every bit the marine he was trained to be.

Coach walked behind his desk. "How long has this been going on?"

"I went to lunch today and—" I started.

"I'm not asking about the damn restaurant, Montclair." Coach lowered his voice. "You messing with Ahlstrom?"

I said "No" at the same time Dan said "She's with me."

I spun and glared at Dan. "I am *not* with you. I never was." The cheating jerk.

"Lying doesn't suite you, Sie."

I hated him and his nickname. "Ditto." It was a stupid retort, but I was too angry to come up with anything better.

Coach rubbed a hand over his head. "You both know the rules." He eyed me. "And it's not his ass that's gonna be on the line. You know how this works."

I did. With my head held high, I stood straight and braced for the worse. "Do what you have to, sir." Jared's hand landed on my shoulder, but I was too proud to push him away in front of Dan and Coach.

"*Christ*," Coach muttered, tossing some papers around on his desk. "You're on leave until the season is over, Montclair. Give your schedule to one of the other girls. And for God's sake, don't do a damn thing unless the lawyers tell you to. You don't breathe without passing it by them first. Understand?"

I understood perfectly. It was the same speech I gave every player who ever got into trouble off the field. I'd said it so many times, I'd lost count after my first month on the job. "Yes, sir."

Dan stood. "Sienna."

Coach jabbed his pointer finger toward him like a weapon. "You're on thin ice, Strom. You're done talking to her." He glanced at Jared. "Get her out of here."

"Gladly." Jared's hand moved to the small of my back.

FIFTEEN

Jared

IN AN ENORMOUS SHOW OF RESTRAINT, I DIDN'T SLAM HER asshole boss's face into his desk or finish what I started with the fucking quarterback pussy.

My phone had been vibrating in my pocket, but I didn't pull it out until I had her safely back in the Mustang. I had one text from Neil.

Media is at her house. The Mercedes is parked. The keys are at your place.

I fumbled through a text back to him.

Thx. Owe u one

His reply was almost immediate.

You owe me more than one.

No fucking shit. I glanced at Red. "You handled that like a boss." She was a rock in that office, and I wanted to kiss her so fucking bad, but I knew I had to earn that right. But it didn't stop me from touching her. I cupped her face. "You okay?"

"Humiliated, but fine."

"You didn't do anything wrong. You didn't cause a scene at a restaurant trying to piss in the sand. That's all him, Red."

"I meant losing my job."

"I didn't hear you get fired."

"It's only a matter of time. By the end of the season, Coach will have another assistant."

I brushed my thumb across her cheek then released her. I didn't want to sit in the parking lot in case her ex came out and I'd be tempted to break both of his fucking arms. "How long have you worked for him?"

"Five years." She leaned back in her seat and sighed. "Since my daddy got me the job."

I glanced at her. "Your dad had an in with the team?"

"Ken DeMarco is my uncle."

Jesus *fuck*. "The coach is your uncle?" And he'd treated her like that?

"Defensive coordinator." She said it all prim and proper.

"Why the hell are you answering phones?" She should be in marketing or some other cushy job.

"I do a lot more than just answer the phone."

Yeah, like take the hit for the asshole quarterback's bull-shit. "What kind of fucked-up family are you from?"

She sighed. "The kind I stay far away from."

"Except every day when you go to work." *What the fuck?*

"I have a different last name. No one knows who I am."

"Is that on purpose?" I was shocked no one had figured it out.

She shrugged. "It's how my daddy set it up."

"And you haven't asked him why?"

"He passed away five years ago." She cleared her throat. "Until then, I'd never met Coach... my uncle."

Jesus, she didn't even think of him as her uncle. "And no one ever said why?"

She glanced at me. "I know what you're thinking, and I'm sure it's easy to see black and white from where you're sitting, but my daddy had just died. I had no one, and he'd told me right before he passed that he'd lined up a job for me. He said to keep my head down, do my work and I'd be taken care of. I wouldn't have to worry about a roof over my head as long as I stayed a good girl and didn't go blabbing who I was related to. So that's what I did." Her voice went quiet. "For four and a half years."

Christ. "Until the quarterback."

"I don't really think you're in any position to cast judgment." She turned toward the window.

"I'm not casting shit." I fucked women for money. Or I did until last night. I fired up the engine. "Except to say you need a vacation."

"Coach said not to go anywhere."

"Do you always do what you're told?" Just the thought turned me on.

"Yes."

"Time to change that." Except where I was concerned. She could take fucking orders from me all day long. I pulled out of the lot.

"I just want to go home."

I shook my head. "I'm taking you to my condo. Media's camped out at your place."

Alarmed, she glanced at me. "At my house?"

"Yeah." I turned in to traffic. "Neil texted after he dropped your car off."

"Shit."

I laughed once. "You do swear."

"This isn't funny." She crossed her arms.

I grabbed her hand. "Hey, it's gonna be okay."

She pulled away. "That's easy for you to say. Your life hasn't been turned upside down. You don't have media stalking you, and you didn't just lose your job."

I didn't say dick. I was bringing a client to my house to shack up, my cock was in a holding pattern and I was probably going to be sued by a professional football team. She was right, I hadn't lost my job—only my fucking mind.

"I'm sorry," she said quietly.

"For what?"

"For getting you involved."

"I told you I wouldn't be here if I didn't want to." Simple truth, I took orders from no one now, least of all the US government.

"So you said. I know the media is at my place, but can you take me there anyway? I at least need a change of clothes."

I didn't want to risk it. "Hold on." I pulled out my cell and dialed. After three rings, my buddy from the Marines who owned his own personal security firm answered.

Luna laughed. "You're calling me. Does this mean you're ready to come work for a living instead of playing with the chicas?"

"No." But I'd been thinking about it. "I need a favor."

"Hold up." I heard a door close and the background noise got quieter. "What's up?"

"I need you to get some things out of a friend's house." I didn't look at Red when I said *friend*.

Luna chuckled. "And by friend, you mean a woman."

"Yeah."

He sobered. "Domestic?"

"No. Media situation."

He whistled low. "All right, fess up, who you involved with?"

"I can bring her keys to you."

"All right, all right, I got it. You can't talk. Where you at? I'm not at the office."

I gave him my location. "But her house is in Coral Gables."

"Okay, meet me at St. Augustus church, back parking lot. You being followed?"

I glanced in my rearview mirror. "Not yet."

"Seven minutes." He hung up.

"Who was that?"

"Friend of mine from the Marines. He does personal security."

"Like a bodyguard?"

"Yeah." Among other things, but his real skill was with a sniper rifle. "I'm going to have him grab some stuff at your place for you."

"I can do that myself."

"This is safer." She didn't say anything, but when I glanced at her, she was pressing her lips together. "What?"

"I don't want some stranger going through my house."

"He's a professional."

She turned in her seat. "And how would you feel if a *professional* went through your underwear drawer?"

She was barking up the wrong tree if she thought I gave a shit about her privacy versus a mob of cameras in her face. "Not a whole lot of privacy in the military."

"Point taken." She turned back to the window.

I drove to the church, and she didn't say another word.

When I pulled into the back parking lot, one of the Luna and Associates black SUVs was already parked. I pulled up to the driver side.

Luna scanned the parking lot as he got out then he shook my hand through the window. "Brandt." He nodded at Red. "Ma'am." All business, he looked back at me. "What do you need?"

"Everything she'd need for a week." He'd figure it out.

"A week?" Red squeaked.

I spared her a glance. "Precautionary. Do you have your house keys or are they with your car keys?"

"I have them separate." She dug in her purse then handed them to me and looked at Luna. "Can you please water my plants?"

Luna took the keys from me. "Yes, ma'am. Is there an alarm? Any items you specifically need? Medications?"

Red's cheeks flamed. "I don't take any medications, thank you. And yes, there is an alarm. The keypad is inside by the front door and the code is one-two-three-four."

Luna frowned. "Understood. If I may suggest, ma'am, when you return home, reset your passcode to something more secure?"

Red blushed then nodded.

"Thank you. Address?" Luna asked.

Red rattled off her address.

"Copy." Luna slapped the top of the Mustang and straightened. "Sixty minutes. Your gate security code still the same?"

"Yeah. Don't drag strays back to my place." I didn't need the media on my doorstep.

He scoffed. "Who do you think you're talking to?"

A marine who could smile like an angel one second, then

blow your fucking brains out the next. "Patrol." I didn't forget the well-earned nickname he'd gotten downrange.

"You know it." He winked then got in his SUV.

Red watched him drive away. "He had two guns."

"I know." A Taurus 9mm on the left side of his waist and a Walther P99 AS in a holster on his right thigh. The fucking scary part? His accuracy was equally deadly, left or right handed.

"I didn't think bodyguards carried weapons."

"He does." Luna didn't go to the fucking john without being armed. I pulled out of the lot.

SIXTEEN

Sienna

J ARED DROVE US TO HIS CONDO AND PARKED WITHOUT another word. He opened my car door and put his hand on my back as he led me to the elevator, but he still didn't speak. We walked into his condo, and he tossed his bloodied T-shirt he was wearing earlier in the trash in the kitchen.

"You're throwing that out?" I noticed my car keys on the counter and set my purse down next to them.

"Bloodstains don't come out," he stated without emotion.

His muscles were so strong and his body was so perfect, it was hard to imagine him wounded in combat. "Is that something you have experience in?"

"Yes." He tossed his keys and his wallet on the counter.

I waited, but he didn't elaborate. "How were you wounded?"

He went to the fridge. "Our Humvee was hit by an IED."

Oh my God. "What happened?"

His hands paused as he pulled two water bottles out of the fridge. It was only for a fraction of a second, but it was enough for me to notice it.

"You don't have to tell me," I quickly amended.

He held out the bottle of water and met my gaze. "Afghanistan. Second tour. I took shrapnel in the back."

"You didn't have any protective gear on?" I thought the military gave all their soldiers protective vests.

"It penetrated my MTV."

I frowned. "MTV?"

"Modular Tactical Vest. Not the music TV channel." His half smile didn't reach his eyes. "You thirsty?"

I took the bottle from his still outstretched hand, and the question popped out before I could stop myself. "Did you feel it? I mean, were you conscious?"

"Yes."

Of course he felt it. I felt like an idiot for asking. I opened the water and took a sip, looking around his condo. Not a thing was out of place. In fact, it was so neat, it was almost as if no one lived there full-time. No magazines on the coffee table, no dishes out, no shoes by the entrance, not even a single framed picture sat on his built-in bookcases. How could someone not have any books?

"Ask," he demanded.

I looked back at him. "Excuse me?"

His stance rigid, he tipped his chin. "Ask what you want to ask."

"You don't like to read?"

He studied me for a moment. "No. What happened with the quarterback?"

I answered how he answered my questions, with frank honesty. "I wasn't enough to hold his interest."

"So you decided paying for it was the way to go?"

I drew in a breath. "I don't see how that's any of your business."

He took his shirt off. Huge muscles rippled across his arms and shoulders. His chest was hard, his abs perfect, and a deep V cut across his hips and disappeared under his jeans. The thin trail of hair from his belly button down was the sexiest thing I'd ever seen. He looked like a Greek god—then he turned around.

Oh dear God.

With no emotion, he started to speak. "The shrapnel ripped into my back, taking half the flesh then burning the rest."

Giant slash marks of scars covered his entire back and neck, like the flesh had been torn off then thrown back on in jagged pieces.

Speechless, I stared.

"It felt like a thousand knives cut me open then a giant branding iron seared the wounds. The blast wave was so fucking loud, my brain shook inside my skull. The pain wasn't intense, it was life changing." He turned around.

Stunned, I didn't know what to say.

His chest heaving, his jaw clenched, he inhaled and told me the rest. "Then I laid in a hospital bed for thirteen months getting addicted to pain meds and counseled on how I was one of the lucky ones. When they couldn't figure out why I was seeing numbers backwards and letters upside down, they declared me medically retired and sent me on my way."

"Jared, I am so—"

He didn't let me apologize for what he'd been through. "Quarterback. Your turn."

I'd never told anyone this story. Being raised by a single dad who was a preacher, I didn't have girlfriends. Gossipy, judgmental church ladies stood in for my peers, role models and support system. I learned early on, if you wanted to preserve your sanity, you said nothing about anything.

"I have a no-fraternization policy at work, so we'd meet at his house or mine." I felt foolish telling him this, let alone right after he'd shown me what he'd been through. "I was naïve and stupid, and I thought it meant something. One night after a team charity event, I waited for him at his house, but he never showed. I went home, and by the next morning, the pictures of him and one of the cheerleaders out at a club started surfacing." I shrugged. "That was it."

"Lot of women get their heart broken."

"Meaning?" He was beautiful. Every muscle rippled with power, and the strength to have endured what he'd been through humbled me.

His gaze intense and never wavering, he studied me like he could read my every thought. "Meaning they don't hire an escort to heal it."

I internally cringed at his spot-on assessment. "Who said I was trying to heal a broken heart?"

"You wanted control."

I didn't tell him that control was the last thing I felt like I had with Alex. "No, I didn't."

"You wanted to initiate, dictate time and place, have the illusion of the upper hand because you held the money and you wanted to be put first." He gaze cut through every single one of my defenses. "That's control."

I nervously took a sip of my water.

He moved around the counter. "But that's not what you need." Taking the bottle from my hand, he placed it on the counter. "Know why?"

Alarm spread through my veins, and I tried to push out

words meant to keep him back, but my voice came out breathy. "I don't need you to tell me what I want."

Like a panther stalking its prey, he moved closer. "I said need, not want." His fingers traced down my neck.

I swallowed and fought the urge to fall into his touch. "I don't need you." Musk and man, he smelled like everything I'd ever wanted.

His fingers slowly moved between my breasts and down my chest. "You need to be taken care of." His hand moved down my stomach. "And I want to take care of you."

I fought for control. "That's sexist and old-fashioned and—" His fingers skimmed over the pulsing ache between my legs and I gasped.

"Exactly why it's going to work. The second I saw you standing on my doorstep, I knew what you needed." He rubbed my mound through my skirt and underwear.

I wanted to rip my clothes off and spread my legs, but something was missing. "I don't need anything."

"You're waiting for the right man to take control." He dragged his mouth across my neck, but he didn't kiss me. "You're waiting for permission."

My nipples aching, my core drenched, my breath short, I didn't want him to give me permission, I wanted him to tell me to spread my legs. "No, I'm not."

"Yes, you are." He nipped my sensitive flesh then leaned to my ear. "Lift your skirt and spread your legs, Sienna."

My eyes closed and I whimpered. Then I did exactly what he told me to do. I pulled my skirt up my thighs and breathed out through my mouth as the cool air in his condo hit my wet underwear.

"Higher." His lips touched my cheek. "Look at me."

I pulled my skirt up to my waist and opened my eyes.

His intense stare swallowed me whole, then his gaze dropped and feasted on my pink panties. "Take those off."

With my skirt bunched around my waist, feeling illicit and more turned on than I should, I slid my underwear down my thighs and stepped out of them.

"Good girl." He brushed his lips across my temple. "Put your hands on my arms."

My fingers tested his rock-hard biceps before my palms settled against the heat of his skin.

He gently stroked through my desire. Then, without warning, he plunged two fingers into me.

"*Ahhh.*" I grasped at him for support and my head fell back.

His thumb on my clit, he thrust his fingers once, twice. "Do you want to come?"

"Please," I begged.

"Look at me," he demanded.

Clutching his huge muscles, I lifted my head up.

His gaze swirled with an emotion I didn't understand, then he buried me with his words. "I did *not* sleep with that client last night."

My legs closed and I jerked back.

As if anticipating my reaction, he caught the back of my neck and drove his fingers deeper. "Sienna," he warned.

"No." Anger and hurt flooded me. "*Let go.*"

His stare, honest and real, didn't waver. "She wasn't what I wanted."

My hands dropped to his wrist and I tried to pull his fingers out of me. "You lied!"

"I did not lie. I omitted." He squeezed my neck. "Take a breath."

I panicked. "Take your hand out of me!"

He did the opposite, he stroked his fingers deep inside me. "I said, take a breath, Sienna."

It felt so good I wanted to cry. "Why are you doing this?"

He didn't release me and his penetrating gaze didn't let me hide. "Because I wanted you here knowing who I was. I wanted you giving yourself to me despite what I was."

His honesty gutted me and tears dripped down my face. I gripped his wrist with all my strength and held on to the only defense I had left. "Do not make me come. Don't you dare."

His forehead touched mine and his voice dropped to an achingly beautiful timbre. "She wasn't what I wanted," he repeated. "She wasn't what I needed." His thumb drew a firm circle. "You give me your body, Sienna Montclair, and I'll give you my word." His lips touched mine. "There'll be no one else between us."

I sobbed for the one impossibility I'd wanted more than anything else since I'd first laid eyes on him.

Holding my neck, he stroked me reverently and gave me a promise I didn't know how to trust. "Just you and me."

"I don't know how to believe you," I cried.

"Let it out, baby." His lips touching mine, he held back the kiss that I both desperately wanted and feared. "Give me those tears." He rotated his fingers and pushed deep inside me. "Stop thinking, beautiful. Just feel."

My mouth popped open and a pressure I'd never felt straddled the line between pleasure and pain. "No! Jared! *Oh my God.*" My legs started to shake. "*Noooo.*"

He bit the sensitive skin below my ear. "Tell me to fuck you, Sienna."

Oh my God, what was happening? "Pleasepleaseplease."

He increased the pressure. "Say it," he demanded.

"*Fuck me,*" I cried.

His mouth crashed over mine and I was coming. But I wasn't just coming. I was mewing like an animal and frantically riding his hand as I followed every stroke of his tongue with a fevered desperation. My body shook, my blood rushed through my veins and the vibrations in my throat turned to grunts as my orgasm fell, but his pace increased.

"Ah, ah, ah, ah, ah." My voice a staccato to his rhythm, my shaking hit a new plateau. A second orgasm didn't build on the tails of the last, it rushed from behind and eclipsed every orgasm I'd ever had as it burst through its finish line with an explosion of colors and heat.

I was the crowd and his hand was the victor.

Over and over, his name fell from my lips, because that's all I had.

Him. Nothing else. Just him.

SEVENTEEN

Jared

MY DICK THROBBING, MY HAND SOAKED, I PULLED a condom out of my pocket. She was so fucking tight, I'd needed to make her come twice so she'd be wet as hell before I took her. Her legs shaking, she looked up at me in a daze.

"Turn around." My need for her hitting a new level of desperation, I barked out the command.

At the sound of my voice, she shivered and gave me her back.

Smooth and round, her ass was so fucking perfect, I wanted to leave my mark on it. Unbuttoning my jeans, I took my cock out and stroked myself as I leaned to her ear. "Do you know what I'm going to do to you?" The anticipation of sinking inside her tight cunt had me shaking.

"Jared," she whispered.

"Right here, beautiful." I rubbed my dick against her sweet ass. Fuck, I wanted to take her bareback. "You on the pill?"

She moved her hips against mine. "No."

"Fucking shame." I sheathed myself then shoved two fingers in her soaking heat. "Because I want to feel this wet cunt all over my bare cock." Goddamn, she was tight. "I want to come so deep inside you, you drip for days."

She moaned and put her hands on the counter.

"That's right, gorgeous." I took the clip out of her hair. Thick red curls cascaded down her back, and I gripped a handful. "Brace yourself."

"What…." She groaned as I stroked her G-spot. "What are you going to do to me?"

I smiled because she remembered the question. My hand in her hair, my mouth on her neck, I licked her ivory skin then bit the bottom of her ear. "I'm going to fuck you so hard, you forget every man who came before me." I shoved in to the hilt.

Her nails scraped across the counter and she screamed.

My eyes rolled back in my head.

Fuck.

Fuck.

My dick pulsing in the tightest pussy I'd ever felt, my mind went fucking blank. Completely, come right fucking now, *blank.*

Sucking in a breath, I put my hand on her arching back and pushed her down on the counter. "Breathe," I commanded.

"No, no, no," she cried. "You don't fit."

"Yes I do, gorgeous." Jesus Christ, she felt incredible. I rotated my hips when all I wanted to do was pull out then slam back home. "Feel that?" I eased back an inch then slowly went deep. "Your pussy was made for me." I fit like a fucking glove. Thrusting deep and slow, I worked her.

She sucked air in through her teeth. "*Oh my God.*"

"You like that?" I reached around and pressed hard on her clit. My teeth against her ear, I bit her once. "Or you like this?" I pinched her clit.

"Ah!" She jerked under my touch then a rush of wet heat soaked my dick.

Fuck yeah. "You like that, Red?" She fucking clamped down on my cock. "You like it rough?" I licked up her neck.

"Please," she begged.

I pulled out then slammed home, bottoming out in her. "Like this?"

She shook like a leaf. "*Yes.*"

I thrust three more times, pounding her hard and grinding my hips every time I hit home. On the fourth thrust, I pulled her hair and brought her back up. "You want to feel my hands on you, Red?" I grabbed a handful of her ass and squeezed. "You want my marks on you?" I wanted to fuck her so hard, I lost myself.

"Don't hurt me." Her voice shook.

I eased my grip on her hair and stroked in and out of her gently once. "Am I hurting you now?"

"No."

"Do you trust me?"

"I… I don't know."

I pulled out, released her hair and spun her around. Grasping her chin, I forced her to look at me. "Say no."

Breathing hard, she swallowed. "I'm not saying to stop."

I put force into my tone. "I said, say *no.*"

"No," she whispered.

"Louder," I demanded.

"No."

Goddamn it. "Yell it."

"No!"

I stroked her cheek and lowered my voice. "You whisper it, you speak it, you yell it, I stop. Any way you say it, I stop." I held her gaze. "Understand?"

"Yes."

"You saying no?"

She shook her head. "No."

"Turn around."

Slow, tentative, she turned.

I put force into my tone, but I caressed her back. "Hands on the counter."

She gripped the edge.

I stilled. "Arms out in front of you. Cross your wrists."

She instantly complied.

My dick pulsed, and I ran both hands over her smooth ass, kneading her flesh. "You ever been spanked, Red?"

"No," she whispered hesitantly.

"Do you want to be?" I held my fucking breath.

"I don't know."

I stroked the back of her thighs. "You ever ridden that edge between pleasure and pain?"

"I don't think so."

My thumbs pushed into the flesh of her ass. "I want to take you there."

She didn't answer.

I waited two heartbeats then I grabbed my cock and stroked the seam of her ass. "I want to make you feel good."

"Okay," she breathed.

I didn't think twice. I shoved in to the hilt and my hand drew back. My palm hitting her virgin flesh echoed through the condo as the cheek of her ass quivered. She gasped and I thrust hard. Her skin pinked, then I slapped the other side and pinched her clit.

Like a fucking awaking, her whole body bowed.

"*Ahhh.*"

"Say my name." *Fuck yes.*

"Jared!"

I slapped her ass. "Tell me you want more."

Her whole body shaking, her voice trembled. "Please, more."

I fucked her.

I fucked her like my life depended on it. Pounding her quivering pussy, spanking her ass, pulling her hair tighter every time she clenched around my hard cock, I fucking took her. I took her innocence, I took her manners, and I fucked them right out of her.

I didn't wait for her to come. I pushed her so fucking hard over the edge, she exploded like a goddamn dream. Back arched, red hair everywhere, guttural moans coming from her throat, she came all over my cock.

I couldn't hold back.

I grabbed both hips and thrust two more times. Then I shoved in to the hilt and lost my fucking mind.

I didn't just fill the goddamn condom.

My chest compressed, my world bent, and for one single moment, my life was Red. All fucking Red. No anger, no bullshit, no scars. Just her.

She was fucking perfect.

My heart pounding, my dick still buried deep, I shoved the crazy shit in my head down deep and swept all her hair aside to kiss her trembling back. "Hold on, gorgeous." Her cunt was still pulsing around me, and I didn't want to pull out. I wanted to fuck her until my legs gave out, but the condom needed taking care of. The last thing I needed to do was knock up a woman like her.

Unwelcome, unexpected, the thought of her with my kid hit my fucked-up mind, and all of a sudden, I was dead in my tracks. I was seeing her with cheeks flushed, hair everywhere, her stomach round, and a smile that said I was her world.

Jesus fuck.

I abruptly pulled out and she whimpered. "Throwing the condom out. Don't move." I yanked the condom off and tossed it in the kitchen trash.

I didn't do kids. Kids were noise. Noise was my fucking kryptonite. I didn't even do domestic, but when I turned and saw her, my chest hurt. Her arms stretched out in front of her on the counter, still crossed at the wrist, she lay with her sweet ass pink and bare and her skirt around her waist. Her heels and jacket still on, she was sexy as fuck, but guilt hit my conscience.

Goddamn it, I was a fucking asshole.

"Come on, sweetheart." I pulled her up.

Her hair fell in front of her face. "I can't walk," she mumbled.

"I got you, baby." I picked her up. "Kick your shoes off and put your arms around my neck."

Her sexy heels hit the floor and her arms, soft and feminine, wrapped around me. "I'm tired."

"I know." I should've regretted taking her so hard, but I was an asshole. All I wanted was to do it again. "You had a rough day." I carried her into my bedroom and set her on her feet.

She peeked up at me. "So did you."

"I can handle rough." I unbuttoned her jacket and pushed if off her shoulders. She didn't have a thing on underneath except a matching bra to the underwear lying on my kitchen floor. I undid the clasp. "Sexy, Red."

She gave me a shy smile. "I like pretty underwear."

"I like you naked." I dragged the bra off and my heart almost stopped. She was so damn gorgeous. Full tits, round hips, she was a wet dream, and I wanted to take her again.

"You're staring."

"Jesus fucking Christ, woman." My cock throbbing, my mouth watering, I shook my head. "Turn around."

"Why?" She crossed her arms over her chest.

"Because I want to see my marks on you." I pulled her arms away from her huge tits. "Don't ever hide yourself from me. You're fucking beautiful." I cupped one of her tits and brushed a thumb over the hard nipple. "Now turn and show me that sexy ass."

She turned.

Flushed, exactly how her face got when she was embarrassed, her ass bloomed with my markings. "So fucking sexy," I muttered, dragging the backs of my fingers over each cheek.

She turned back around, and green eyes full of doubt stared up at me. "You spanked me," she whispered.

My heartbeat faltered and I locked down my expression. "Yes, I did." I wasn't sorry. Not for one second, but I'd be a fool not to recognize she was the most innocent woman I'd ever touched. "You got a problem with that?"

She didn't hesitate. "No." Heat hit her cheeks. "I think I liked it."

My dick throbbed, and I pulled back the covers as I stepped out of my boots. "Get in."

She crawled across my bed with her ass in the air, the little vixen. "No comment?" She looked at me over her shoulder before sliding under the sheets.

I fought a smile. "Put your head on the pillow and close your eyes before I decide to fuck you again."

She stared up at me. "What if I want that?"

My doorbell rang.

I winked at her. "Hold that thought."

I fastened my jeans as I walked to the entryway. I checked the peephole then opened the door to Luna.

He waltzed in with a suitcase. "That was more than a few media, bro. You wanna tell me what's up?" He set her shit down and glanced around my place. His gaze landed on her underwear, and he smiled as he tipped his chin. "Besides you?"

"Asshole."

He grinned. "Still waiting."

Fuck. "Her ex was at a restaurant we were at for lunch. He caused a scene, and I took him down."

"Since I didn't recognize her, it must be the ex. Who is he?"

I drew in a breath and let it out. "Dan Ahlstrom."

Luna's eyes went wide as fuck. "She dated Miami's quarterback?"

"She didn't date him." I hated that fucking prick.

"But you took him down?"

"Him and the linebacker, Sunshine. That defensive end, TJ, was there too, but he stayed out of it."

"*Dios mios.*" He exhaled. "You break anything?"

"Strom's nose, the linebacker's too."

"Fuck, Brandt, you know that's a felony."

115

"Self-defense. I wasn't charged."

"You got a lawyer?"

"I said I wasn't arrested."

"I wasn't talking about for when you get arrested, which by the way, you're lucky you didn't get booked. I was talking about when you get sued. If you took him out of the lineup, he'll come after you."

"Fucking pussy, let him. Twenty witnesses were filming the whole damn thing. And it's preseason."

"Doesn't mean he won't sue. Professional football teams have whole rooms full of lawyers with nothing else to do."

Goddamn it. "There a point to this conversation?" Red was naked in my fucking bed.

"Yeah. You're dumb as shit."

"Fuck you."

He glanced at Red's underwear again and smiled like he always did, like a damn saint. "Looks like you got that covered."

Christ. "Thanks for getting her stuff. I owe you."

Luna sobered. "The media was on a warpath, my friend. They're going to find you next. You step foot out of your place, you're going to need a detail."

I dragged my hand over my face and the sweet scent of Red filled my head. I knew he was right. I didn't want someone on my ass, but this wasn't about just me anymore. "Can you spare someone?"

"Yeah, but that's not going to solve your bigger issue. You need a lawyer to get ahead of this."

"I'm not hiring a lawyer."

"Your funeral, amigo. Don't say I didn't warn you."

Shit. "Fine. You know someone?"

"I know a lot of lawyers, but someone dumb enough to

take this on? No." He thought a second. "Well, maybe." He pulled his phone out and scrolled through the contacts. "His name's Mathew Barrett. I just texted you his contact info. Call him."

Fuck, I didn't want to deal with this. "Thanks."

He nodded as he messed with his phone. "I'll post my guy Tyler out front and leave him on you for three days. Keep your head down until the media moves on." He glanced back up at me. "How's everything else?"

Out of all the brothers I served with, he was the only one who ever asked. Not that I saw Luna often, he was busy running his company, but he always asked how I was whenever I saw him. Not that I told him or anyone else a fucking thing. "I'm fine." It didn't escape my notice that the redhead in my bed had gotten more out of me in the past twenty-four hours than my buddies had in nine years.

Luna smiled and slapped my shoulder. "One day I'll get it out of you."

"There's nothing to get."

His smile disappeared. "Right. And I don't lie awake at night counting kills."

EIGHTEEN

Sienna

I DREW MY KNEES TO MY CHEST AND PULLED THE SHEET UP to my chin. His friend's words bounced around in my head like warning bells. *Counting kills.*

Shirtless and all muscles, Jared strode back into the bedroom. His intense brown-eyed gaze on me, he stripped off his jeans and crawled into the bed naked.

I tried to not stare at the size of him but it was impossible. His length, his width, he was huge. I still couldn't believe he'd fit inside me, let alone what we'd done. What I'd let him do.

"Let it out," he demanded, snaking an arm under my knees and another behind my back. He lay down and brought my back to his chest.

"Let what out?"

"What you need to say. You heard our conversation."

It wasn't a question, so I didn't pretend to answer it. "Your friend's right. Dan will sue you." I didn't work with the team lawyers much, except to pass correspondence between them and Coach, but I knew how things worked. They'd tell Dan to sue Jared to keep him from suing Dan.

118

"I'll handle it. What else?"

"You can't take on the league by yourself."

"I'm not taking on the league. What else is bothering you?"

"I didn't say anything was bothering me."

"You didn't have to. You were curled in a ball with the covers at your chin like a terrified kid." He stroked my tender backside. "Are you sore?"

Desire swirled low in my belly. "I'm fine," I whispered, not sure I was ready to talk about that or how it'd made me feel.

"Don't lie to me, Red."

I exhaled. "I didn't want to like you hitting me, but I did. I shouldn't have felt safe or even turned on, but you just touching me now…." I sucked in a breath as I trailed off. "Your friend said he counted kills."

"He was a sniper in the Marines," Jared answered matter-of-factly, as if this was a common occupation. Then he lowered his voice. "You're always safe with me. You enjoyed it because you didn't have to think. I took control and gave you a release your whole body would feel."

"What did you get out of it?"

"Control and your trust."

He said it reverently, but I didn't know how to take any of it. I felt weak for enjoying the way he'd touched me. And I knew our military protected us and I knew I was living a free life because of the sacrifices so many like Jared had made. But I'd never been this close to it. This wasn't a torn ligament or a bloodied face on football Sunday. This wasn't about the millions of dollars that poured through an industry whose sole purpose was to entertain. This was real life, real death, real people sacrificing everything they had to protect what I took for granted.

"I've never been around someone who served before. This is… new to me."

A hint of defensiveness crept into his tone. "I'm no different than anyone else."

I looked up at him. "You're very different." Alpha, aggressive, guarded, protective, even the way he carried himself. It wasn't just confidence, it was the knowledge of capability behind that confidence. He didn't posture or assert himself to prove a point or to make it look good for the cameras on Monday night. He did it because it was ingrained in who he was. "You're a hero." A true hero.

"I'm no fucking hero, Red." He rolled to his back and rubbed his hand over his face. "You hungry?" He started to get up.

I grabbed his hand. "That bothers you?"

The angles to his face went sharp and he turned on me. "I'm not some saint who wanted to make a difference. I was an eighteen-year-old kid who wanted a stable job. I didn't enlist to protect my country. I signed up to get a paycheck and shoot shit. Then I got blown up and the Marines dropped me faster than you can say *wounded*. So don't glorify what you think I am. I'm a damaged ex-marine who likes to fuck hard." He threw the covers off, grabbed his boxers and walked out. A few seconds later, I heard pots banging in the kitchen.

His anger should have scared me, but it didn't. I should've been running, not walking out the door, but I wasn't. I was pulling open dresser drawers full of perfectly folded clothes and borrowing a T-shirt that smelled better than any article of clothing I'd ever put on.

I walked into the open-plan living space and saw my suitcase by the front door.

Without turning around to look at me, Jared spoke. "You eat eggs?"

I stared at the scars on his back as I walked up behind him. Aching to touch them, I turned the burner down under the pan. "If you don't burn them."

He whisked a bowl of eggs to within an inch of their lives. "I wasn't going to."

I went to the fridge. "Do you have bread?"

"Yeah." He dumped the eggs in the too-hot pan.

I pulled bread, butter and a package of cut-up cantaloupe from the fridge. "Toaster?" There wasn't a thing on his pristine counters besides a coffee maker.

"No."

I looked at him. "How do you make toast?"

He jabbed at the eggs, breaking them up into little bits. "I don't."

I took the spatula from him and gently folded over the cooked parts. "Like this." He stood so close, I could smell his scent, strong and masculine and tinged with sex. My core ached for his touch.

His breath landed on the side of my neck. "Nice shirt."

"Nice boxers. You can turn the oven broiler on and we can make the toast that way."

He didn't move. "You telling me what to do?"

I hid a smile. "Yes."

Quick and precise, he punched the buttons on the oven then grabbed my shoulders and spun me. His lips were on mine before I could gasp, and his tongue sank into my mouth. Pulling me against his hips, he devoured me. His hard cock pressed into my stomach and he thrust in rhythm with his tongue.

SYBIL BARTEL

I didn't melt into him, I fell apart at the seams.

His dominant hold on me, and the memory of him inside me, had me so turned on that if he touched me once between my legs, I would've come. But he didn't.

He pulled back and spun me. "You're burning the eggs."

Breathless, I looked at the pan. "Right." His strong body behind me, he slowly rubbed his hard length against my backside.

His lips touched my ear. "Stir."

I shivered. Then I did exactly what he told me to do. The spatula still in my hand, I stirred.

His voice softened. "Good girl." His hand traveled up my shirt and his thick fingers grasped my nipples through the material and pinched.

My back arched and I moaned.

He squeezed my nipples harder, then abruptly let go and his palm made contact with my ass.

The sting followed by the ache in my nipples made me gasp as his hand slid down my stomach and two of his fingers shoved into me. "*Oh my God.*" I dropped the spatula and blindly reached forward.

His arm came around my waist and he spun me so fast, my head swam. His fingers thrust inside me, touching a spot so deep and so personal as his palm ground against my clit that I stopped caring about anything else.

Overnight, he'd turned me into someone else. Someone who let a stranger spank her. Someone who left her home, not to avoid the media, but to be with a man she didn't know. Someone who wanted a male escort to be hers.

"*Stop,*" I cried.

He froze, but then his fingers rotated deep inside me. "Tell me you don't want to come and I will."

I started to shake. "I don't."

"You're lying. Tell me you don't want me inside you."

Oh God. I wanted him. I wanted him so badly I could taste him. "Why?"

"Because you want to come, you want me inside you, and you want to be exactly where you are. Stop thinking and let go." His strokes slowed, but he increased the pressure as he pressed into my front wall. "Grab those hard nipples and come."

The sound that crawled up my throat and spilled from my lips wasn't as shocking as the sheer freedom of doing exactly what he said. My own fingers slid under my borrowed shirt. Pinching my tender nipples, my body aching for release, I cried out as the orgasm slammed into me. My muscles burning with exquisite tension, my core grasped at his fingers and I completely fell apart.

I came so hard tears slid down my cheeks.

His fingers still deep inside me, he pulled my head back to his chest and stared down at me. For three heartbeats, no words passed between us. We just stood, connected.

Then he leaned down and kissed my tear-stained cheek. "I own those."

NINETEEN

Jared

I SWEPT MY THUMB ACROSS HER CHEEK AND SHIT FUCKED with my head. I didn't want to pull my hand out of her body, I didn't even want to let her go. This woman was better than me in every possible way. I needed to leave her the fuck alone, but I couldn't bring myself to.

My dick pulsing, I eased my fingers out of her swollen pussy. "You burned my eggs," I deadpanned.

Her chest heaving, she barely nodded. "Yeah."

"Need a minute?" My arm still around her waist, I held her up, but the kitchen was starting to smell like burned shit.

"The burner," she managed.

I reached over and turned it off. Her back still up against my body, she started to shake. "Hey, you okay?" I brushed her hair away from her face.

A smile curving her lips, she held back laughter. "My legs don't work."

The corner of my mouth twitched.

Eyes bright with laughter and tears, she looked up at me. "I'm not sure I care."

I smiled.

Soft and feminine and so fucking beautiful, she laughed. "You do smile!"

My childhood, enlisting, getting hit, the hospitals, the women, everything in my life flashed and culminated into this one single moment. Red hair, green eyes and a smile so fucking beautiful, my heart hurt.

I cupped her face. "Yeah, Red, I smile."

She turned serious. "You're so very handsome."

I was a demanding, scarred fuck. And the second she realized I couldn't balance a checkbook, let alone read it, she'd leave. "You're too good for me."

She frowned.

I released her and changed the subject. "You gonna make me food?"

She cleared her throat. "I'm sure you worked up an appetite."

Like she wouldn't believe. "I'll feed that after I eat." I tossed the pan of burnt eggs in the sink and grabbed another pan, handing it to her.

She took it, smiling shyly. "Will you, now?"

My dick a fucking rocket, I stared at her until her cheeks flushed. "You have to ask?"

She pulled more eggs out of the fridge. "I have no doubt that your appetite is—"

"Insatiable?" I stared at her. I liked her in my kitchen.

"I was going to say voracious." She turned on the burner and bent slightly to make sure it was on, giving me an eyeful.

My dick throbbed for release. "With you it is." I realized the hole I'd dug myself into the second the words left my mouth.

"Right." Her tone went instantly formal as she cracked eggs into a bowl.

"I don't bullshit, Red." At least not with her I didn't.

"Mm-hm." She poured some milk from the fridge into the eggs. "Where are your spices?"

"You got something to say, say it." I opened a cupboard and handed her salt and pepper.

She set the salt and pepper down. "I meant spices. Herbs? Seasonings?"

"I don't have any. Why are you avoiding the subject?"

She whisked the eggs and her prim and proper voice returned. "I'm not avoiding it. I have nothing to say."

"Bullshit." I grabbed the bread and started to open the bag.

She snatched it from me. "Wash your hands."

Slow, deliberate, I lifted my hand to my mouth and sucked the fingers that'd been buried deep in her pussy. My gaze on her, my dick got even harder.

"Stop it," she squeaked.

I licked one finger then the other, loving the hell out of her shocked expression. "I'm just getting started."

She turned the water on. "Wash!"

Half my mouth tipped with a smile. "You telling me what to do again?" I'd fuck her on the kitchen counter this time.

As if knowing my thoughts, she turned the water off and schooled her features. "Suit yourself."

I chuckled. "Giving up so easily?"

"There's nothing to give up, and even if there was, I'm not a quitter."

I seized the opening. "You walked out on me last night."

"That was… different." She poured the eggs into the pan.

I wanted this cleared up, once and for all. "You told me to call a client, Red," I reminded her. "That was you quitting."

Her shoulders stiffened. "We hadn't started anything *to* quit."

"The second you showed up at my door, something started." I wasn't going to let her deny it.

"No, it didn't. And I'd changed my mind is all."

Right. "Was that before or after I kissed you? Or was it when I made you come for the first time?" I stepped closer to her and lowered my voice. "You felt it. I felt it. Why deny it?"

She turned the burner off and spun on me. "Because I don't want to like you, okay? Is that so hard to understand?"

I grabbed the back of her neck. "Why? Because you think I don't like you? You think I'm lying about what I promised?"

Her face twisted as if with grief. "*You're an escort.*"

I knew it was coming. It had to. I sold sex. I wasn't an idiot, I knew at a fucking minimum, she'd be insecure about my past. It'd be an uphill battle to get her past it, and I didn't have a fucking clue how to address it except with the hard truth. "Now I'm your escort."

"What does that mean? I don't even know what that means! You sleep with me until you decide you're bored? You tell me I'm yours but you still go make money at night with, with, *with them.*"

"It means I own every fucking orgasm of yours and you own mine." I reached for her.

Hard and fierce, I kissed the fuck out of her.

When she kissed me back, I growled and grabbed her ass, lifting her up. Her arms wrapped around my neck, her legs went around my waist and I was walking us to the bedroom without a single thought except getting inside her. Tossing her on the bed, I yanked my shirt over my head then pushed my boxers off. I fisted my cock, crawled on top of her and rubbed the head around her soaked entrance. My jaw clenched in restraint, I forced words out. "This isn't going to be gentle," I warned.

So soft, I barely heard it, she whispered, "I like you rough."

I shoved to the hilt in one thrust.

She gripped my arms, her head fell back and her mouth opened with a gasp.

Hot, wet, and tight as hell, she clamped down on my dick and I saw stars. *Motherfucking hell.* I grabbed two handfuls of her hair. "You pulse on me and I'm gonna come so fucking hard, you won't know what hit you."

A sexy half gasp, half moan escaped her lips. "You don't," she panted, "have a condom on."

"I know." *Goddamn it, I knew.* "You want me to pull out?" God fucking help me, I wanted her to say no.

"Just, please…." Her eyes fluttered shut and her hips tried to move under my weight.

I gripped her chin and barked, "*Hey.*" I didn't have self-control. I didn't have restraint. I was a loose fucking cannon waiting to detonate and she was the fuse.

"*Jared?*"

My name, said like that, from her? *Jesus.* My grip on her softened. "Yeah, baby." I touched my lips to hers.

Her green-eyed gaze landed on me. "I need you," she whispered.

My heart climbed up my chest and lodged in my throat.

Her small hand cupped my face. "Just like this."

Slow and deliberate, I eased back then thrust deep, once, twice. "Trust me?"

"Yes," she breathed, holding my gaze.

"I'm gonna make you feel good, but I'm not gonna come inside you. You good with that?" Christ, I never wanted to pull out.

She sucked in a breath and glanced down to where I was slowly riding her. "I don't do this." She looked back up at me. "I've never done this." She bit her bottom lip.

I tugged the lip free with my thumb. "I'm clean." I slid home and rotated my hips.

Her chest rose and fell twice. She looked at me like no other woman had ever looked at me. "You're so big."

I forced a half smile and gave her a slow burn as I ground my hips. "Answer my question, Red." I sucked lightly on one of her nipples.

Shy and so damn sexy, it hurt to look at, she smiled. "You're being gentle."

Air locked out of my lungs and I stilled. Not because I was being gentle but because I was losing my fucking mind over it. Hard as shit, my dick ready to explode, I could've thrust one more time and simply let go. Inside her.

I fought the tremor that started at the base of my spine.

"Jared?" Her fingers slid into my hair.

"Yeah?" Fuck. Fuck, fuck, fuck.

She looked alarmed. "What's wrong?"

"Nothing." And that was the problem. Not a fucking thing was wrong. I wasn't pissed the fuck off. I wasn't hearing a distant ringing in my ears, my back didn't fucking burn, my head wasn't screwed sideways. I was fucking slow. *And I was enjoying it.*

"Okay." Small and hurt, her voice crawled into my head.

I lowered myself to my forearms and dragged my nose

across the sweet scent of the heat on her neck. Better than any whiskey, she was intoxicating. My hips keeping the slow rhythm I'd only ever done with her, I kissed her jaw. "You want the truth?"

Her hand let go of my hair. "I don't know."

I gave it to her anyway. "I've never fucked like this."

She said nothing.

I sunk myself deeper. "I could get addicted." I sounded like a fucking pussy, but I gave zero fucks. I was riding a sweet woman I had no business fucking with, but my heart and body were drawn to her in a way I couldn't explain. I knew I should let her go, but I'd never done the right thing.

Her hands landed tentatively on the back of my neck. Slowly, her fingers brushed across my flesh and moved to my shoulders. "Is this okay?"

Forcing my breath to stay even, I stilled. "Yeah."

She traced the scars over my shoulders and across my back. "Does this hurt?"

Fighting the urge to pin her hands down, I stared at her. "No."

Her fingers glanced over the deepest scar. "Do you like it?"

I liked everything she did, but not this tender bullshit. "I'm not made of glass, Red." I had too much scar tissue to feel shit except the pressure of her touch.

"I know."

No, she didn't. I didn't want her fucking pity. Ever.

Her hands moved to my ass and she pushed down as she brought her hips up. "I have a confession."

Concentrating on not coming inside her, I thrust once. "Confess away."

"I love your cock." She grinned.

Caught completely off guard, I fucking laughed.

"That's not funny!"

"Trust me." I smiled down at her and all the bullshit about her touching my scars evaporated. "Hearing you say 'cock' is fucking funny, gorgeous."

She tried to push me off her.

"No way." I held on to her hips. "You're not getting rid of my cock until you come at least once." I thrust deep and ground against her clit.

Her growl turned into a moan. "I hate you."

"Good." The little liar. "Take it out on me."

She tried to look serious. "There is something wrong with you."

"You're right. I've got my dick buried deep in a beautiful woman and I'm fucking talking to her instead of pounding her into submission."

Her expression sobered. "Is that what you like to do?"

"What?" I brushed her hair from her face. "Make you submit?"

"Yes," she said quietly.

"You not been present the past few orgasms, Red?"

"What's that supposed to mean?"

I didn't know whether to laugh or be fucking alarmed at her innocence. "Yes, I like to make you submit to me."

"But what exactly does that mean?"

"I'm in control." No more or no less complicated.

A small, shy smile touched her lips. "I think I'm okay with that."

I didn't return the smile. "I know."

She frowned. "But that's good, right."

Really fucking good. "Yes." Still balls deep in her, I was up to my neck in this conversation, and I needed to get out of it, but I stupidly did the fucking opposite. "You want kids?"

She went so still, I was surprised I could still feel her heart beat. "Why?"

"Because I'm inside you without a condom." It was a simple fact what that led to.

Her pulse sped up and she blanched. "I don't know you."

That made two of us. The second I stuck my dick in her, I didn't know myself. I hovered a fraction of an inch above her mouth and said the only thing I knew to be true. "I'm the asshole who's gonna fuck you to tears."

TWENTY

Sienna

IS MOUTH CRASHED OVER MINE AND I KNEW HE WAS right. I already wanted to cry. The gentle way he was moving in and out of me, the hard exterior he held up despite his scars—my heart was breaking because he was breaking it.

His kiss was nothing like the way he'd come at me in the kitchen the first time. Hard and fierce and breathless, he'd taken me like a man possessed. But now? His tongue slowly stroking through my mouth, matching the rhythmic rocking of his hips, he kissed me like a completely different man.

His hand grasped the side of my face, but he wasn't gripping my hair or holding me down. He wasn't barking commands while he drove me mad with lust. His kiss was so far from that, I felt desired and needed and cherished. I felt loved. And it terrified me. Because Jared Brandt, with his gentle hold and questions about children, wasn't going to make me cry, he was going to break my heart.

A tear slid down my face.

Without breaking his rhythm, his thumb brushed across

my cheek as his lips moved to my ear. "Save those for when I make you fall apart." He pressed deep inside me.

A spot I never knew existed before last night blossomed into a need so consuming, I wanted everything he was offering. "I don't want to fall apart." I wanted to believe the fairy tale he was selling.

"Yes, you do." His mouth, his lips, they sucked my neck as his tongue swirled promises across my flesh.

His hips steadily taking me past the point of no return, I didn't respond. Holding on for dear life, I closed my eyes.

His fingers slipped between us. "Eyes on me, *right now.*"

With no willpower to go against him, my gaze found his and oh my God, he was beautiful. So beautiful, I didn't have any words. Only one thought climbed across my vulnerability and took up residence. I was going to be crushed by this man.

His thumb pressed down on my clit as his hard length caressed deep inside me. "Come," he demanded.

The wall I'd built around my heart shattered into a million pieces as I started to come apart under him. With my core humming, and my body shaking, he pulled out and pressed the head of his cock against my swollen clit.

Hot semen pulsed against me and I saw fireworks.

TWENTY-ONE

Jared

FISTING MY COCK, PRESSING HARD INTO HER CLIT, I fucking exploded. Her pussy still contracting, her body shaking, I watched her fall apart. Coming harder than I ever had, I covered her mound with my release and spread my seed all over her red curls.

One singular thought sank into my fucked-up brain.

Mine.

She was mine.

I didn't have any other words. I only had fucked up shit running through my head as green eyes full of emotion stared up at me.

"That," she whispered, "wasn't fucking."

I didn't lose it.

I broke.

TWENTY-TWO

Sienna

WITHOUT A WORD, HE TURNED ME ON MY SIDE AND lay down behind me.

My heart hammering a warning, I pushed. "Did you hear me?"

"I heard you." His arm snaked under my head.

His release dripped down my thigh. "Your sheets."

"I don't give a fuck about the sheets," he snapped.

"You didn't answer," I said quietly.

"It wasn't a question."

"Fine." Inhaling, I turned as much away from him as I could.

Either pretending not to notice or not caring, he snaked his arm across my waist and pulled me back, then his hand landed on my breast. Rough fingers twisted my nipple and desire shot between my legs despite me having just come.

"Stop it." I shoved his hand away.

The arm under my head folded across my chest and he rolled me toward him. "You don't want me to touch you?" His tone was accusing.

"I don't want you to lie to me."

His nostrils flared and his chest heaved, but his words came out even. "It was more than fucking, is that what you want to hear?"

"You're the one who started this. You called me to meet you, you hit Dan, you brought me here and *you* made me promises. Don't turn this around like I'm saying something I *want to hear*." My finger jabbed into his chest. "This is what you started." I sucked in a breath. "You did this." There. Let him deal with his own truths, the mercurial bastard.

His tone turned to liquid sexual seduction. "What did I do?"

I eyed him. "Are you smiling?"

"No." He fought a smile then turned serious again. "Minus your hair pinned up and the pink suit, I like the feisty Red almost as much as I like the innocent Red."

Wait, what? "What's wrong with my hair up and my pink suit?"

"I hate them."

I bristled. "That's a nice suit, and I always wear my hair up to work. It's called being professional."

"I don't want you professional."

I leaned back. "That is sexist, Jared Brandt."

"If not wanting you to work with your ex and a bunch of steroid-driven ballers is sexist, then I'm fucking sexist."

I blinked and a silly kind of relief that he didn't find me unattractive with my hair up and in a suit washed over me. "So, it's not the suit?" My traitorous heart danced around in my chest.

"No, Red, it's not the suit." He stroked my cheek then brushed my hair behind my ear. "It's what you do in the suit."

"Just so you know, steroid use is illegal in the league." I hated how much I liked what he'd said.

"You know exactly what I mean."

"I have a mortgage." I had bills to pay, and working for Coach was the best-paying job I'd ever get without a college degree.

His intense stare burned into me, and then he said something I never saw coming. "I don't."

Before I could open my mouth and sink myself so far over the edge, someone pounded on the front door.

Jared jerked like he'd been hit, then he was out of bed so fast, I had whiplash. "Stay here." He grabbed a clean pair of jeans, stepped into them and headed for the door.

"I need my suitcase." I wanted more than just his T-shirt or we'd wind up right back in bed and I was sore.

With only a nod, he disappeared then returned with my suitcase as whoever it was pounded on the door again. "Wait here." He closed the door behind him.

A few seconds later, I heard angry male voices and I didn't wait. I grabbed some yoga pants and the T-shirt I'd borrowed from Jared, threw them on, then I opened the bedroom door and stepped into the hall.

"You were supposed to be stationed out front," Jared growled.

"Understood, sir. As I said, I was not authorized to serve the papers myself. My only choice was to let the process server—"

"Letting him up here was *not* your call," Jared bit out.

I stepped into the living room. A dark-haired guy with almost as many muscles as Jared stood military straight in front of Jared. His gaze cut to me and he nodded with a clipped smile. "Ma'am."

Jared spun. Anger contorting his features, he scanned my outfit then looked back at the guy. "Read it," he demanded.

"Sir?"

"Read. It," Jared enunciated.

The guy, who was dressed exactly like Jared's friend, André, in the same type of black logo polo shirt and black cargo pants, looked uncomfortable. He glanced at me.

I walked over and took the paper from him. It was a complaint. I was surprised the lawyers had gotten this filed so quickly, but I was shocked when I read how much Dan was actually suing Jared for. I looked up.

Jared's jaw clenched. "*What* does it say?"

My stomach bottomed out. "Dan's suing you." I swallowed. "Twenty-five million."

Jared looked at the other guy. "Leave."

"Yes, sir." He nodded then turned to me. "I'm Tyler, ma'am. I'll be your protection detail for the next few days. Please let me know if you need anything."

"*Leave*," Jared barked.

Tyler walked out.

I handed the paper to Jared. "You need to call that attorney your friend André told you about."

He threw the paper on the kitchen counter, picked up his phone and dialed. A second later he was telling someone to order takeout food.

I waited until he hung up. "I'm sorry." Guilt was eating me alive. If I hadn't agreed to meet him at the restaurant, none of this would have happened, including me and him.

"For what? Are you going to sue me next?" He walked into the bedroom.

I followed. "That's not fair." I didn't tell Dan to be a jerk and I certainly didn't tell Jared to hit him.

Pulling a shirt out of his dresser, he didn't say anything.

I stood there feeling helpless. "What are you going to do?"

"Shower." He walked into the bathroom and shut the door behind him.

I grabbed my purse from the kitchen counter where I'd left it and fished out my cell as I walked back into the bedroom. When I turned it on, texts started coming in from Dan.

Where are u?

What the hell are you doing with that jerk?

Y did u leave?

Turn ur phone on!

Damn it Sie, I love u, u know I do

Don't do this

You gave me ur virginity, that meant something!

I cringed at the last one. Then I let my indignation get the best of me and texted back.

25 million. Really? What's wrong, is your cheerleader girlfriend blowing through your money?

The three little dots that said he was texting back appeared immediately.

Nothing HAPPENED! I told u that!

I didn't believe it then and I didn't believe it now. The simple truth was that Dan Ahlstrom was a self-entitled coward. I stupidly texted back.

Whatever.

His reply was almost instant.

Put the ring on and the lawsuit disappears

My stomach bottomed out then anger, red-hot and furious, blossomed. My thumbs flew across the screen.

Blackmail? That's how you get women now? You're pathetic.

I didn't know what I'd gotten myself into with Jared, but I knew he would never do to me what Dan was doing. Jared had defended me at the restaurant. He'd gone with me to Coach's office. He'd quietly let me know he was there for me. He would never blackmail me.

But now Jared was getting sued—because of me.

As I sat on the edge of the bed, holding my phone, another text from Dan came in.

Wear the ring

I knew what I wouldn't do. I was never going back to Dan. But that wasn't my only option.

Jared came out of the shower.

I didn't even look up, because if I did, I wouldn't have the courage to say what I needed to say. "This is my fault. You would never be in this situation if it weren't for me. I'm going back to my house. You can get on with your life." My heart breaking, my stomach in knots, I stood. "I know words are just letters strung together, but I'm truly sorry." I picked up my purse.

"Who were you texting?" he asked, no intonation in his voice.

I glanced up. His rugged features were so stoic, I couldn't tell if he was angry and I told myself it didn't matter. "Dan."

"What does he want?"

I stared at Jared a moment. In a simple gray T-shirt and jeans, his hair wet, he was the most beautiful man I'd ever seen. I wanted to fall in his arms and forget everything except how it felt to be the object of his desire. Instead, I told myself to toughen up. I swiped to unlock the screen on my phone

SYBIL BARTEL

then held it out. "Here." Maybe if he saw what I'd stupidly given Dan, he wouldn't respect me.

Jared made no move to take the phone. "I'm asking you."

"He wants the same thing he wanted a month ago." Me, pathetic. "And if I go back to him, he'll drop the lawsuit."

Jared snorted out a laugh.

"This isn't funny." I turned my phone off and put it back in my purse.

"No, it's not, but he's a fucking pussy."

A pussy who would drop the lawsuit if I stopped seeing Jared. I wasn't going back to Dan, not for anything, but I would back away from Jared if that's what it took to save him from my mess. I took a step towards the door.

"Hey," Jared snapped.

"This is best. If I'm not around, Dan will have no reason to sue you."

Jared stepped in front of me and dropped his voice. "Do you know the difference between me and the asshole quarterback?"

"Everything?" His scent, clean and so, so him surrounded me, and it hurt to stand there looking at him. All I wanted was to reach for him.

Warm and firm, his fingers grasped my chin, and his intense gaze speared my heart. "I know what's standing in front of me."

Oh God. Why was life so difficult? "Jared—"

"I don't give a shit about the lawsuit. You're not going back to him. Let him fucking pay lawyer's fees for the next decade, I don't have twenty-five million. I've got something better." His thumb stroked my cheek. "And I'm not letting her walk away without a fight."

142

I fought emotions that threatened to break what was left of my resolve. "Some fights are better left alone."

"Not this one."

Every word he said was perfect. He was perfect. Perfectly broken and heroic and rough, and there wasn't a single thing I would change about him, but I couldn't let him do this. "What if I asked you to walk away?"

"The Marines didn't train me to be a coward, Red."

I saw the subconscious flex of his shoulders and the slight movement of his back muscles, and I wanted to cry for him, for what he'd been through. But I also understood what incredible strength it'd taken for him to survive. You couldn't teach that kind of resolve. "I'm pretty sure you were a fighter before you enlisted." I smiled, but all I felt was sad.

He dropped his hand. "Food will be here soon. You're staying." As if life bent to his will, the doorbell rang.

TWENTY-THREE

Jared

"YOU NEED TO EAT." I PUT MY HAND ON THE back of her neck, because I couldn't not touch her. There was no way I was letting her go back to that asshole. I was already jonesing like a fucking junkie to be inside her again.

"So do you." Despite her T-shirt and leggings, her voice was all pink business suit.

Any other woman, I would've had her on her knees the second she told me what to do. Or kicked her to the curb. I didn't take orders from women, ever. But this woman? I was tripping all over myself for her. I didn't even give a damn about the lawsuit. I knew what the video footage would show. It was self-defense. Let that asshole come at me. He wouldn't find my money.

I led her to the kitchen where I'd fucked her and my dick stirred. "Sit."

I grabbed my wallet and answered the door for the old guy the condo association paid to watch the lobby weekdays. "Thanks, Con. How much?"

Con's face wrinkled up in a smile. "Jared, my boy. How are you?" He handed the bag over.

"Good. Did you get something for yourself?" That was our deal. I called him, he dealt with calling whatever takeout place I wanted, he got something for himself, then I paid.

"Yep, Chinese spicy chicken. It's not Cuban spicy." He chuckled. "But I'll take it. Saves me from cooking later."

I nodded. "How much?"

"Forty-seven because you asked for extra." Despite being a foot shorter than me, he tried to look over my shoulder. "Do you have company? There's a bodyguard who keeps walking through the lobby. He's not very talkative. I saw he works for André though." He pointed to his chest. "He has the shirt."

Shit. I should've warned him about Luna's guy. "His name's Tyler. He'll be around for a few days." I debated not telling him about Red. I'd brought her up from the garage level. Con could check the security feeds if he was curious, but I was counting on him being glued to his soaps. "I have a guest who's avoiding the media."

Con's expression turned grave. "Yes, I saw you and your lady friend had a problem with the quarterback."

Christ. "Something like that." I handed him three twenties. "Thanks for the food."

He pocketed the money then clapped my shoulder. "Stay strong, my boy, stay strong."

"Always." I shut the door and found Red sitting at a stool right by where we'd fucked. I was perverse enough to get off on it. "Chinese." I set the food down and grabbed a couple of plates and forks. "What do you want to drink?"

"Water, please." Her formal voice was back.

I set a plate, napkin and utensils in front of her. "What's wrong?"

"You buy your doorman dinner?"

I grabbed waters. "A few times a week."

She folded her napkin and placed her fork on it dead center. "That's very nice of you."

What a joke. If she only knew the real reason was because I couldn't dial a number without getting it wrong fifteen times first. I sat down next to her and threw food on my plate.

"Thank you for…." She glanced at the clock in the kitchen. "Dinner." She put food on her plate like a girl.

"You're welcome." I took one of the containers and dumped half on her plate. "Eat."

She opened her mouth to say something.

I cut her off. "Don't even try it. We missed lunch, your ass is fucking perfect and you need to eat." I pointed with my fork to her plate. "All of it."

Her hands folded in her lap as she looked at me. "You're bossy."

"And you're fucking gorgeous. Stay that way. Eat."

A shy smile hit her lips and she picked up her fork. "I would like you to call the attorney."

"I'd like you to eat naked."

Her fork froze halfway to her mouth. "I hardly think this is something to joke about."

"I wasn't joking." Fucking starving, I shoveled in a huge bite.

"Protecting yourself isn't a game."

"I'm not playing games." I wanted her naked. I wanted to stare at her tits while I ate. Next to fucking her, it'd be my new definition of nirvana.

She stood up.

"Going somewhere?" I raised an eyebrow and took another bite.

She took off my T-shirt and started to sit back down.

I pretended not to choke on my food. "That's not naked." Fuck, her tits were gorgeous.

With a huff, she placed the T-shirt on the stool, slid her hands into her waistband and pushed down over her hips and lush thighs. Then she stepped out of her pants and sat her ass back down on the stool. I took one look at my dried cum in her red curls and my dick was rock-hard.

She picked up her fork. "Call the attorney."

Fuck me. I smiled, seriously smiled. And it felt fucking good. I shoved my phone toward her then I drew a finger around one of her nipples. "You dial."

She glared at me but her nipple pebbled. "Fine. But you're talking to him."

I leaned in and put my mouth on her. Swirling my tongue around her hard nipple, I waited until her fingers were swiping across the screen, then I bit.

"Ah!" She dropped my phone.

I quickly lapped the sting and brushed a finger through her curls. "Dial."

Fumbling with my phone, her legs spread a few inches wider and she shifted in her seat. "It's ringing."

I sucked hard and pulled back until her nipple popped out of my mouth. As I took the phone, I rubbed her clit.

"Barrett," a clipped voice answered.

Red gasped.

I fucking loved that gasp. "Hey, this is Jared Brandt. I'm a friend of André Luna. He suggested I give you a call."

"What can I help you with, Mr. Brandt?"

Red sat still as fuck as I dragged my finger through her wet heat and circled her clit. "I'm being sued by Dan Ahlstrom and I need representation."

Pause.

Red held on to the counter and her eyes fluttered shut.

I glanced at the phone to make sure the call was still connected. It was. "Hello?"

Barrett's professional tone was replaced with disbelief. "You're the guy on the videos who hit Strom?"

"I was provoked." I increased the pressure and a small sound escaped Red's gorgeous lips.

Barrett cleared his throat. "I see. How much is the suit for?"

"Twenty-five million."

"Do you have that much?"

"Not even close." I slipped a finger inside Red's tight pussy.

"Were you injured?" Barrett asked.

"I'm a marine." Red's lips parted. If I weren't on the phone, my mouth would've been on hers.

"Yes, I understand from the media coverage that you're a combat-wounded veteran, but when Mr. Ahlstrom provoked you, were you physically harmed?"

I snorted. "No." I wanted to fuck her into tomorrow.

"You're not giving me a lot to work with, Mr. Brandt."

"It was three against one." I wanted Red to climb on my lap and sink down on my cock as I bit her nipples.

"Yet, that hardly seemed a problem for you."

"It wasn't." I could've taken three more of them.

Barrett inhaled. "I'm not sure how I can help you, Mr. Brandt."

"Luna said to call you." Red's hair fell across her shoulders as she rocked forward on my hand.

"Yes, and I appreciate his vote of confidence, but maybe a bigger firm with more experience with the league would have better success in negotiating a settlement you could afford."

Jesus, Red was beautiful. "I'm not being sued by the team and I don't intend to pay Ahlstrom shit."

"Understood. All I'm saying is that—"

"Are you interested or not?" I needed to make Red come and I didn't want to be holding my fucking phone when it happened.

Barrett exhaled slowly. "All right. Come to my office tomorrow morning at—"

"You need to come here. The media is still camped out in front of my place."

"Okay, I can be there tomorrow morning. Is eight too early?"

"That works." I eased my finger in then out.

"My fee is two hundred and fifty an hour and I take a retainer upfront of two thousand."

He was in the wrong business. "Fine."

"Your address?"

I rattled it off. "There are a couple visitor parking spots below the building. The gate code is nineteen ninety-nine. I'm on the seventeenth floor."

"Got it. See you tomorrow, Mr. Brandt."

I hung up and curled my finger. "You're not eating, Red."

With her eyes squeezed shut, and her head down, her hands tightened on the counter. "You're incorrigible."

"The fact that you're spewing big words while I'm

149

finger-fucking you means I'm not doing my job right." I increased the pressure.

Her head fell back and she moaned.

"That's better." I circled my thumb over her clit, and right as she started to clench around my finger, I eased out. Kissing her cheek, I picked up my fork. "You need to eat."

Her eyes popped open. "You…." Her chest rose and fell. "You did that on purpose."

I forked a hunk of beef and chewed slowly. "Did what?"

She looked down between her legs, and I could practically read her thoughts.

"Go ahead." I smiled. "Finish yourself off." My dick throbbed at just the thought of it.

"You'd like that, wouldn't you?"

Like she wouldn't believe. "You have no idea." I shoveled food in. "Start eating."

"You're not naked."

"Remember that next time you tell me what to do."

Her back straightened. "I didn't tell you. I asked."

"Same thing."

"Is that why you're so good in bed, because you're a sexist, bossy jerk and you need to make up for it somehow?" She picked up her fork.

I didn't fucking smile, I grinned. Like an idiot. "Woman, if I take my clothes off, you won't be eating fried rice, and I've already kept you from a meal twice today. Not to mention you're probably sore as hell. Eat the fucking food."

"Coward." She daintily took a bite.

TWENTY-FOUR

Sienna

I couldn't believe I'd taken my clothes off like that, let alone ate all the food he'd heaped on my plate. I'd never been comfortable naked around anyone, including myself. My hips were too wide, my stomach wasn't flat, and my thighs touched in the middle. But Jared made me feel like I was beautiful.

If I stopped to think about all the women he'd slept with, how he probably made them all feel special, I'd start to hyperventilate.

"Spill it," Jared demanded.

"Excuse me?"

"You say that every time you stall. You heard me." He picked our plates up and put them in the sink, but then he didn't come back and sit by me. He stood on the other side of the counter and stared me down.

I inhaled and started with the obvious. "I know what you said earlier, but if I walk out the door, the lawsuit goes away."

"Not happening. The lawyer's been called. He'll deal with it. I'm done discussing that bullshit. Next issue."

I slipped his T-shirt over my head, not sure if I was impressed with his confidence or afraid of it. "I don't understand… this." I didn't understand what was happening between us or how he knew I had more than one issue on my mind. I picked up my leggings and pulled them on. My core still humming from his touch, I ached for more of him, but I couldn't look at him. If I did, I wouldn't want to tell him the rest of what I was thinking.

He stepped around the counter and got in my personal space. Lowering his voice to a deep cadence, he was all at once seductive and mesmerizing yet totally demanding. "Start talking."

I breathed in. "How do you do that?"

"Do what?" he asked in the same voice.

"That. Your tone. You make me want to tell you every thought I ever had, but at the same time, it's demanding, like I don't have a choice not to tell you, except I'm not sure I even care, because you're focusing all your attention on me and it makes me feel…." I stopped myself.

"Special?"

I exhaled. "Yes."

"You are. Now tell me why you were frowning when you were eating."

All of a sudden, I wasn't standing in front of the demanding Jared, or even the angry Jared. This was a different side of him, but I couldn't gauge it. I didn't know what was going on. I'd only known this man hours. I was uncomfortable in a way that made my stomach flutter and breath catch, yet I was more relaxed than I'd ever been around any man. It was my excuse for asking what I asked next. "How many women have you been with?"

"I'm not going to tell you that."

Oh God. It was because it was a lot. I knew this. I told myself I knew this. He was an escort, for goodness' sake, but oh my God, this didn't feel good. "More than a hundred?"

He studied me for a moment. "Is the answer going to change how you feel?"

I thought about that. Would it? Would I walk out that door if he'd slept with five hundred women? I would. I knew myself. I wouldn't ever get past that. But a hundred? A hundred and fifty? Could I live with that? What was my threshold? I didn't even know, because having this conversation was already so far past my comfort zone.

So I told him the truth. "Yes."

He didn't hesitate. "No."

A breath I didn't know I was holding released from my lungs and my chest eased for two whole seconds before I started fixating on numbers. Fifty? Seventy-five? Was he lying? Could I trust him? Would I ever trust him? What would happen if his past came out and everyone at work knew I was dating a former male prostitute? What if Coach found out about his past? Would I lose my job? How long could I live off the little bit of money Daddy left me? Okay, I could live awhile if I was careful, but that wasn't the point. Was Jared's past even in the past? He'd had a client at his beck and call within minutes last night. Which, I mean, I got it, he was incredible. I didn't know any woman who didn't want exactly what I'd just had all afternoon. But still.

"*Sienna.*"

My name rolled of his tongue like he was the only man ever meant to say it and it made my chest hurt. "I like you," I blurted. "But this is hard, and I'm confused, and I thought I would understand a hundred, but I don't. Not really. I don't get why selling yourself for money was appealing, but what's worse is that I just don't see you doing it. I know you said not to bring up Alex, but he's different. He's all about the money. You can tell that. But you're not like that. You didn't even flinch when I said you were being sued for twenty-five million. It's like you don't even care about money."

"I don't."

"Then why be an escort?"

"I told you."

"Because more than your back is scarred? What does that mean? I don't understand. And I want to understand because I don't want to just walk out that door and never see you again." I hated thinking it, let alone saying it, but I wasn't stupid. Healthy, stable relationships didn't start with two strangers having sex. Did they?

His nostrils flared and his jaw ticked and his tone went from zero to clipped in two seconds flat. "I'm not going to give you a number, and I'm not going to bitch about Afghanistan or getting wounded. You want a fucking pussy who cries on your lap, then you should get the fuck out."

I bristled, but then I saw it. I wasn't seeing the marine who'd taken down two football players who had fifty pounds on him. I was staring at a man who looked as unsure as I felt. So I ignored his tone and I ignored his words about leaving, and I focused on the one thing I thought would be my biggest obstacle. "I hardly think crying on my lap constitutes effective communication."

"Don't pull that pink suit bullshit work attitude with me. You know exactly what I'm saying."

I stood my ground. "I want a number."

"I didn't fucking count."

"Then how do you know it's less than a hundred?"

He exhaled. *"Jesus fucking Christ."*

I didn't say anything.

His hands went to his hips. "You gonna wait me out?"

"If I have to. But I would prefer a straight answer so I can go shower." I was testing him, same as he'd tested me in the elevator last night. I may have not had much experience with men, but I did know my limitations, and I couldn't handle someone I couldn't talk to.

He raised an eyebrow and the side of his mouth twitched. "You feeling dirty?"

The change in his tone from irritated to pure sex made me want to bite my lip, but I stood perfectly still. "If you must know, yes."

"I like you dirty." He smiled.

My knees wobbled. "I'm getting that."

He grinned. "Still waiting me out?"

His smile, unfiltered and devastating, was incredible. But when he looked how he looked right now, like he wasn't carrying the weight of world on his shoulders? Oh my God, I had no defense to protect my heart from him. "Yes."

"Good. Go shower."

Pretending my heart wasn't wildly skipping and my stomach wasn't fluttering, I raised an eyebrow. "Then you'll tell me?"

He lowered his voice. "Then I'll take you to bed."

That tone, his intent stare, they were my undoing. "I'm not going to sleep with you," I fibbed.

"Who says I'm letting you sleep?" He winked.

Faking it, I put a hand on my hip. "You're lucky I don't know your middle name."

"Jacob."

Was there anything that wasn't sexy about this man? I fake sighed. "Fine, Jared Jacob Brandt. I'm going to shower. Then you'll tell me what I want to know."

Mischief lit up his amber-brown eyes. "Are you bossing me again?"

Oh God. I thought about saying no but the muscles in my core were suddenly throbbing. The memory of the heat of the sting on my backside was making me want to pull my pants down and beg him to spank me until I orgasmed. "I wouldn't dream of it."

His eyes narrowed as his head tilted. "You know I can tell when you're lying, right?"

"No, you can't." Back straight, expression locked, I didn't have any tells. After years of experience with church ladies and then football players, I'd learned not to.

"Body language, Red." He lightly slapped my backside. "Go shower."

"I don't have any—" I never got the rest of the sentence out.

Someone pounded on Jared's front door. "Sienna!"

Jared's face contorted with anger as his phone started ringing.

My stomach bottomed out. "It's Dan."

"I know who it is." He picked up his phone. "Get in the bedroom."

What? No. "I'm not hiding."

He gave me a warning look. "You want to talk with this asshole, do it on your own time. But when he shows up on my doorstep, this is *my* call." Turning away, he answered his phone. "How the fuck did he get past you?... I don't give a shit if there're ten of them. Do your fucking job!" He hung up and stalked toward the front door.

"Jared, *wait.*" Oh my God. I didn't want him answering that door.

He didn't even pause. He threw the door open. "Just give me a reason, you fucking asshole."

His hair a mess, his chest heaving, his eyes black and purple, Dan looked over Jared's shoulder. His frenzied gaze landed on me, and the second he took in my outfit, his face fell. "Sie, don't *do* this." He gripped the doorframe.

"She's not doing shit," Jared growled. "But I will if you don't back the fuck up."

I stepped forward.

As if he had eyes in the back of his head, Jared ground a command out in warning. "Not another step, Sienna."

"I can fight my own battles." I looked at Dan. "A lawsuit and blackmail? What's happened to you?"

"Come on, Sie. Just talk to me. Just come with me and we'll work this out." He pleaded like a broken child. "You don't have to do this. You told me you love me. You know I love you. You still have my ring. We both know what that means. Don't betray us like this."

Jared growled.

I'd be lying if I said I didn't have a twinge of sympathy for Dan. I knew what he was looking at. I knew what that kind of hurt felt like. But I only knew it because of him. I wasn't betraying Dan. I was betraying the man with scars on his back who'd risked everything for me today. Inhaling, I did what I should've done the second Dan pounded on the door. I walked into Jared's bedroom.

TWENTY-FIVE

Jared

"**S**IE!" HE CALLED AFTER HER WITH HIS BULLSHIT nickname.

About to lose my fucking restraint, I bit words out. "Leave while you can still fucking walk." I wanted to kill him.

The asshole's face contorted with anger and he dropped the pussy begging routine. "*I* was her first. I know who the fuck you are. You think she's going to pick some unemployed, broke veteran over me? Go ahead." He jabbed a finger at my chest. "Count your days with her. I already gave her a ring. She's coming back to *me*."

Enraged, I grabbed his wrist.

The stairwell door burst open and Tyler, Luna, and some other fuck in a Luna and Associates shirt rushed out.

"*Brandt*," Luna snapped. "Cameras."

My nostrils flaring, anger raging, I ground my teeth and tightened my hold.

Luna stepped up next to the fucking quarterback. "On second thought, go ahead, amigo." His hand rested on his holstered gun.

"Yeah, go ahead," the quarterback snarled. "See what happens when you get arrested and aren't around to play house with her."

He was her first? *This fucking asshole was her first?* Enraged, I couldn't speak.

"Or?" Luna shrugged. "You can let him go. He's already screwed himself."

I let go.

"Days," Ahlstrom taunted. Turning, he shoved Tyler in the chest.

Tyler stumbled back and held his arms out. "Boss?" he asked, as Ahlstrom stalked toward the stairwell.

"Stand down." André tipped his chin at the cameras. "We got what we need." He pressed the com on his earpiece. "Stairwell. Detain… copy." He nodded at me. "We'll get him. Cops are on the way."

She had his goddamn ring. She'd said nothing when he'd told her he loved her. Nothing. *She had his fucking ring.*

I slammed my fist into the wall. The plaster crushed in and a picture crashed to the ground.

She came running out of the bedroom. "What happened?" Shocked green eyes took in the wall and my scraped knuckles. "Jared?" She stepped toward me.

"Don't," I barked.

She glanced at Luna and Tyler and her face pinked, exactly like her ass had under my hand.

Rage twisted my voice. "What did you give him?"

She crossed her arms over her braless tits. "What?"

"*What did you give him?*" I yelled.

"Brandt," André warned.

No. Fuck him. Fuck her. *She gave that fucking piece of shit her virginity and told him she loved him?* I was losing my fucking mind. I didn't give a shit about virgins. I never wanted that responsibility. I fucked and I fucked hard. But Red with that fucking asshole? *Wearing his ring?* That wasn't some sixteen-year-old back seat car fumbling. She'd fucking saved herself. *She'd saved herself for him.*

Her back straightened like she had her fucking suit on and she was talking to her goddamn boss. "I didn't give him anything. You were standing right there."

"How long where you with him?" I ground out. "How long ago did you date him?"

Confusion clouded her face. "For three months, a couple months ago, but I don't see how that—"

"You're twenty-fucking-four!" Rage engulfed me. She'd given herself to that asshole then hired Vega like she was some well-played piece of ass. I wasn't furious, I was enraged. Enraged it wasn't me taking her innocence. Enraged she'd slept with Vega, and diabolically pissed at the glaring truth Ahlstrom threw in my face. I was an un-fucking-employed hustler who couldn't goddamn read. I'd never be good enough for her.

Unhinged, I barely looked at André. "Get her out of my place."

"Copy that." André nodded once.

"Jared!"

The sound of my name pleading from her lips sliced into me like a fucking knife, but I didn't acknowledge her. I was already halfway to the kitchen. A second later, the bottle was in my hand and I was chugging.

TWENTY-SIX

Sienna

I STOOD IN THE BEDROOM, NOT EVEN REMEMBERING
having walked there.

"Ma'am." André maintained deliberate eye contact.
"I'm going to need you to come with me." Standing with his
legs apart, one hand grasping the wrist on his opposite arm,
he looked the way Jared had looked in Coach's office.

My stomach churned. "What is he doing?"

"I'm taking responsibility for your safety now, ma'am."
He tipped his chin at my suitcase. "Please get your things."

I got angry. Pound *my* fist into the wall, angry. "The hell
you are." I aimed for the door before I could think about
what was left of my dignity.

André stepped in front of me. "I wouldn't do that if I
were you."

No, I wasn't going to let him do this. "I'm going to speak
to him, *right now*." I tried to sidestep him, but he pivoted and
full-blown panic set in. "Get out of my way!"

He inhaled, and for a moment, his military mask slipped
and he looked at me with a look I knew so well, I wanted

to vomit. "I'm sorry, ma'am, he's chosen not to engage with you."

Engage? *Engage*? Like I was some mission or objective or whatever the hell they called it in the Marines? "I'm not some object he can toss away. You tell him to come talk to me!" My world was crumbling faster than I could hold it together.

"This is a done deal, ma'am. Please hurry and get your things. I'd like to clear you of the premises before the police arrive."

"The police?" Oh my God. "What happened between him and Dan?"

"Clothes, ma'am."

"Tell me what happened!" My heart crushing a thousand times worse than it ever had with Dan, I couldn't breathe.

"Everything's under control, ma'am, but it's time for you to leave."

I sucked in a breath. Then another. This was my fault. I'd put myself here. How stupid had I been to trust him? To think for one minute that I was going to change who Jared was? After knowing him for *hours*? What did I think would happen? That'd we screw like rabbits as the sun set on a perfect little happy life? I wasn't crazy, I was clinically insane. Worse, I was exactly what I never wanted to be. Pathetic.

Fighting tears, I snatched clothes out of the suitcase and my zippered toiletries bag I used for traveling that André must have taken from under my bathroom sink. I rushed back into the bathroom, feeling like every corner of my life had been violated. My heart, my pride, my privacy, my job, *everything*. Nothing was left untouched, and I had no one to blame except myself.

I brushed my hair. I covered my freckles with makeup. I

did what I'd always done when my life fell apart around me. I put on a façade. The same one that I'd put on at my daddy's funeral. The same one I wore to work the day after Dan broke my heart. But those times, my lip wasn't quivering. Those times I had somewhere to be on a weekday morning. Those times, I didn't know what it felt like to have brown eyes looking down at me like I was someone special.

I'd sworn to myself that I never wanted to be that to anyone again. Losing Daddy broke me. The grief was missed hugs and Sunday dinners and no more crinkly smiles. It was knowing I was alone in this world.

But stepping into jeans that someone had carefully folded and put in a suitcase for me, this wasn't that grief. This was crushing my chest. This was a kind of panic that made me want to run to arms I knew were out there. Arms that were out there but didn't want to hold me. This wasn't grief. This was desperation.

And I hated it.

A knock sounded on the door. "Ma'am? You ready?"

My shaking hands buttoned a silk blouse I used to love. "Yes." I opened the door and my toiletries bag slipped from my hands. The mirror in my compact shattered on the marble and hair pins scattered.

"Don't move." A man I'd met in a parking lot a few hours ago plucked me off my feet, lifted me out of the bathroom and set me on the carpet as if he cared what happened to me. "Get some shoes." He grabbed the T-Shirt I'd left on the counter then squatted and used it to clean up my mess.

I stared at the door.

I knew he was out there. I could feel him just like I could feel the memory of his hands all over my body.

"Chica," André said quietly.

I was looking at a man with short, neatly cut brown hair and brown eyes, who was every bit as handsome as Jared, but my heart didn't react.

André glanced at the door then inhaled. "He's protecting you."

"From what?"

"Himself." He put my bag in my suitcase, zipped it shut then took the handle. "Come on, let's get you out of here."

I didn't want to go. I wanted to understand why he was shutting me out. I wanted to know what'd happened and I wanted to take back walking away before Dan left. I wanted a lot of things, but I was out of choices.

With a hand on my back, André led me down the hall and toward the front door, but when I saw him, I froze.

On the balcony, he stared at the ocean. The moon cast a million sparks of light across the rippled surface of the water, but it cast shadows across his scarred back. My throat burned, my eyes welled and I didn't want to give him the satisfaction of seeing me upset, but I was moving toward the balcony before my good sense could tell me to stop.

The slider door was open and the salt air blew lazily in like it didn't know my life was in shambles. I didn't step out on the balcony. My hand fisted and I pounded on the glass. Then I spit out the one thing I thought would hurt him most. "You're a coward, Jared Jacob Brandt."

The words broke my heart and the impact stung my hand, but Jared never looked up.

His scarred back to me, a tattoo covering his right bicep, he didn't even flinch.

I had no dignity left, but I squared my shoulders anyway.

Biting my tongue to keep from sobbing, I shoved past a shocked André and Tyler and walked out.

I jabbed at the elevator call button without a clue as to what I was doing. André's hand closed over my shoulder, squeezed once, then he let go. I felt like I was falling.

I didn't remember the ride down to the garage. I ignored the police cars pulling in and the media at the gate yelling my name. I didn't know how Dan had gotten past all of them, and I didn't care. I hated him. He'd said something to Jared, I was sure of it, but I told myself it didn't matter. I told myself a man who was so easily swayed wasn't a man worthy of me anyway.

André led me to a black SUV with tinted windows and put me in the front passenger seat before sliding behind the wheel. "I'm taking you to Luna and Associates."

"I want to go home."

"I have secure apartments for clients. You'll be safe from the media there."

"I'm not your client." I hadn't paid him five thousand dollars to sleep with me.

He spared me a glance. "Brandt is my brother."

I looked out the window at the media snapping pictures as we drove past. "I didn't know he had any brothers."

"Not biologically. The Marines, ma'am." He pulled onto the street and gunned the engine.

"What happened to him?"

"That's something you'll have to ask him."

"I did. He said it was an IED."

André nodded. "It was."

"Where you there?"

"Not in the Humvee, no."

I let it go because I couldn't figure out why I was asking or what it mattered. "What happened to Dan?"

"Ahlstrom is being detained. What happens now is up to the police."

I scoffed. "They'll let him go."

"Possibly." He drove fast, but he commanded the large vehicle.

"If you take me to your office, then what?"

"You sleep." He said it so succinctly, like it was the answer to everything.

"That isn't going to fix anything." I wanted the comfort of my own bed, but I also didn't want to deal with the media.

"I'm not sure what there is to fix, ma'am. The media will find another scandal to stalk in a day or two."

Now I was a scandal. "And until then?"

He smiled, wide and charismatic and all white teeth. "Until then, you're the woman who scorned Miami's favorite quarterback."

TWENTY-SEVEN

Jared

MY HEAD FUCKING POUNDING, I STARED AT MY phone. Regret ate at me like a festering wound.

"Mr. Brandt, did you at any time engage with Mr. Ahlstrom when he showed up here last night?"

The lawyer, Mathew Barrett, looked young as shit, and he was a dead ringer for fucking Clark Kent. "How old are you?"

"What I lack in age, I make up for in experience. Please answer the question."

She hadn't called. Not that I expected her to. "I didn't fucking touch him." The quarterback was lucky he was still alive.

"Mr. Luna said you grabbed his wrist in self-defense?"

"Watch the tapes." I was sure Con had them. "The door-man downstairs can get you a copy." Why the fuck did I send her away? I should've fucking talked to her. I should've done a lot of shit I didn't.

"Yes, he's working on it as we speak."

Fucking great. "Anything else?" I stood up. I couldn't fucking sit still anymore. I needed to know where she was. I needed

167

to touch her. One night without her and I didn't give a fuck who took her virginity.

"In light of last night's events, I think we have a solid argument in getting the lawsuit dropped. If not, I'm going to recommend a countersuit. In the meantime, I'm advising you to file a temporary restraining order."

"No." I needed to go to her.

"Mr. Brandt—"

"I'm not filing shit." What a joke. I could take care of myself.

"It's a simple process that will ensure—"

"I said no." Was he fucking deaf?

He put his pen and his damn yellow pad of paper down and looked at me like he was about to tell me someone was dead. "One last question."

I knew what was fucking coming. I tipped my chin.

"What is your occupation?"

I didn't even blink. "I'm medically retired from the Marines."

His elbows on his knees, his hands clasped, he nodded. "I understand that. What else do you do for income? And may I remind you that you have attorney-client privilege. Anything you say is in confidence."

Confidence my ass. "Who told you?"

"It's my job to defend you, but I cannot be effective if I am not armed with the truth."

"Fucking Luna." I didn't have to guess.

Clark Kent sighed. "He suggested you may be at risk."

Jesus Christ, what a prick. "What kind of risk?"

"He didn't elaborate, but I assumed he meant the kind that could land you in jail. I'm not sure what you do, and that's why I'm asking. I need to know if this will impact—"

"Escorting isn't illegal." But my past was a big part of why I sent her away last night. Shit would escalate for her in a fucking heartbeat if it came out who she was dating.

He frowned. "Is that what you were doing with Miss Montclair?"

"*No.*" I jumped down his throat. "She has nothing to with this."

"With all due respect, she has everything to do with this."

"She's not a client," I ground out.

The placating fuck nodded. "Understood." He held up a finger then paused for a second. "But I do have concerns that your... occupation will become an issue with regards to this suit."

"How the fuck does what I do in my spare time affect any of this?"

"Mr. Brandt, a ten-minute search last night netted me evidence of your biannual trips to the Cayman Islands, and in light of your recent admission, it's not a far leap to assume you're putting money in an offshore account. I'm sure Mr. Ahlstrom's legal counsel could find the same information."

What the fuck? He'd looked into me? "So I like to go on vacation." With six months' worth of cash that I deposited into an offshore account that was the only fucking numerical sequence I'd forced myself to memorize.

"For twenty-four hours every January and June?"

Goddamn it. "I don't have twenty-five million, and if I did, that pussy quarterback would be the last person I'd give even a single cent to."

Clark fucking Kent held up a hand. "Understood." He tossed his pen and paper in a messenger bag and stood.

What kind of lawyer had a damn messenger bag? "Just do your job."

"I will." He eyed me. "Refrain from any sexual interactions in exchange for money until this is over."

"I'm not a fucking prostitute." Not anymore. My dick hadn't even been hard since she'd called me a coward and walked out.

With his piss-ass grave expression, he nodded. "Next time something arises like Mr. Ahlstrom breaking into your building, or any other football player for that matter, call me." He walked to the door. "I'll be in touch."

"You do that." I knew I was being a fucking asshole. Problem was, I just didn't care.

The second I shut the door behind him, I was reaching for my work phone. Turning it on, I ignored all the texts that started popping up and glanced at the forty-seven numbers I'd painfully entered over three years. I'd spent two grand on a fake identity to get this fucking phone. A phone you couldn't trace to my real name. A phone that'd been my life for three years.

I pulled the SIM card out and crushed it. Then I walked out on the balcony, broke the phone into pieces and hurled them over the fucking railing. The past three years of my life fell seventeen stories and mixed with the debris littering the beach from the hurricane.

TWENTY-EIGHT

Sienna

A NDRÉ TURNED INTO MY NEIGHBORHOOD. "FOR THE record, chica, I think this is a bad idea."

"You already said that." He'd told me a dozen times that going home was a bad idea. I'd wandered into his offices early this morning looking for him because I hadn't slept a wink. "I appreciate your hospitality, but I need to get home." I didn't want to be around twenty men all dressed like André who acted like the former marines that they were. All they did was remind me of Jared.

"You could've stayed at the apartment until this died down."

"Thank you, but I've already put you out enough." A news van gunned their engine and passed us.

André slowed down. "Something you're not telling me?"

Another news van pulled up behind us and honked. "No." I looked out the back window as dread started to creep in. "What's going on?" The second van raced past us and turned onto my street.

"Hold on." André picked up his phone and dialed.

"What's your location? I need assistance. Recon." He told the person on the line my address. "Copy. Holding back." He hung up and made a U-turn.

"Where are you going? My house is the other way."

"I'm circling until I find out who those news crews are chasing."

My stomach twisted. "You gave someone my address."

"Just doing my job, chica."

He'd stopped calling me ma'am last night after he'd dropped me off in a fully furnished apartment. I'd asked him what Dan had said to Jared but he wouldn't tell me. He'd just squeezed my shoulder and said, "*Get some rest, chica.*"

"I didn't hire you," I reminded him. I didn't even know if I could afford him. With his fleet of SUVs in the garage of his building, and all the men wearing Luna and Associates polos, I was sure if you had to ask how much André charged, you couldn't afford to hire him.

"I'm still gonna protect you as if you had." His phone buzzed and he answered with a command, "Report." He listened for a moment. "Copy. One support, one backup, separate vehicles. One shadow on perimeter. Five minutes. Switch to coms." He hung up. "You have company at your house."

My stomach dropped. "Who?" I asked, but I could guess.

He took an earpiece from the center console and put it in his ear. "Plates are registered to Kenneth DeMarco."

Surprised, I frowned. "It's not Dan?" What was Coach doing at my house?

"I don't have confirmation. The vehicle is idling in your driveway, but the windows are tinted out." He glanced at me. "And the team's general manager has called a press conference."

Oh God. "For what?"

"We're about to find out." He circled the block and two black SUVs identical to the one we were in turned onto my street. Like a well-coordinated marching band routine, one pulled in front of us, the other behind, and with bumpers practically touching, we all pulled up to my house.

A dozen news crews, with their vans and equipment and reporters, blanketed my street. "Oh my God," I whispered, staring at them all.

"Listen to me, chica."

I started to panic, like seriously panic. My heart racing, my breath short, a dozen scenarios started running through my head, not the least of which was that I was being fired for hiring a male prostitute.

André touched his earpiece. "Twenty seconds." He grasped my shoulder. "*Chica.*"

I dragged my eyes away from the circus that'd become my life. "I'm in trouble." My voice shook.

"You don't know that. I'm going to get you out of the vehicle then I'm going to take you inside. Do not look up, do not answer any questions, do not pause. Walk quickly but normally. Do you want DeMarco to have access into your residence?"

Did I? Coach had never been to my house. I'd never even seen him outside the complex. "I guess."

"I need an answer."

"Okay."

"Keys." He held his hand out.

My hands shaking, I fished them out of my purse.

He took the keys and gave me a warning look. "I don't know who else is in the vehicle."

I understood what he was saying and I wasn't going to let Dan into my house. "Just Coach can come in."

"Copy that. Wait for me to open your door." André pressed his earpiece as he quickly scanned the street and Coach's SUV in my driveway. "Advance. DeMarco is allowed access." He got out of the vehicle, and at exactly the same time, the drivers in the other two black SUVs got out. Both in the same outfit as André, they flanked him as he opened my door.

Lights flashing, my name being yelled, the reporters rushed us.

"*André.*" I panicked.

"Perimeter," André barked over his shoulder.

The two men turned toward the reporters. One said "Private property" as the other said "Back up." They both held their arms out like I was a government official.

André took my hand and helped me out of the vehicle. Without letting go of me, he put his arm around my shoulders and led me toward my front door. The reporters barked questions at me about Dan, about Jared, about the team, about the owner.

We passed Coach's old Ford Expedition and all four doors opened at once.

The reporters flew into a frenzy as Coach, Dan, TJ and Sunshine all got out.

"Dios mios," André muttered, then he barked out for one of his men. "*Tyler.*"

"On it." Tyler veered off.

Coach and his players walked toward my house. Their strides were all relaxed but purposeful, as if they dealt with this type of media frenzy all the time, but I could see the tense set to Dan's shoulders as he shoved his hands in his pockets.

Tyler cut him off. "DeMarco only."

Dan halted, but he looked at me, and for a moment, it was the man I'd lain in bed with late at night and talked to about his upbringing in Oklahoma. "Sienna," he said, quiet enough for just us to hear. "This is important. Please let me and Coach in. I'm not here to cause trouble." His eyes blackened, his nose still swollen, he wasn't desperately pleading like he was last night at Jared's.

I glanced at André as he unlocked my door.

"Your call, ma'am." He ushered me to just inside the front door and punched in the alarm code that I'd given him.

I made a rash decision. "Dan can come in only if you stay."

"Understood." André nodded at Tyler. "DeMarco and Ahlstrom only." He gently pushed me against the wall. "Stay here while I do a sweep." He disappeared while Coach, Dan and Tyler stepped into my foyer.

Tyler shut the door and the shouting from the reporters muted to a dull murmur. Dan started to move toward the living room, but Tyler stopped him. "Until the house is secure, you need to wait here, sir." He paused just enough before he said *sir*.

Dan didn't notice Tyler's tone of contempt and Coach stood with his back to the wall and his eyes on his feet. I didn't know which upset me more.

André returned from the hallway that led to the bedrooms and started closing my plantation shutters. "All clear."

Coach spoke for the first time. "I need to talk to Sienna alone."

Dan took two strides and kissed my cheek. "I'm here."

I didn't have time to hate him for the way he thought he could kiss me after everything he'd done. Coach, with his shoulders dropped and his head bent, nodded at me to follow him as he walked into my kitchen.

He pulled out a chair at my small table. "Sit."

I glanced back toward the foyer where Tyler stood in front of the door like a guard and André peered through the shutters of the front window as he spoke quietly on his phone. I looked back at Coach. "They can still hear us." Desperately holding on to what little dignity I had left, I didn't want to be fired in front of them all.

"It's going to be all over the news in an hour anyway." He looked at me without raising his head. "Please sit."

I lowered to the edge of the seat.

He pulled the other chair out and set it in front of me. Sinking into the seat, he rested his elbows on his knees. Hazel eyes that were red rimmed and tired focused on me. "Jed Burrows died last night."

Confusion clouded my mind. "The owner of the team?" Why was Coach coming here to tell me this? I was sorry Mr. Burrows had passed, but I didn't understand what this had to do with me.

Coach took my hands and closed his eyes for a second. When he looked back at me, it was with the most emotion I'd ever seen him display. "Your father never told you."

It wasn't a question, it was resignation, but my heart beat too fast for me to breathe normal anyway. I fought not to jump out of my seat and yell at him to stop looking at me like that. "Told me what?"

He exhaled. "Jed was your grandfather."

I blinked.

I blinked again.

Anger pulsed, my mind scrambled and tears of shock

welled. "No," I whispered. "I met my grandparents before they died." They weren't Jed Burrows. They were kind and smiled and my grandma had made me cookies.

"Jed was your mother's father."

I sucked in a shocked breath as the reality of it sunk in. "But… then that makes you...." *Oh my God.* "You're the owner's son?" How could this happen? How come he never told me? No one ever told me. *My own father never told me.*

"Stepson," he explained.

"You have a different last name." It came out like an accusation, and part of it was because I couldn't believe what was going on.

"My mother was Jed's second wife. I was fifteen when he married her."

I knew Jed Burrows had survived two wives and a daughter, it was in his bio, but no names were ever given and I never made the connection. Why would I?

Confusion warred with anger. My father knew. He knew when he put me in touch with Coach who my grandfather was.

Coach squeezed my hands. "I know this is a lot to take in. You're going to have to reconcile it however you need to, but in the next few weeks, there's going to be a lot of press." He inhaled. "And they're going to read Jed's will, probably tomorrow."

My back went ramrod straight. "What does that mean?"

"You're his only living heir, Sienna."

Denial burned in my throat, and more anger than I knew what to do with threatened to boil over. I pulled my hands away from his fake comfort and lying secrets. "You're his son," I bit out.

"Like I said, I was his stepson. I wasn't his blood relative. That meant something to him."

Means something? I didn't mean anything to Jed Burrows. I was nothing to him. He'd never so much as looked at me. Five years working for his team and countless events and all his monthly walk-throughs to make sure everyone was "doing their job." He'd seen me. I'd been introduced to him. He hadn't even shaken my hand or so much as acknowledged my presence.

Coach looked at me with pity and maybe something else that said he knew what I was going through, but I didn't care. I hated him. I hated him right then more than I'd ever hated anyone in my whole life.

I pushed my chair back and stood. "Get out."

André glanced up from his phone call. One look at my face and he was behind Coach, his hand on his weapon. "Time for you to leave, DeMarco."

Sad, like a middle-aged man who'd been defeated by life, not like a coach who yelled at three-hundred-pound men to sack harder, he stood and nodded. "Call me when you calm down, Montclair."

"Get out of my house." I was sick. Not even my house was sacred anymore. I'd bought it with money I'd made working for a liar. Money that'd come from my grandfather's beloved football team. A team that meant more to him than family.

André ushered Coach to the door as Dan stood and watched me.

"Did you know?" I demanded.

"I'm sorry," he said quietly.

"*Did you know?*" I yelled.

His hands still in his pockets, he glanced down at his feet. "Jed told me to keep an eye on you." He looked up at me with guilt all over his bruised face. "I didn't figure it out at first, but, Sie, come on, you have his eyes."

Oh my God. "Leave." Gulping for air, I turned my back. A thousand emotions flew through my head, but all I kept thinking was that I'd gained and lost a grandfather in two sentences. *Jed Burrows died last night. Jed was your grandfather.*

"Come on, baby." Dan wrapped his arms around me like he had a right to touch me. "We'll get through this. Just put my ring back on and we'll do this together, you and me."

Shocked, infuriated, I shoved his arms off me and spun. "*Together?*" Was he insane? "There is no us. There will *never* be an us. You're a lying, cheating bastard and you can take your ring and shove it!"

"You're upset right now. I get it." He glanced at André as André moved to my side. "I'm not going to hurt you." He half laughed. "Come on, you don't need protection. It's just me, babe."

"Get out of my house," I ground out, furious.

His hand on the gun in his holster, André stared Dan down. "She told you to leave. I'm not as polite." He tipped his chin toward the door. "You have two seconds."

Dan's face twisted into a sneer. "Who the hell are you to tell me what to do?" He dropped the fake caring voice. "You screwing her now too?"

Dan didn't even get the last word out.

André moved lightning fast. Drawing his weapon, getting in Dan's face, he grabbed his shoulder and aimed his gun point-blank on Dan's balls. "Apologize," André demanded.

Like the coward he was, Dan threw his hands up. "Relax."

"In case you're wondering, the safety's off. Your next breath better be an apology."

Dan scoffed. "She knows I didn't mean it."

André's voice went lethally quiet. "All she knew was a man who has a hundred pounds on her grabbed her from behind after she told him to leave. From where I'm standing, that's aggravated assault."

Dan's face paled but his tone was belligerent. "And a gun to my balls isn't?"

"Two choices. Apologize and walk out." André paused for half a second. "Or don't."

Dan ground his jaw then spoke without an ounce of remorse. "My apologies."

"Step back, two paces, turn and walk out. You ever return, I'll be waiting." André let go of Dan's shoulder only to hold his gun with both hands and raise his aim to Dan's chest.

Dan smirked at André then glared at me. "This isn't over." He stormed to the door then slammed it shut behind him.

André glanced at me as he holstered his weapon. "You okay, chica?"

My heart in my throat, I could only nod.

TWENTY-NINE

Jared

MY PERSONAL CELL PHONE RANG AS I WATCHED THE carnage of my work cell fall seventeen stories. It stopped and three seconds later it started ringing again. I didn't look at the display. With my head fucked up, the letters would've been jumbled anyway. I didn't think for one second it would be her. If I did, I would've answered it immediately.

In a fucking war with myself, I was half a second from driving to Luna's to see her. But the last ounce of rational thought I still had told me to wait until the lawyer resolved the lawsuit.

The phone rang again and I picked it up. "What?"

"I've been calling you," Luna barked.

My chest tightened. "She okay?"

"Now you care?"

Adrenaline kicked in. "Goddamn it, what happened?"

"Something's going down at her house. The coach is here, so are your punching bags and their sidekick."

"*What the fuck*, Luna?" I growled, grabbing my keys. "You

let them into her house? And why the hell is she home? You were supposed to keep her safe." I'd sent Tyler away because Red wasn't here anymore, but the media was still camped out in front of my place. I couldn't imagine what kind of shit show was going down at her place.

"Calm down, she's secure, but she wanted to go home this morning. Only the coach and your boyfriend are inside."

I didn't bother with the elevator. "If that fucking pussy touches her, kill him."

"You kicked her out, bro."

I ground my teeth, barely refraining from telling him off. "What are they saying to her?"

"Don't know, but the team's general manager scheduled a press conference for nine o'clock."

Jesus Christ. "What the fuck for?"

"That's what I'm trying to figure out. Get over here."

"I'm on my way." I hung up and jogged down seventeen flights. I was sweating the fucking alcohol I'd drunk last night by the time I hit the garage level.

Gunning the engine, I peeled out of my garage and sped past two news vans still parked by the front of the building. I didn't know if they knew which car was mine and I didn't care. I was only intent on getting to Red.

If her asshole ex was trying to drag her into the lawsuit, or if her fucking uncle was going to fire her, or worse, make an example out of her, I was going to level them both.

Breaking every speed limit, I made it to her neighborhood in record time, but when I gunned it around a corner and turned onto her street, my stomach bottomed out. There weren't a few news vans on her street, there was a fucking parade of them.

Braking so I didn't plow into one, I glanced at her house in time to see the coach getting behind the wheel of an SUV. I swerved around a news van blocking the street and was contemplating driving across her neighbor's lawn when I saw her asshole ex walk out of her house. Ahlstrom got in the front passenger seat of Coach's SUV as Luna stepped out her front door and scanned the street.

Seeing me, Luna glanced at the SUV then nodded at the driveway. I fucking got it. Wait till they pulled out then drive into their spot. One of Luna's company SUVs that was parked behind their vehicle backed up and the coach pulled out.

I waited in the street to fucking glare at the asshole quarterback as they passed then I gunned it into Red's driveway.

Luna met me at my car, but the second I got out, the cameras were going off and my name was being shouted. I ignored all of it and aimed for Red's house as Luna shadowed me. "What's going on?"

He didn't respond as he walked me to the front door. Right before he opened it, he quietly answered. "Team's owner died last night. Your girlfriend was his only living heir." He pushed her front door open, shoved my shocked ass inside and closed the door behind me.

The silence of her house was deafening compared to the fucking circus outside, but neither that nor Luna's bomb could compare to the hit my chest took seeing her. Standing next to her dining table, her head down, her arms curled around herself, she swept at her face, but she didn't turn around.

"Thank you for getting rid of them, André." Her voice shook. "You can go now."

I stepped up to her back and her scent washed over me

183

like a fucking drug. It took every ounce of self-control not to pull her into my arms. "Red," I said quietly.

She sucked in a sharp breath, and backed up as she turned. "What are you doing here?" Tears running down her face, her makeup a mess, she wasn't asking the question, she was throwing out an accusation.

I forced my feet to stay put. "What happened?"

"Did André call you? Is that why you're here? You wanted to get in on the spectacle?"

She looked so fucking hurt, I wanted to kill someone. I'd get to what was going on, but first I needed to address the shit that went down between us last night. "I thought I was doing the right thing last night."

She laughed bitterly. "Oh, that's rich. Now that I might have something to offer, you're interested, is that it?"

I refrained from snapping back at her. "I don't know what happened." I wasn't going to assume shit.

"Right," she scoffed. "Like your Marine buddy didn't tell you everything." She moved toward the kitchen with none of her usual grace.

"Yeah, he called me, but that only sped up the timeline. I was coming to you no matter what." I sounded like a fucking pussy, but I didn't give a shit. It was the truth.

"Why, so you could screw me on my kitchen counter then leave without an explanation?" Her hand shook as she reached for a kettle on her stove.

The acidity in her tone left a bitter taste in my mouth because I was the one who put it there. I knew I'd fuck her up, but I stupidly didn't think I'd do it in such a short amount of time. My only saving grace was she hadn't kicked me out yet. "I wasn't coming here to fuck you." I was coming to apologize.

Again. Because deep down I knew what she was. I'd known it the second I'd laid eyes on her. It wasn't her designer purse or fucking Mercedes, it wasn't the cost of the shit she wore, or anything you could buy. It was her. Gracious and kind, her manners weren't a fucking act, she simply didn't have an agenda. You couldn't fake what she had. I'd known enough women who tried. But Sienna Montclair wasn't one of them. She was the real deal, and she was too damn good for me.

She laughed, but it wasn't a laugh I wanted to hear. "Even better. A male prostitute who doesn't want to sleep with me." She filled the kettle with water and dropped it on the stove. "You can leave now." She grabbed a box of tea bags then she went on her toes to reach for a bottle of Jack Daniel's high up in her cupboard.

I stepped behind her small frame and grabbed the whiskey. "No."

"This is *my* house."

She was so fucking defiant, I wanted to do exactly what she accused me of intending to do. I wanted to bend her over the counter and fuck, finger and spank her until her tears were from an orgasm I'd given her and not the fucked-up shit Luna had thrown at me.

I held the bottle just out of her reach. "You don't strike me as the type of woman to drink at nine o'clock in the morning."

"You don't *strike me* as the type of man who cares." She made a play for the whiskey.

I pulled back and she fell into my chest. "I fucking care."

"Give me that!"

Jesus, she smelled incredible. "Talk to me."

"Screw you!"

I couldn't stop myself. My arm curved around her back

and I fucking held her for all I was worth. "You wanna hit me? Do it. I'll take it. You wanna fuck this out, fine. I'll make you come so hard it'll be tears from me you're crying and not whatever the fuck just happened. But know this." I moved my arm up her back and cupped the back of her neck. "You'll still tell me what happened and I'll still care about you."

"You don't even *know* me." She spat the words out, but her face wasn't angry, it was hurt.

I dropped my voice. "I know how to make you blush. I know how to make you smile. I know how to make your eyes flutter shut. You're smart and pure and so fucking gorgeous, I don't deserve you." I laid it all out. "You're right, I don't know everything about you. But I know enough that walking away from my life just to have a single chance to wake up next to you is the best fucking decision I ever made."

"You threw that away last night," she accused.

"You didn't deny loving him." I shot right back.

Her eyes widened with shock. "*I walked away.*"

I didn't say shit. I just stared at her. If she didn't know what the fuck that looked like, then I was in the wrong fucking house.

Her face fell. "That's why you sent me away? Because you think I love him? You're blaming last night on me?"

I'd never said those three words to anyone, but she'd said them to that fucking asshole, and not years ago, weeks ago. "I'm not blaming you, but you have his ring and he was your first. What the hell was I supposed to think?"

She blanched. "That's what he told you?"

"You denying it?"

She pulled away and I let her go. "I don't see how that's any of your business."

"I offered you something I've never offered to another woman." I might as well have been standing there with my fucking dick hanging out. "An hour later, your ex is on my doorstep professing his love and you're not denying him. That makes it my business."

She dropped her head and the attitude in her tone disappeared. "I didn't know how serious you were."

"Dead fucking serious." I wasn't playing games.

The kettle whistled and she turned her back to me. "You know that's not normal?"

Neither was the complete mindfuck that happened the second I laid eyes on her. "Do you think I give a shit?"

"No." She took two mugs out.

"You're right." She might be getting to know me after all. I watched her put tea bags in the mugs and my hands went to my hips. "I don't drink tea."

She filled the mugs halfway with hot water. "And I don't jump into relationships five minutes after meeting someone."

"Neither do I." I didn't fucking do relationships, period. She was either mine or she wasn't. "Why were the coach and that asshole here?"

She ignored my question and put her manners back on like a fucking shield. "May I have the whiskey, please."

I'd forgotten I was still holding it. I set the bottle on the counter next to her. "Luna said the owner of the team died."

Her back stiffened. "Jed Burrows passed away last night." Her voice lowered to a whisper. "Apparently he was my grandfather."

If Burrows was her grandfather and the coach was her uncle... *Christ.* "DeMarco's his son."

"Stepson."

"And you never knew?" Un-fucking-believable.

She shook her head and poured three fingers of whiskey into each mug.

Jesus, her family was fucked. I waited until she set the whiskey down then I turned her to face me. "Red."

Her head bent, her arms at her sides, she wouldn't look at me.

"Hey." I tipped her chin and her eyes welled. "How did you not know?"

A fresh tear slid down her cheek. "My daddy never told me."

Hearing the despair in her voice, seeing the hurt in her eyes, it made me want to fucking pound her dead father and grandfather *and* her uncle. "Where's your mom?"

"She had Huntington's Disease. She passed away when I was ten."

Jesus fuck. I couldn't not touch her anymore. I pulled her into my arms. "I'm sorry, baby."

She choked on a sob then pushed me away. "I'm not some forlorn orphan." She swept at her face.

Seeing her sad was fucking killing me. "No, you're not. You've got a shit uncle who lies to you." I was going to have words with the fucker when I saw him. "Who else?"

She fished the tea bags out of the mugs, put them in the sink and inhaled. "Who else what?"

"Who else knew about this?"

She picked the mugs up and walked into the living room. "I don't know. I have no living relatives left to ask besides Coach. Well, any that I know of." She perched on the edge of the couch and set one of the mugs on the coffee table.

I sat down beside her and went for practical. "So in reality, what's changed since yesterday?"

She gave me side-eye.

I was just fucking thankful she wasn't still crying. "I'm not talking about us. I'm asking how this information changes anything from yesterday or last week or last month for you."

She sipped her drink. "There's an us?"

"You really want me to answer that?" Because I'd lay it all out. I didn't give a shit. I knew it was fucking crazy, but I wanted this woman. My past would come between us, some-way, somehow, but right then, just being next to her after missing the hell out of her last night, I didn't give two fucks. I'd figure it out.

"No. And nothing's changed except everyone I ever loved lied to me."

"Maybe there was a reason for it." And I was going to do what I could to find out for her.

She looked at me like I had two heads. "It's family. You may have a big family with a mess of siblings, but I grew up with no one except my daddy. If I knew I had other family, I wouldn't have taken that for granted." She took a big swal- low of her tea-flavored whiskey like she was intent on getting shitty.

The fucking crazy truth, we weren't that different. "It's just me and my dad." But the second I was old enough, I'd enlisted.

She cupped her mug in her lap. "I'm sorry to hear that."

I shrugged. "Life is what you make it, Red."

She took another huge swallow. "Then what were you making it when you decided to sleep with women for money?"

"You drunk yet?" She'd poured a triple into that mug.

"Why? You gonna lie to me too?" She tipped her drink back again.

"I never lied to you."

"Give it time."

I gripped her chin and she sucked in a shocked breath. "I have not, nor will I ever outright lie to you. You want to throw insults, make it count."

Her face crumbled. "What if I inherit the team?"

I stroked her cheek then cupped her face. "Then you'll be the quarterback's boss and you can trade the fucker." I didn't know jack shit about how the league operated, but I wasn't above planting the seed.

"That's not what I meant."

"You won't have to work for DeMarco." That prick would work for her.

Her voice went whisper quiet. "I'm scared."

I held her gaze. "I'm not going to let anything happen to you."

"That kind of money changes everything. People will want things from me. I won't know who to trust."

"First, you have no idea how this is going to play out, so don't worry about it yet. Second, trust is a bullshit relative term outside the military. Don't trust anyone. And third, sell the fucking team if you don't want the headache." I didn't care what she did as long as she was happy.

She stared at me for two heartbeats. "You don't care about money, do you?"

I brushed her soft hair from her face. "If I had none, I probably would."

"You make everything seem so easy."

I tipped the corner of my mouth up. "You overthink shit."

"Are you insulting me?"

"No, stating fact. It's part of who you are." And I wouldn't change a damn thing about her.

Her gorgeous green eyes took me in. "You have money, don't you?"

She wasn't asking about the size of my bank account. Her shoulders tense, her hands gripping the mug, she was looking for something from me. But all I had was the truth. I tipped my chin toward the door. "You want to walk out of this life right now? Let's go." I was all in for that plan. "I have plenty to take care of us."

She exhaled. "That's crazy."

"I can think of a lot crazier shit." Like sticking around to see how all this would play out.

"I think you were looking to escape your life before I showed up."

I picked up the fucking tea and chugged half. "You want the truth?"

She shrugged.

"I haven't been able to escape shit since that fucking IED hit our Humvee. I laid like a weak piece of shit in that hospital bed and I had no control. Not over my thoughts, my body, my treatment, nothing. I hardly sleep at night, I can't read, I can barely dial a damn phone. Half the time I'm pissed off, and the other half I want to control something. I found fucking and working out. It was keeping me sane, but it wasn't an escape." My head down, my elbows on my knees, I looked at her. "Then you showed up in a yellow dress like a ray of hope."

She swallowed. "Jared—"

I wasn't finished. "I don't give a fuck who your family is or was. I don't care about football or money or your asshole ex. I just want to breathe the same air as you."

She closed her eyes and a tear slid down her cheek.

I forced myself not to touch her. "I'm no good for you. I'll fuck you up in ways you never imagined. You're probably better off with a goddamn baller. But I'm selfish enough to try and convince you otherwise."

She looked at me. "I shouldn't want to let you."

I didn't hesitate. "No, you shouldn't, but I'm hoping you will."

"I don't love him," she whispered it like a confession.

I tucked a strand of her hair behind her ear. "You waited a long time to give yourself away, Red."

"I was… hoping I would meet the right person." She dropped her head. "Then I got tired of waiting."

"I'll never be careless with you." You didn't have to be a genius to realize what sex meant to her. But she hadn't gotten what she'd wanted from it, so she was trying to numb herself to it. If anyone could understand that shit, I could.

She was quiet a moment. "You said I was vanilla."

I didn't blink. "You are."

She stared into her mug. "You said it like it was a bad thing."

"There's nothing wrong with you, Red."

"You've been with a lot of women."

I didn't deny it. I'd been with countless women, but none were her. "Enough to know what I want."

She looked up at me. "Why me?"

I cupped her face and stroked her bottom lip with my thumb. "Because you make me nervous." I couldn't explain it any better than that. Not with words. I leaned down and brushed my lips against hers, and for the first time since she'd walked out of my place last night, I could breathe past the heavy weight on my chest.

My forehead to hers, our eyes locked, I didn't need a single other thing in that moment. I didn't even need to pound her into submission. Holding her face, seeing the trust in her eyes, feeling her pulse race, it was better than any fucking drug.

THIRTY

Sienna

M Y HEAD SWAM, FROM HIM AND FROM THE ALCOHOL, and my thoughts bled out of my mouth. "You make me more than nervous."

His intense gaze cutting into mine, he didn't hesitate. "Good."

My eyebrows drew together. "Why is that good?"

"You know why."

I struggled through my whiskey blanket to understand which way he meant that. But my head was murky and hazy, like I was swimming through lake water. "I think I need to save that thought for when I'm sober."

He smiled and his face transformed. "Noted."

"You're beautiful when you smile." So, so beautiful. In a way I had no words for except that deep in my soul I knew his real smile was rare, and that broke my heart as much as it gave me joy to see it.

He shook his head like he was humoring me. "Men aren't beautiful, Red."

"You are, when you smile."

He smirked. "Appreciate it." His expression turned serious. "You're gonna be okay."

"I'm always okay. I have to be. I have a mortgage and house plants to take care of." I sighed. "And maybe a professional football team." I frowned again. "Do you even like football?"

"Except for quarterbacks."

I laughed, but then it hit me. "Who do I have to hate?"

The backs of his fingers stroked my cheek. "No one, baby."

"How can I feel both really insecure around you and safe? But not safe like your friend André makes me feel safe. That's nice and all, but that's a different kind of safe." All my thoughts kept coming out of my mouth unchecked. I glanced at my empty mug. "Maybe I shouldn't have finished my whiskey tea."

Amusement danced in his eyes. "I like you drunk, Red."

I smiled. "Are you going to take advantage of me?"

He turned serious. "Never."

Shame flushed my cheeks and I looked down at my lap. "I didn't mean—"

"I know what you meant, but I'm telling you that I won't ever take what you're not giving. You hear me?"

"Yes," I whispered.

"In and out of the bedroom," he clarified. "Understand?"

My cheeks burned. "Yes."

"Look at me," he commanded.

I lifted my head and I was struck all over again by how handsome he was. Mercurial and dominant, his face all hard angles and his eyes never anything less than intense, he was the most attractive man I'd ever met. And it scared the hell out of me.

His gaze held me as sure as his touch. "You're perfect, Sienna, exactly how you are."

"No one's perfect." Least of all my family. Hurt lanced at my heart, but the whiskey dulled it. Or maybe it was Jared and his deep voice and golden-brown eyes. Or the T-shirt straining across his huge biceps.

"That's the beauty of human perfection, Red. It can lay down in a bed of lies and still be fucking perfect. Imperfection makes life real."

Because I had no filter right then, I said the first thought that popped into my head. "Maybe you're talking about yourself."

"No doubt."

He was so grave, I remembered my morning wasn't the only thing he had going on. "Did you talk to André's attorney?"

He lifted his chin once.

"What did he say?"

"That he'd work on it."

His tone was so even I couldn't tell what he was thinking. "What does that mean?"

"If he's any good, he'll resolve it."

I nodded, suddenly overwhelmed. Putting my mug on the coffee table, I exhaled. "I should make us some breakfast." I stood and my knees wobbled.

Jared was up in a heartbeat and scooping me up. Cradling me to his chest, his strong arms held me as if I weighed nothing. "You're going to bed." He strode toward the hallway to the bedrooms.

"I'm a little tired. I couldn't sleep last night," I admitted, inhaling the scent of him. Soap and man and the whiskey I'd poured us wrapped around me like comfort and safety. More than anything, I wanted to crawl under my covers and feel his body curve around me.

"Which door?" His chest rumbled as he spoke.

"On the left."

He pushed the door open with his shoulder then kicked it shut behind us. After gently setting me on the bed, he started to walk away and I panicked.

"Where are you going?"

He gave me a half smile over his shoulder. "Nowhere, just closing the curtains."

My plantation shutters were closed, but I also had drapes in my bedroom. He pulled the curtains shut, and I ignored the reason he had to shut us in as the room fell into an unnatural darkness.

"I'll be right back. I'm going to talk to Luna for a minute." He brushed a kiss on my forehead and was gone.

I'd forgotten André and his employees were outside guarding my house from the media. If I did inherit a professional football team, I was sure it would only get worse for a while. Not to mention what would happen if the lawsuit between Jared and Dan escalated or the media got wind of it. The thought of losing my anonymity made me want to cry.

Before I could sink into despair, Jared was quietly walking back into my room. A part of me knew I should be more protective of my heart, now more than ever, but the second I saw him in my house this morning, I'd wanted to forgive him.

I had no reason to trust him, but my heart was past that. I wasn't sure I had a choice anymore how I felt. I just wanted to be with him.

I tucked my hand under my head. "That was quick. Is he leaving?"

Jared stepped out of a pair of boots that looked combat ready. "Tyler's staying. I called the lawyer I spoke with this morning. He's going to come here this afternoon to talk to you."

I watched him pull his T-shirt over his head with one hand. "Why?"

"Because you may need representation." He stepped out of his jeans.

The security, the attorney, I should have thought to handle that myself. And I definitely shouldn't have liked Jared taking care of me, but I did. "Thank you. Please let André know he can send me a bill for all of this."

"You're welcome." He pulled back the covers. "And you're not paying for shit."

"I can pay my own way."

"I'm sure you can, Mercedes SLK, but that's not happening." He snaked his arm under my head and pulled my back to his chest.

I turned to look at him. A sliver of light from between the curtains shone across his face, and I struggled to remember what I was going to say. "I could be rich, you know."

"Wouldn't change anything between us."

I hadn't known I was waiting for him to say that, but I was. My entire body let out a breath and I fought and failed to not compare him to Dan. "Dan told me Jed Burrows told him to look out for me."

Every muscle in Jared's body went rigid. "How so?"

"I'm not sure. Dan looked guilty after my uncle talked to me. And it struck me as strange that he came with Coach to begin with, after what happened in Coach's office. So I asked him if he knew what was going on and that's when he told me that."

Jared exhaled, but he didn't say anything.

"He said Jed never said anything but he figured we were related."

"That fucking tool," he ground out.

"Yeah." I regretted ever having feelings for Dan. Every second I spent with Jared made me realize just how much of a jerk Dan really was.

Jared brushed my hair aside and kissed just below my ear. "Close your eyes and forget about all that shit for now, beautiful."

"You have such a way with words."

"I'm a fucking poet."

In the dark of my bedroom, with the media camped outside and an uncertain future hanging over my head, I peered up at the one person who was making me feel both grounded and crazy in lust. "Every time you touch me, I want you."

"If you hadn't thrown back a triple whiskey, I'd be inside you right now."

Desire flared between my legs and I wanted more than just a quick brush of his lips against my neck. "You gave me wine the other night."

"That was different."

"How?" The alcohol gave me courage to ask.

"I wasn't trying to keep you then."

My heart melted. "You're trying to keep me?"

One hand fisted in my hair, the other gripped my chin, and he turned my head away from him as his mouth touched my ear. "You're pushing my restraint, Red."

The delicious growl to his voice made my toes curl. "I like you better without it."

Like a tidal wave, he surged.

THIRTY-ONE

Jared

I DROVE MY TONGUE INTO HER MOUTH.

Her sweet little body pushed against me and she moaned.

I thrust against her ass with my aching cock. "You want me buried inside that tight little cunt?"

"Jared," she pleaded.

Releasing her face, I cupped one of her full tits and squeezed the nipple. "That's all you got, Red? Just my name?" The second I touched her, she melted. From the moment I first kissed her, hell, from the second I opened my front door, I knew she was different. She eclipsed every woman I'd ever been with, and I couldn't even say why. I fucking loved it and I hated it. I wasn't in control of the shit running through my head, and for the first time in years, I didn't a give a damn about it.

"Please," she begged. "Touch me."

I was going to do a hell of a lot more than just touch her. Moans crawling out of her throat, her cunt soaked, her legs trembling as she came, I was going to make her body fucking sing. "I want you out of these clothes." I pulled her dress over her head, and the fucking doorbell rang.

Goddamn it. "Stay." I tossed her dress aside and grabbed my jeans.

"Who is that? I thought you said Tyler is outside."

"He is." But if he'd let a reporter through, I was going to fucking throat punch him. "Don't worry, I'll handle it." Adrenaline spiking, I stepped into my jeans and strode out of the room, closing the door behind me.

Two feet before the front door, the knocking started. I looked out the peephole and saw Tyler, but behind him was the defensive end, Terence Joyner, and whole fucking slew of reporters.

I cracked the door. "What?"

Tyler stood guard, not letting TJ get by, and lowered his voice. "You need to hear what he has to say, boss."

"He alone?"

Tyler nodded. "Affirmative."

I stepped back, belatedly wishing I'd thrown my T-shirt on as the cameras started snapping pictures and the reporters started calling my name. Tyler moved just enough to the side for TJ to pass, then inclined his head at him.

TJ smiled casually like this was an everyday occurrence for him, and slapped Tyler on the shoulder as he passed. "My man." He stepped into the house and offered me his hand. "What's up, marine?"

I stood back out of the line of sight of the cameras, but I shook his hand because he'd done me a favor at the restaurant. "Close the door."

He shut the door and dropped the smile. "Where is she?"

"Resting. Keep your voice down."

The giant defensive end put his hands on his hips and sighed. "I need to talk to her."

"Not happening. Anything you have to say goes through me first." I fucking hoped she stayed put until I knew what the fuck this was about.

Skeptical, he eyed me. "She never told me she had no boyfriend."

"She never told me you sexually harass her at work." It wasn't a wild fucking stab, I saw the way he'd looked at her at the restaurant.

He held his hands up. "Hey, man, just letting a pretty woman know she's got it going on. Nothing harassing about that. Besides, you know, Miss Sienna can handle herself."

Yeah, I'd seen how she'd fucking scolded him, but that didn't mean I wanted the asshole eye-fucking her every time she stepped foot in that complex. "What do you want?"

He looked down at his feet then back up at me. "I got no beef against no man. You hear what I'm saying?"

"Just fucking tell me." I didn't care what his agenda was, I wanted to know the content.

"Strom's got a hard-on for something he ain't got no right to. He was in bed with the owner long before he set his sights on Red."

"Keep talking."

"I didn't put it together until he called me and Sunshine this morning, saying he needed backup. That corn-growing Oklahoma farmer got an arm on him for sure, but a Super Bowl ring ain't all he's after."

"Speed this up." I didn't care what the hell kind of aspirations that asshole quarterback had as long as it wasn't Red anymore.

202

"He's been acting like Burrows's long-lost son for a while now. He'd go have dinner with him, talk about hanging out at his place. He even said they went over his footage."

Okay, now I was fucking listening. "And?"

"And he told Coach just now that Burrows promised him a piece of the team. He said it'd come out at the will reading but that he and Coach needed to strike fast and get Red on board before the body was cold."

My back fucking teeth ground in anger. "What'd DeMarco say?"

"Nothing. He didn't say a word, and if you knew Coach, you'd know that meant something was wrong." He glanced toward the hallway leading to the bedrooms. "You gotta tell her. I tried calling, but her phone's turned off."

That motherfucking asshole, Ahlstrom. "You knew who Coach was to Burrows?"

He shrugged. "A rumor went around when I first signed. A few of the players speculated, but you didn't mess with Coach. He was the only thing between you and a bench, and I just wanted to play. That family shit ain't none of my business."

Bullshit. I scoffed. "So you weren't hitting on my woman thinking you were going to score big?" What a fucking liar.

He held a hand up again. "Think what you want, man. I ain't got no reason to lie to you, but you'd have to be one blind motherfucker not to see that woman is smokin'. I asked her out, is all. I wasn't looking to give her the keys to my kingdom."

What fucking kingdom? He was goddamn defensive end. "You asking to be hit?"

He smiled. "We're good, man, we're good."

For a professional football player, he was a fucking pussy, but as human being, I couldn't deny he was being decent. "Anything else?"

"I'm no family shrink and I don't know nothing about all this 'cept what I overheard Strom telling Coach. But if you ask me, if Coach really was Burrows's family, there should've been a little more love."

No fucking kidding.

"You tell Miss Sienna I came to see her. That woman's never been nothing but a friend to me. She's good people, man. You hear what I'm saying?"

I did. She had a heart of fucking gold, but she needed new friends. "You eye-fuck her again, I won't stop at a broken nose."

He smiled and slapped my shoulder. "Wouldn't expect nothing less, marine."

"Keep setting the edge, Miami."

He grinned and punched my shoulder. "I *knew* you were a fan."

"Not of your fucking quarterback."

His smile dropped. "I don't like no one messing with Miss Sienna. She don't deserve that."

No, she fucking didn't. "I'll let her know you stopped by." After she talked to the Clark Kent lawyer.

"Thanks, man."

I opened the door a crack and nodded at Tyler, then stepped back.

TJ watched the interaction with curiosity. "He a marine too?"

"Yeah."

He nodded slowly. "I bet you all were some bad motherfuckers in uniform."

Christ. "Get the fuck outta here."

"Don't gotta tell me twice." He stepped around Tyler and his easy smile slid into place as he walked toward his car.

I glanced at Tyler. "No more interruptions. She's sleeping. I'll let you know when she's up."

"Copy that."

I locked the door and strode back into the bedroom, wondering what the hell I was going to tell Red. Turned out, I didn't have to say shit. When I opened the door to the bedroom, she was sound asleep.

I stepped back into the hall, pulled my phone out and scrolled to Luna's number.

He answered on the first ring. "What's up?"

"I need a favor."

"They're piling up."

"I know." Fuck, I knew. "I'll owe you."

"Come work for me and we'll call it even."

"You've got enough jarheads. You don't need me."

"I've got no one who can do what you do."

Shit. I rubbed a hand over my face as I exhaled. "I'm retired."

"Un-retire. I need someone who can't be seen."

"That's not gonna happen with my face all over the news."

"You know what I'm talking about."

Our buddy Talon had nicknamed me Ghost. I couldn't fucking read shit like maps to save my life, but I made up for it in other ways. I memorized locales, all the ways in, all the ways out, all the places you could breach. I learned to blend in, and I'd watched the way Neil never made a fucking sound. By the end of my first deployment, I had a rep for being a ghost—getting in and getting out with the recon we needed without ever being seen or heard.

I caved. "What kind of terms are we talking about?"

He named a price that was more than triple what I was thinking.

"Bullshit. You can't be making that much to pay me that." I didn't need the money. It wasn't about that. It was about something to channel my shit into. As much as I wanted to fuck Red twenty-four seven, I'd need something else.

"I can't handle all the business coming in. You'd be doing me a favor."

"I'd only be interested in field work." Fuck any office bullshit.

He didn't hesitate. "Understood."

"I'll think about it."

"That's all I ask. What do you need?"

"I want you to see what you can find out about Sienna being Burrows's granddaughter. What's in his will, what the fuck happened to split the family apart and why the asshole quarterback was kissing up to the owner before he died." And shit, the news conference. "And find out what the team is saying about Burrows's death."

"How much time do I have?"

"Couple hours." Red would sleep for a while.

"Damn, amigo." Luna exhaled. "I'm good, but I'm not that good. I'm not going to get anything on Burrows's will."

"Just do what you can." His computer skills were hacker level.

"Copy that."

"Thanks." I hung up and called the lawyer.

Six hours later, I was crawling out of my fucking skin. Worse than a motherfucking sand trap in Afghanistan, I had no rational out. I couldn't shoot my way out of the media shit-storm out front, and I couldn't take the four walls of her house up seventeen flights.

I stood against the fucking wall and alternated between watching her and the asshole news crews out front waiting to pounce. Tyler held his position, but I didn't fucking care. I wanted out of her house.

"Jared?"

I whipped my head toward her. "Yeah, right here." I let go of the curtain.

Sleep rough and husky, her voice traveled across my nerves. "What are you doing? What time is it?"

With her red hair sprawled across the bed, she looked like an angel. Inhaling, I told myself to suck it the fuck up. I could fucking hang. "You should get dressed. The lawyer will be here soon."

She sat up and looked at me funny. "What's wrong?"

Every fucking thing about me playing house, not to mention the pain I wanted to inflict on Ahlstrom. "Push the covers off." I tried and failed to make my tone sexual.

"Answer my question and I will."

I crossed my arms to stop myself from looking out the fucking window again. "You really want to play it like that?" I stalked toward the bed.

She sat up but brought the covers with her. "I think I do."

Six fucking hours I'd watched her sleep while more re-porters showed up. I hadn't turned on the TV nor done an Internet search, but I'd bet my fucking Mustang it'd leaked who she was, and my money was on a certain asshole quarterback.

I dragged my gaze from her suspicious expression to her

chest and lingered until she pulled the covers tighter around herself. "Spread your legs and push the covers down slow."

"Not everything is about sex," she said quietly.

I sucked in a breath and counted to ten. "You're right." It was about distraction and control and mind-numbing orgasms. It was about a woman who was going to break my fucking tenuous hold on sanity. "Sometimes it's about desire, and I want to see your gorgeous cunt."

She flinched. "I don't like that word."

"Pussy is vulnerable, fragile. Cunt is strong and powerful. And trust me, what your cunt does to me has nothing to do with defenselessness." I tipped my chin at the bedspread. "Push the covers down."

"What if I say no?"

I stilled because I hadn't anticipated that. "Are you?"

She hesitated. "No."

I whipped the covers off, grabbed her ankles and pulled her to the end of the bed. I spread her legs wide, and she shrieked as I loomed over her. "Here's the thing you need to remember about me." I gently pushed her ankles to the backs of her thighs and kissed her forehead for reassurance. "I'm predictable." Still holding her legs, I swept my tongue through her wet, exposed cunt and swirled around her clit. Then I forced myself to release her. "Get dressed."

"That wasn't predictable." Her voice a breathy moan, she held her legs where I'd put them. "And I didn't say no."

Jesus fuck, she had no idea how hot she was. I stroked myself through my jeans. "You asking for something?" She had to be sore as fuck. "Because that pussy still looks swollen."

"You said pussies were weak." Her cheeks flamed when she said *pussies*.

"I said fragile, not weak." I slowly dragged a finger through her desire.

She groaned. "I don't have an off switch around you."

I stroked her again. "Good. But you're not getting my cock in your cunt right now."

Her hands on her ankles, she whispered, "Please."

I dropped to my knees and latched on to her clit. I needed to come as much as I wanted to make her come. My head a fucking mess, her scent settled in, and for the first time in six hours, I was grounded. I swirled my tongue before biting her clit, then I sucked away the sting. Unzipping my jeans, I gripped my shaft and fucking stroked as I sucked the sweetest cunt I'd ever tasted.

Her hands dug into my hair and her thighs pressed against my face. I didn't like it, I fucking loved it. Sucking her off, stroking my rock-hard dick, it took seconds to make her come. Desire dripped out of her as her cunt started contracting. I wanted to bury myself to the hilt and come inside her, but I didn't even stick a finger in her. Hooking an arm around her waist, I rose as I pulled her ass over the edge of the bed. Then I pressed my cock to her clit and fucking exploded.

"*Fuck yeah.*" I rubbed semen all over her mound. "Whose tight cunt is this?"

Gripping my arms, her pussy still quivering, her nipples hard as shit, she looked up at me and licked her lips. "Yours."

"Whose?" I wanted her to fucking shout it.

"*Yours.*"

I leaned closer. "Say my name."

Her voice turned breathy and soft. "Jared."

"You're fucking mine, Red." I kissed her.

THIRTY-TWO

Sienna

K NEELING IN FRONT OF MY BED, JARED SWIRLED HIS tongue through my mouth and held my legs as my ass rested on his thighs. I was half on, half off the bed, my core still contracting with aftershocks, as his semen dripped down between my legs.

I reached between us and did something I'd never done before. I spread his seed all over my lower stomach.

"Fuck," he growled.

I tasted my finger and he lunged.

His hand threaded in my hair and he yanked, hard. "You do that again, and I'm not going to come on that sweet cunt next time."

"Promise?" I wanted him to come in my mouth.

His nostrils flared and he kissed me once. Fast and hard and with a single thrust of his tongue in my mouth, then he retreated, only to leave me wanting more. "Be careful what you ask for."

I didn't want to be careful. I wanted him to come inside me. I wanted to taste him. I wanted to run away with him just because it was something a preacher's daughter would never, ever do. I wanted so many things, but they all had a single thread in common. And that thread was a six-foot-three ex-marine, ex-male escort, who'd told me he couldn't read.

I looked down at his still-hard cock, the tip glistening with my desire as it rested against my folds and my thoughts scrambled. "What does it feel like?"

"What does what feel like, gorgeous?" He ran a gentle hand through the length of my hair.

"Coming inside a woman."

"I'll let you know when I come inside you."

I looked up at him? "You've never come inside a woman?"

He brushed my hair over my shoulder then trained his gaze on me. "Not without a condom."

My pussy pulsed.

He smiled, slow and wicked. "I can read you like a book, Red."

A fresh wave of desire for him surged between my legs, and my breathy voice gave me away. "I didn't say anything."

"You didn't have to."

I remembered what he'd told me earlier. "What do you mean you can't read?"

His smile and his gaze dropped, and he fisted himself. With deliberate slowness, he dragged the head of his cock through my folds and pressed against my entrance. "Do you want me to come inside you?"

My heart leapt and my body hummed. I didn't hesitate. "Yes."

He swirled his cock in a tight circle. "Do you know what a blast wave is?"

"No." I bit my bottom lip.

"Do you know what could happen if I come inside you?"

I knew he wasn't asking what would happen physically. He was asking if I knew what that would mean for us. "Yes," I whispered.

He looked up. "Are you giving yourself to me?"

In that second, in that moment, I knew what had been set in motion the minute I'd first laid eyes on him. I wasn't giving myself to him. I'd already given what I had to give. He had my heart. I didn't know if it was when he'd called me his woman in front of Dan or when he kissed me in the bar at Pietra's or when he'd said I made him nervous, but I was his. I'd never felt like this, and I'd never wanted anything more in my life. It was crazy and way too soon and any psychologist would have a field day with this, but I didn't care.

So I leapt. With both feet. "Are you giving yourself to me?"

He cupped my face and looked into my eyes like no man ever had. "Already a done deal."

But I had one fear. "What if you get sick of me?"

"Never happen."

"How do you know?"

One of his eyebrows arched. "You really want me to answer that?"

I barely nodded.

"I've fucked enough women to know."

My heart stung with betrayal as I tried to hold on to the simple, straightforward honesty of his response.

His hand on my face gripped me harder. "Don't fucking go there, Red. I see that look. You have nothing to be jealous of."

"All those women had you." How could I not be jealous?

"No," he said fiercely. "They *never* fucking had me. Not where it counts. Understand?"

A tear slipped down my cheek, and I hated the emotional wreck I'd turned into in a matter of days. "What happens when we run into one of them?"

"What happens when we run into the asshole quarterback?" he countered.

"You get mad?"

His jaw ticked. "Besides that?"

There were a hundred ways I could have answered, but suddenly, only one made sense. "We keep walking and go home together."

The tension in his muscles relaxed only marginally. "Can you handle that?"

He wasn't asking if I could handle seeing Dan. He was asking if I could turn away from his past. I didn't have a perfect answer. I couldn't say I wouldn't be jealous. I couldn't say I would handle it well. But I could say this—I didn't want the alternative. I didn't want to throw away my chance of being with him.

I cupped his face like he was cupping mine and I smiled. "Yes."

His thumb stroked my cheek. "I will always put you first."

"I'm going to be a jealous girlfriend." I never thought about it before, not even when I saw Dan with that cheerleader, but I knew it now, and I knew it was because of what I stood to lose.

The whisper of a smile tipped the right side of his mouth in a way that I was becoming addicted to seeing. "Wouldn't have it any other way."

I smiled wider. "Maybe even crazy jealous."

The other side of his mouth tipped up. "I'll fuck you in front of them to prove you're mine."

I feigned shock, but in truth, I was getting used to his outrageous dirty talk. "Maybe just kiss me."

"Cunt or nipples?"

"Jared Jacob Brandt!"

"Fuck, you sound like a mother."

My heart stumbled. "Do you want children?"

He inhaled sharp and fast. "I never used to."

I held my breath. "And now?" Because even though I'd told myself after my father died that I didn't want a family, I did. I'd always wanted one. I wanted a house full of laughter and the sound of little feet. I wanted Sunday family dinners and I wanted a family to call my own.

He stared at me and time stopped. "Now…" The head of his cock eased an inch inside me. "I'm thinking about it."

"I want children." I bit back a moan. "I want my own family."

"I want to fuck your virgin ass. I want to come inside your tight cunt. And I want to hear my name moan out of your mouth as my semen drips out of your pussy."

Heat flamed my cheeks as I desperately tried not to pulse around him or show a reaction. "I wasn't talking about your sexual fantasies."

"I know. I'm fucking distracting you."

I let myself pulse around him. "It's working."

He threw his head back and laughed like I'd never seen him laugh.

My heart filled with so much joy, I didn't know where to put it, but I still teased him. "You're incorrigible." I smiled wider than I had in a long time.

He gripped the back of my neck and kissed my forehead. "You're right." He lifted me by the waist and set me on the bed then he effortlessly rose to his full height. Taking my hands, he pulled me to my feet. "Come on."

I stood naked in front of him without an ounce of self-consciousness. "Where are we going?"

"Shower."

"I thought you liked me dirty."

My hand in his, he kissed me once. "Like you wouldn't believe." He led us into the bathroom and let go of my hand to turn the shower on, but when he glanced at the window, he frowned.

I moved around him to peek out between the blinds. I couldn't believe I'd fallen asleep for hours with them all out there, but having Jared here had made me feel safe. "They still camped out there?"

"They're fucking there." His hand raked through his dirty-blond hair. "We'll move to my condo after you talk to the lawyer."

"You don't like my house?" I joked.

"It's a house."

His bitter tone and his resigned expression gave me pause. "What's wrong?"

"Nothing." He tested the water then stepped out of his jeans. "Get in."

I stared at the broad expanse of his shoulders and his perfectly sculpted abdominal muscles and remembered exactly what he'd been doing when I'd woken up. "You said you wouldn't lie to me."

His chest rose and fell. "It's a nice house, Red, but there aren't enough stories between me and the world to ever be comfortable here."

My heart sank. I loved my house. My home was my sanctuary. Well, not when there were news vans parked out front, but otherwise, it was what I was most proud of. Every inch of my house had been carefully, painstakingly renovated or painted or improved with my blood, sweat and tears. "You couldn't live here?"

He shook his head.

How could you raise a family in a condo on the seventeenth floor? Or even have a dog?

"Say something," he demanded, his nudity as natural to him as breathing.

"Oh." I stepped into the shower.

Frustration all over his features, he followed. "Let it out. I know you've got something to say."

"I don't have anything to say." I was processing too many scenarios at once, but at the forefront was one that stood out above all else. How much was I willing to give up for this man? I picked up the shampoo.

"Goddamn it, tell me what you're thinking."

Water streaming down my back, steam swirling around us, I picked the least inflammatory thought running through my head. "This isn't how I envisioned what showering with a man would be like." I'd read romance novels, and this wasn't even close.

His hands went to his hips and his head fell back. "*Fuck.*" He intense gaze cut back to mine. "You never showered with a man before?"

My gaze traveled below his waist, and I still couldn't believe he'd fit inside me. Even at rest, he was long and thick. Just looking at him did things to me. I wet my hair single-handed as a now familiar dull ache persisted between my legs. "I've never been naked in front of a man in daylight hours before yesterday, let alone showered with one." I flipped open the cap on the shampoo.

His arm wrapped around me and he plucked the shampoo out of my hand. "Jesus Christ, woman." He reached behind me and set the shampoo back on the shelf, then held me in both of his arms. "You need to tell me these things."

I couldn't breathe when his naked body pressed up against mine. "You don't tell me everything." Like what a blast wave was. Or why he couldn't live on the ground floor. Or why sleeping with a bunch of women made him sure he'd never tire of me.

His hand smoothed over my wet hair. "You're even more gorgeous like this, naked, wet, no mask."

"Mask?"

"Makeup."

"You don't like me in makeup?"

"No."

To say I was surprised was an understatement. Didn't men like women all made up? "Why?"

His thumb dragged across my bottom lip. "I like you like this, innocent and pure."

"I'm not innocent." A twinge of regret hit me about Alex. I'd been so upset over Dan that one of the women in the office had joked that I looked like I needed a night with a willing male with no strings attached. The idea had struck and taken hold. When I'd asked her where you found a guy like that, she said you didn't, you paid for it. She told me about the "dates" her friend went on with a gorgeous guy. A day later, she handed me a piece of paper with a number. I'd laughed it off and tossed it out in front her, but when she'd walked away, I fished the number out of the trash. A week later, I'd called.

"When you're naked in my arms, Red, you don't get to think about other men."

I started. "I wasn't."

"Yes, you were."

"How can you tell what I'm thinking?" I didn't know how the hell he did that.

"Body language, facial expression, but mostly I pay attention. I know you've been with two men before me, and I know who they are. I said you were innocent and you denied it. It didn't take a fucking genius to guess you were thinking about Vega."

"I don't regret that." I dipped my head. "I met you."

"I'm not holding it against you."

"You just don't want to talk about it."

"Ever."

I nodded. "What is a blast wave?"

He grabbed the shampoo and squirted some into his hand like he needed a distraction. Once he was lathering it into my hair, he started to speak. "When an IED detonates, the aftershock is called a blast wave. It's fucking loud, and if you're close enough, the wave itself can kill you. Same principal behind not being close to a rocket launch. Bursting your eardrums is the least of your worries. Blast waves can scramble your fucking brain." His hands worked through my hair like a professional.

"The blast wave from the fucking IED worked me over. Now I have trouble with numbers and letters. I'll see them sideways and upside down. Even though my brain knows it's wrong, I can't always focus. I'm shit for reading or dialing a phone."

"You texted me. And called."

"Not without effort."

I didn't know which emotion was more prevalent, my heart aching for him for his struggles or for the fact that he'd made the effort to text and call me. "Is that why you have so few numbers programmed into your phone?"

He studied me. "I threw out my work phone. The phone I had you hold on to is my personal cell."

"You threw out your work phone?" I should be happy, but I wasn't ready to trust it.

"Crushed the SIM and tossed the phone." He leaned my head back under the hot spray.

His hands on me and in my hair felt better than good. "So there's no going back for you?"

"I told you I wouldn't." He said it without irritation.

I questioned it anyway. "Just like that?"

"Yes."

Tension eased out of my body as his strong hands ran through my hair. "How long were you…?" I didn't want to say prostituting.

He watched what he was doing with the same intense stare he used on me. "Three years."

Oh God. "That's a long time." A really, *really* long time.

"Too fucking long," he agreed.

"So…." I hesitated. "It wasn't just me that made you change your mind?"

His gaze cut to mine. "You got a problem with being the catalyst?"

Did I? "No." I didn't think so.

"Good." He tilted my head back up and amber-brown eyes I could get lost in studied me. "You got his ring?"

"Yes." I would be lying if I said I didn't think what it would be like to belong to Jared, to wear his ring.

"How come you never gave it back?"

"I tried." Several times. "He refused to take it back. But it wasn't an engagement ring."

Reaching for the soap, he paused. "There's another kind of ring?"

"It was more of a promise ring."

His eyebrows drew together. "What the fuck is that?"

"A promise of an engagement?" I didn't actually know, now that he'd asked.

"What a fucking pussy. You either ask a woman to marry you or you don't."

I fought a smile. "You swear a lot."

"You denying he's a pussy?"

"No." The next question bled from my subconscious. "Have you ever thought about getting married?"

"Not as much as you." He lathered the soap in his hands and ran them over my shoulders. "Turn around, gorgeous."

It didn't escape my notice that he hadn't said he didn't think about marriage. "Maybe, when I was younger."

His hands ran over my back, massaging my tight muscles. "You're still young."

"I'm five years older than my mother was when she had me." Oh my God, I loved the way he touched me, bold and dominant but also gentle. "How old are you?" I couldn't believe I'd never asked him.

"Twenty-eight." His hands ran over my ass and squeezed, then he turned me back to face him. "Did you stop thinking about getting married after your dad died or after the asshole quarterback?" He picked up the soap again.

He was incredibly perceptive, shockingly so. "Why do you ask?"

"Curiosity." He soaped the small patch of curls between my legs that I kept neatly trimmed.

Something I'd noticed about him, he never shrugged or made unnecessary body movements. He didn't gesticulate when he spoke. He didn't have a swagger when he walked. It was as if every movement was purposeful and calculated. "Do you know you don't shrug?"

"Yes."

I wanted his hand to move lower, but he swept across my stomach and over my hips. "Is that purposeful?"

He stared at his hand as he rubbed a thumb over my nipple. "Observation happens with stillness."

I bit back a groan. "Do you like to be an observer?" His other thumb found my neglected nipple and, oh my God, that felt good.

Cupping both breasts, he brushed his thumbs rhythmically back and forth. "I was trained to be observant."

"By the Marines?"

"Yes." He increased the pressure on my nipples, and I felt it in my core. "Do you want to come?"

So, so bad. "Not yet. What did you do in the Marines?"

"Recon."

"I'm not sure what that means."

"We hunted bad guys."

I couldn't figure out if it was a flippant comment aimed at a civilian or simply another one of his statements of fact. "Did you enjoy it?"

"Combat is addicting."

"You didn't answer the question." Desperately rubbing

my thighs together, I ached to feel the kind of release only he could give me.

"I didn't enjoy it as much as I'm about to enjoy making you come this way."

"Is that possible?" The burning ache in my core was almost intolerable.

"Your legs are trembling, your nipples are dark and hard as shit, if I tongue you right now, you're gonna fucking detonate."

"Tongue me where?" I panted.

His mouth latched on to one breast, his fingers twisted the other nipple, and he pressed his cock against my pussy.

My head fell back, a guttural cry ripped from my lungs and I exploded. "*Ahhhh.*"

Pleasure-pain shot from my nipples and traveled to my core where the pulsing effect was secondary to what was happening to my breasts. Unlike every other orgasm I'd had with him, this one wasn't a release. It was as if a switch had been hit and I became singularly focused on getting him inside my body, but at the same time, I didn't think I could take any more. "What are you doing to me?" The blood drained from my head, and if I weren't gripping handfuls of his hair, I would've sunk to my knees.

His tongue swept across one nipple then the other before he brought his lips to mine. "You're so fucking beautiful, Red."

Heat hit my cheeks as warmth curled in my stomach. "You're turning me into an addict."

"As long as I'm the drug."

Oh, he was my drug. I smiled and he kissed me.

Slow and sensual, he swept through the heat of my mouth. With his huge hands holding either side of my head, it was the gentleness of his touch and his kiss that sent me over the edge. For the first time in five years, I wasn't thinking about steeling myself against hurt by blocking my feelings to anyone and everyone. I was thinking about a future. With him.

He pulled back and looked into my eyes. "I hear you thinking."

I wasn't ready to tell him how I felt yet. I wasn't sure I was ready to even acknowledge it out loud, so I brought up another question I had. "Why don't you like my house?"

He eyed me for a moment like he knew I was deflecting, then he picked up the soap. "The house itself is fine. It's the location and the elevation of it."

"So you're not against ever living in a house? It just has to be the right house?" I was trying to wrap my head around this, but I was missing something.

He scrubbed the soap across his chest. "I don't talk about Afghanistan and I don't fucking dwell on my time in the Marines, but I will say this. Once you've been in a war zone and you see how fucking easy it is to breach a home on the ground level or even on the second or third floor, you wouldn't feel fucking safe in your house either."

I didn't belittle him by telling him Coral Gables wasn't a war zone. How could I? He was right. Anyone could walk up to my front door and kick it in. If living higher up made him feel more secure, who was I to take that away from him? "I never thought of it like that."

"No, you were probably thinking kids and dog and a yard in a high-priced zip code."

I didn't deny it. "I was." Watching him wash himself felt almost more intimate than having him inside me.

"That a deal breaker for you?"

Was it? Did it matter where I lived? I didn't have an easy answer. My whole world was changing faster than I could blink. I took the soap from him then casually pressed on his side to get him to turn. "What about a big sprawling ranch on forty acres?" He didn't move.

His muscles tensed under my hand. "You got something you wanna tell me?"

I smiled, but it didn't reach my eyes. "I don't have a ranch." Would he let me wash his back?

He studied me. "But you want one."

I half laughed, half sighed. "Did I have a tell just then?"

"Fake smile."

I held the soap up and went for a more direct approach. "May I?"

"Why?"

"Because I want to make you feel good like you made me feel good."

"Then you should put the soap down."

His expression was so serious, I couldn't tell if he was teasing. "I don't know if you're serious or not."

"I don't need my back washed, Red."

"Ever?"

He didn't hesitate. "No."

"So it does hurt?" I regretted my stupid question as soon as I asked it.

"It's fine."

"That's not what I asked." I put the soap back on the caddy.

"Christ, you're working me. You want to touch my scars, go ahead. You want to drag your nails down my back while you fucking come on my dick, bring it. But if you want to wash my back like I'm some goddamn infant that needs coddling, forget it. I have scars, I'm not a goddamn broken pussy who needs a woman to lick my wounds."

"Well, when you put it that way."

He brushed my hair off my face and changed the subject. "Why a ranch?"

I didn't even think of not answering or bargaining for the answer I wanted out of him. "Growing up, I always wanted to learn to ride horses, but Daddy couldn't afford it. He promised me one day, but after my mother passed away, I stopped asking." Jared had a way of peeling back my layers with unmatched deftness. I couldn't tell if it was because he was cunning or simply bossy.

"I'm sorry you lost your mom."

"Thank you. What happened to your mother?" He'd said he'd grown up with only his father.

"Another man caught her interest. She decided she didn't like being a plumber's wife and a mother."

Wow. "Do you ever see her?"

"I saw her before I enlisted. I made peace with her in case I didn't come home."

I couldn't imagine being an eighteen-year-old and having to say goodbye to my family in case I didn't come home. "She didn't come see you after you got injured?"

"I never told her."

"Your dad didn't call her?"

"He wouldn't do that."

I struggled to understand how his injuries couldn't bring a family together, but then again, I was only finding out I had a family after my grandfather was dead. "I'm sorry."

"I'm not. Let's get you dried off." He shut the water off.

"One day, I want to wash your back."

He paused. "Are you telling me what to do?"

Excitement coursed through my veins. "No, I'm making a request."

"Noted." He grabbed a towel and wrapped it around me.

"Is it always going to be like this?"

"Like what?" He wrapped a towel around himself, and I couldn't help but notice that he was still aroused.

"Talking like this…." Naked and intimate and no holding back.

"Don't know. Never done this before. But I will tell you this." He reached under my towel and between my legs. Sliding his fingers back and forth, a smile tipped the corner of his mouth. "When talking stops working, I'll start fucking."

THIRTY-THREE

Jared

"I SHOULD BE APPALLED BY YOUR CRASSNESS." SHE pulled the towel tighter and it pushed her tits together.

My dick a goddamn rocket, I wanted to tit fuck her. I breathed through the need for her that was only getting worse every time I touched her. "You should."

"But I'm not." She smiled the shy smile that was becoming my favorite thing to see, next to her face when she came.

"Good." I was conditioned to fuck. I'd fed the beast for three years, and before that, I wasn't a damn monk. But this constant hard-on was fucking new for me. Nothing eased it. I came with her, and five seconds later, I was ready for more.

She glanced around her bathroom. "I, um, need to get ready."

"So get ready." She could take a piss in front of me and I wouldn't care.

"Okay." She exhaled. "I get that you're not shy and perfectly comfortable being around me, but I need a little privacy to do my hair and makeup."

She looked fucking gorgeous just how she was. She didn't need to do a damn thing, but I needed to check if the lawyer was here. "I'll be in the living room." I turned to go.

"Jared?"

I loved my name on her lips. "Yeah?" I glanced over my shoulder.

Heat colored her cheeks. "Did you… shower with any of the women?"

Fucking hell. I turned and grabbed the back of her neck. "You can ask me any damn thing you want. But I am never going to discuss what I did or didn't do with a client." I didn't want to fucking say what I had to next, but I couldn't leave it hanging anymore. I was already in neck-deep, and if she was going to walk, it needed to be now. "I need a clean slate, Sienna. If you want this to work, you're gonna have to trust me on that."

"Trust is earned."

I couldn't fault her for being right, but she was missing the point. "Then give it time to grow. I'll never give you a reason to be jealous."

"Your past makes me jealous. I can't help it."

The sick part of me wanted to smile. If she was jealous, it was because she gave a shit. But I also knew a festering wound when I saw one, and I didn't have a fucking clue how to close this one.

I ran a hand through my damp hair. "All right, here's the deal. You get two questions." She opened her mouth and I held my hand up. "Two fucking questions, *total*. You can ask whatever the hell you want, and I'll answer, but after that, I'm done. So think about what you want to ask and make it count."

She barely waited until the last word was out of my mouth. "Did you ever have feelings for any of your clients?"

"Is that your first question?"

She nodded. "Yes."

"No."

Her eyebrows drew together. "No, you're not answering or no you didn't have feelings for anyone?"

"You said clients, not anyone, and the answer is no."

Her face scrunched up in confusion and disbelief. "Really? Not at all?"

I dropped my hold on her and my hands went to my hips. "It wasn't about the clients, Red." I couldn't touch her and talk about other women. It felt fucking wrong.

She looked even more confused.

Fuck me. "It was never about them. It was always about me. Yeah, they fucking smelled nice or looked good or even felt good for five fucking seconds as I got off, but it wasn't about them. It was about me having control. I wasn't looking for a fucking girlfriend. My aim wasn't some bullshit domestic fantasy. I played rough, I fucked harder, and I breathed in the control. I used it to escape." I saw every fucking judgment in her shocked expression, but I went on because she asked. She'd fucking *asked*.

"War is a trigger. Violence gets under your skin and you can't un-live it. You don't want to. The Marines trained me for combat, but I own it. I own every skill I honed to kill and I live it. I'm not fucking perfect, but I don't regret who I am and I don't regret fucking women for three years for money. It served its purpose." I stared her down. "What's your second question?" I demanded.

She swallowed. "I—" Her voice cracked. "I don't have one."

"Get dressed." I strode out of the bathroom, not sure who I was more fucking pissed at, myself for talking to her in that tone or her for not recognizing what we had between us as fucking special.

I didn't have a damn second to think about it because she followed me.

"You're angry I asked the question."

"Goddamn it, Red. I'm not angry about the fucking question."

"Then what are you angry about?" She held the towel around herself like a shield.

I felt fucking guilty because even though she was smart as hell, she didn't have the experience with sex that I did. But I also knew myself. If I backed off or lied to her now, it would be pointless to stay another goddamn second in her place. "I was pissed that you didn't recognize that shit between us is different."

I saw the change in her expression before she opened her mouth and her pink suit voice bled out. "I grew up with a hardworking minister father who left my day-to-day care to a whole mess of church ladies because he had a parish to run. When those ladies weren't putting the fear of God in me, they were busy telling me how the devil was in all the young men in the parish. They said they were just waiting to get the milk for free. So I stayed away. Turned out, they should've just warned me to stay away from male escorts." She turned tail and slammed the bathroom door.

Inappropriate as hell, I fucking smiled and grabbed my jeans as my phone buzzed. I answered without bothering to look who it was. "Yeah."

"The lawyer is here," Tyler said.

"Send him in." I hung up and threw on my clothes. I was walking into the living room when I heard the knock on the front door. Turning the deadbolt that wouldn't do shit to stop an intruder, I opened the door.

"Mr. Brandt." Clark Kent aka Mathew Barrett nodded at me with a grave expression that I was beginning to despise.

I didn't say shit. I glanced at Tyler and all the fucking leech news crews yelling for my attention, then I closed the door.

Barrett exhaled and pulled his messenger bag off his shoulder. "That's a lot of press."

I cut right to the chase. "Did you do what I asked?"

The lawyer leveled me with a look. "Yes, and unfortunately, your day just went from bad to worse."

"Sienna's getting dressed. You have thirty seconds."

He dropped his bag on the coffee table but neither of us sat. "Ahlstrom's filed assault and battery charges in addition to the lawsuit. I've drawn up a testimony based on the video I saw and a friend of mine who is on the police force will be here soon for you to file your own charges. Assault and battery for the restaurant and assault charges for when he showed up at your house. Additionally, you're going to file an order of protection."

Motherfucker. "I told you I'm not filing a fucking restraining order." I didn't care what charges that asshole filed. The videos everybody and their mother took showed it was self-defense.

"You're out of options. If you want me to represent you, then this is how we're doing it."

Goddamn it, I wasn't going to be strong-armed by a Marvel Comics-looking motherfucker. "I'll think about it."

"If you want to retain your personal wealth and freedom, then I suggest you do more than think about it. I get paid either way."

Fucker had some balls. "I'm not getting arrested."

He shrugged. "That's up to the prosecutor's office now. But the quicker we file our own charges, the better it is for you." He reached for his bag. "However, I have a feeling this news is going to pale in comparison to what else I found out."

Every muscle in my body tensed. "What?"

"Jed Burrows's will is being read tomorrow, and not only are Mr. DeMarco and Miss Montclair requested to be at the reading, but so is Mr. Ahlstrom."

"Jesus *fuck*."

THIRTY-FOUR

Sienna

IS HEAD DOWN, HIS HANDS ON HIS HIPS, JARED SWORE. A tall man with jet-black hair and black-framed glasses stood next to Jared. "I don't know the particulars, but he must be named if his presence is being requested." In a pressed dress shirt and what had to be custom-made trousers to fit his height, the man bore a striking resemblance to Superman.

I stepped out from the hall and both men immediately looked up.

"Hello." The handsome man with the glasses stepped forward. "You must be Miss Montclair." He extended his hand. "I'm Mathew Barrett. I'm Mr. Brandt's attorney."

His voice was deep, but he looked too young to be an attorney. "Mr. Barrett." I shook his hand as Jared took in the exchange with narrowed eyes.

"Come, have a seat. I believe we have some things to discuss."

Jared stepped between us. "Give us a minute." He ushered me into the kitchen and dropped his voice. "I hate milk, Red."

"Meaning?" He was using my nickname, staring at me like he wanted to devour me, and I knew what he meant. He was

233

referencing the analogy I'd told him the ladies in the church had warned me about. He was saying he wasn't going to use me. But I wasn't letting him get off that easy. He needed to say the words because I needed to hear them.

"I'm not going to take advantage of you." Strong, decisive, his words were as potent as his tone.

"Taking advantage isn't limited to only the physical."

"You're right. Physically I'm going to take full advantage of you and your gorgeous body, every damn chance I get. But I'll never intentionally belittle you for your lack of experience. I fucking love that innocence. I wasn't trying to hurt your feelings with what I said earlier."

Hearing him say *love*, my heart melted and my stomach fluttered. I wanted to rush at him so bad, it hurt not to touch him. "Okay," I breathed.

He stepped closer. "What you're feeling right now?" His fingers dragged through my hair then gently held the strands at the end for a pause. "What we've got going on?" His hand traveled down my arm to my hand and he laced his fingers through mine. "It's fucking special."

"I know," I whispered.

"Then trust it."

"Okay." I didn't care if the attorney was watching, I willed him to kiss me.

A storm surged in his golden-brown eyes, making every streak of brown go dark gray. "I'm not giving Clark Kent a fucking show. I'm gonna wait till he's gone, then I'm going to touch you." He squeezed my hand. "Understand?"

Heat flooded between my legs and the air left my lungs. "Mm-hm." I pulled my lips into my mouth.

"Do you know how good I'm going to make you feel?"

His thumb stroked slowly across my knuckles, feeling every ridge and valley as if it were my most erogenous zone.

Nervous, not sure how to say it, I hinted at what I wanted. "I want to make you feel good."

His heated gaze went to my lips and his voice dropped. "You ever sucked a man off, beautiful?"

"No," I shyly admitted.

His eyes closed for a brief moment, and when they opened again, they were almost black with desire. "You're so fucking perfect, Sienna Montclair."

Warmth swirled in my stomach and spread to my veins. My cheeks heated, and I dropped my head.

His finger tipped my chin. "No," he said in a fierce whisper. "Never shy away from me."

His utter dominance, his natural scent, musk and man and all-consuming, fell around me like a barrier to the outside world. "Okay."

He studied me a moment. "I need to tell you something. I don't want you to hear it from the lawyer."

The intensity of the moment bent to make room for doubt. "Was this all a distraction leading to this moment?"

"I asked you for trust," he reminded me.

I dipped my chin. "I'm sorry. You're right, you did." But I no longer felt sexy and wanted by man so far out of my league sexually. I felt like I was drifting.

He searched my face. "What just happened?"

I hesitated. "Nothing."

"Don't lie to me."

I gave him the truth. "I'm not trusting. Not by nature or by circumstances. Just as you're asking me to trust you, I'm going to ask you to be patient with me."

"Fair enough. Tell me what made you frown like that."

"I felt… alone."

His eyebrows drew together. "And?"

"And like you were only being nice to me to butter me up so you could tell me something bad."

"No, I needed to clear the air between us from before you went to change."

"Okay." I was beginning to understand that he didn't like to leave things hanging between us.

"But I do naturally like to dominate you, Red. That's never going to change."

"I like that part," I admitted, heat flaming my cheeks.

The hint of a smile touched his face. "I know."

The one tip of the corner of his mouth was all it took. I didn't feel alone anymore. I smiled. "I pretty much forget whatever we were talking about when you smile at me."

"Did I smile?" He smiled.

I swooned. "Okay, I'm good. Tell me what you need to tell me."

His face instantly sobered. "Ahlstrom's going to be at the will reading."

It was as if someone turned out the lights. I completely shut down emotionally. My mind conjured up crazy reasons why he would be in Jed Burrows's will, then, just as quickly, I dismissed them as Dan's confession this morning settled into place and tainted everything I never knew I had in a grandfather.

"Red?"

"I'm good." I pulled my hand away. "I should go talk to your attorney."

He pulled me back with a hand around my nape. "Remember what I said."

He'd said a lot of things, things about touching me, not taking advantage, he was giving up his clients, he couldn't read, he wanted me to trust him. Forcing air into my lungs, I looked up at him. "Nothing's changed since before I knew who Jed Burrows was." I didn't know if I was telling him or myself.

His knees bent, he dipped his head and got closer to my eye level. His huge hand caressed the back of my neck. "We got this."

But there wasn't a *we* for this. There was me and this was my screwed-up family and I wished none of it was happening. The headache started right between my eyes. "We shouldn't keep him waiting." The attorney was probably billing Jared for every minute we wasted talking to each other.

With only a nod, Jared led me back into the living room.

Barrett gestured at my couch as if he were in charge. "Miss Montclair, I don't know if you've had an opportunity to check your messages today, but the law firm representing your grandfather is requesting your presence tomorrow in their offices to read the will."

I'd kept my phone intentionally off since yesterday. "I didn't know he was my grandfather until this morning. Do I need some sort of DNA test to confirm this?"

Superman glanced at Jared as he sat down next to me. "It's certainly your right to request it, but I am going to assume a man as wealthy as Jed Burrows would not request your presence at the reading of his will if he were not absolutely certain of who you were to him."

"How did he die?" I'd forgotten to ask my uncle.

"Congestive heart failure. His attorneys can tell you more tomorrow." He sat in a chair opposite the couch and rested his elbows on his knees. "If you would like my presence with you tomorrow, I can accompany you to the reading."

I glanced at Jared. He nodded. "Thank you. I would appreciate it."

"I don't know what's going to happen, or how I will be able to alter any terms of the will, but I am glad you're choosing to have representation."

"I don't need to alter any terms. I'm not expecting anything from him, nor am I sure I want it." I didn't know the first thing about owning a professional football team, and if the reporters camped outside my house were any indication, then I certainly didn't want this life. "In the highly unlikely event that I inherit any part of the team, I will need to figure out how to sell it." I'd already made my mind up.

Superman looked at Jared again, and it was starting to make me angry.

"I assure you I can make my own decisions, Mr. Barrett. You don't need to look to Mr. Brandt for conformation or acknowledgement of any decision pertaining to my affairs. If I wish to confer with him, I will."

"Right, of course, my apologies."

Jared's arm snaked behind my back and his hand landed on my hip. "I think what he's getting at, Red, is that a professional football team is a lucrative business to own. Maybe you might want to wait till tomorrow to make any decisions."

Trying not to be pissed at the messenger, I attempted and failed to rein in my tenuous hold on my temper. "How much money?"

Jared looked at Superman. "You got a figure?"

Superman looked at me. "The team's revenue last year was 391 million. They've exceeded that so far this year."

My heart stopped and a ringing buzzed in my ears.

"Red?"

Oh my God.

Jared's hand moved to my nape. "Breathe, beautiful. Deep breath."

I sucked in a breath.

"That's it, baby. Another."

My body listened to him. I pulled air into my lungs. 391 million. In dollars. *391 million dollars.*

Superman rattled on as if I weren't losing it. "If you were to sell, I am not sure what the sale price would be, but the team was valued last year at two-point-five billion. Of course, Mr. Burrows upon his death only owned fifty-two percent of the team, so roughly half that."

I barely heard what he was saying. My head spinning, my breath short, thoughts scrambled. How could my mother and father never tell me about this? How could they keep such a secret? *Why* would they keep such a secret? What was half of two-point-five billion?

Jared snapped at Superman. "She fucking gets it, Barrett." He gripped my nape, hard. "Sienna, look at me. Fucking look at me." He enunciated each word.

Golden-brown eyes swam into focus and thoughts started bleeding out of me. "I don't want that kind of money. I don't even need it. But I could pay off my mortgage and not ever worry about a utility bill, but then I wouldn't even be able to live in my house because there's no gate. This isn't a gated community, and that's part of the reason I love my house. I never wanted to live in a cage, but this would be worse than a cage. It'd be a fishbowl, and I would need security. You would need security. My children, if I had any, would need security. I would need a Tyler around the clock."

"You have me," he calmly stated.

I didn't even hear him. "Everywhere I went, it would be like this. I would have to move. Maybe out of state, but I love Florida. Florida is my home, and one day I wanted to raise children here. I wanted them to grow up by the beach and breathe the spring air when the orange blossoms are in bloom and swim with dolphins and see the beautiful colors of the sunsets. But I can't do that if someone is always going to want something from me because I have money. How is that going to work? I'm not a princess, this isn't a fairy tale. *There's not going to be a happy ending to this story.*"

Jared stood and scooped me up. "Get her purse and her keys," he ordered Superman. "Lock the door and follow us close to my Mustang."

"Jared?" Alarmed, I squirmed. "What are you doing? Put me down!"

He held me tighter to his chest and strode toward my front door. "Not a fucking chance."

"I don't want to go out there," I shrieked.

"You promised me trust." He reached the door. "Head down, arms around my neck. Hide your face."

He opened the door, and I didn't get a second to react. Lights flashed, people yelled, so much yelling, my name, his name, even the lawyer's name. And questions, so many questions. My heart hammering, my lungs burning, my limbs shaking, I gripped Jared's neck hard and held on as he issued commands.

"Tyler, call Luna for extra security detail as you follow us to the condo. Keep formation, no separation. Tell Luna I want twenty-four seven, double guard. Barrett, open the passenger door. Meet us at the condo tomorrow morning at nine." Jared gently put me in the passenger seat of the Mustang.

Barrett handed me my purse and keys. "I'll see you tomorrow morning, Miss Montclair. I'll have paperwork for you to sign, retaining me on your behalf."

"She fucking gets it." Jared closed the door and moved around the front of the car as reporters came up on my lawn.

Tyler tried to hold them back, but there were too many of them and only one of him. Superman stood behind Tyler until Jared roared the Mustang's engine to life. Then he moved into Tyler's position as Tyler got behind the wheel of a giant black SUV.

With no regard for the reporters spilling across my property like vultures, Tyler drove the SUV across my lawn and paused on the street.

Jared backed up in front of him, then we were off.

THIRTY-FIVE

Jared

I WANTED TO HIT EVERY FUCKING NEWS VAN ON THE street. I floored the Mustang and she came alive under the hood. Steering one-handed, I wove in and out of the traffic jam that'd become her street and grasped her hand with my free one. Bringing her delicate fingers to my mouth, I kissed her knuckles. "Inhale, baby." She'd gone white as a ghost in her living room.

She didn't respond, but she drew in a breath.

My phone rang, and I hit the answer button on the steering wheel. "Speaker," I warned.

"Copy." Luna switched to Spanish. "Can she understand me now?"

We were both silent a beat, but Red didn't say anything.

Luna continued in Spanish. "I'm three blocks ahead of you. Turn right on University Drive. I'll be halfway down the first block. Ease up and give me lead. We'll lose your tail before going back to your condo."

"Got it. Did you get what I wanted?" I asked in English.

"Mostly."

"Anything stand out?"

"Besides the fact her family was crazy, her father was controlling and both her mother and her grandmother died of the same genetic disease?"

My fucking guts seized up, and I almost drove off the road. "Elaborate, *now.*"

He knew what I was asking. "She doesn't have it."

"Are you sure?"

"Yes."

I exhaled and my heart started again. "Anything else besides the details?"

"No."

The fucker was lucky we were in two different cars. He'd given me a fucking heart attack. "You can brief us both at the condo."

He switched back to English. "Copy that. I see your car. I'm pulling in front of you." He hung up.

"You know Spanish?"

Luna pulled in front of me. "Enough to understand Luna."

She looked out the window. "I never learned."

Her voice had gone from a panicked shrill to sad. I hated both tones.

"Spend some time around Luna, and you'll pick shit up, mostly swears."

"Do you know any other languages?"

"Some Danish."

"Danish?"

"Yeah, from Neil. If he gets pissed enough, he'll stop talking English altogether."

"You served with him?"

I was so glad she was talking, I almost didn't give a shit

what the subject matter was. "More like lateral deployments and a common enemy."

"You said Alex saved your life."

"Both him and Neil."

"How?"

Fuck. I exhaled. "Vega pulled me from the Humvee as Neil laid cover fire and Luna picked off a couple of those fuckers. His unit was caught in the same firestorm. His medic, Talon, triaged me and our buddy Dane and some of the other guys. We didn't lose anyone that day because of Vega, Neil, Luna and Talon." I needed to change the fucking subject. "Now we all live in Florida." I glanced at her. "Those brothers are my family." I squeezed her hand. "Family is what you make it, Red."

She turned away from me. "I wouldn't know."

"You will." I vowed then and there to show her. "Luna's coming upstairs to talk to us." I pulled into my underground parking behind Luna.

"Why?"

"I asked him to look into a few things." Luna took a visitor spot, and I parked in my assigned space. "Hold up, I'll come get you." I cut the engine and went to her door, but when I opened it, she just sat there. "Red?"

Staring at her lap, she didn't look up. "How long am I going to be here?"

She looked so damn vulnerable, it fucking hurt to see her like this. "As long as you want. Come on." I started to lift her out.

She pushed my hands away. "I can walk."

Luna stepped up next to us. "Ma'am, Brandt."

I nodded and took Red's hand. I led us to the elevator,

and none of us spoke until we were inside my condo. The floor-to-ceiling ocean view hit me, and I felt like I could fucking breathe again. I led Red to the couch. "Sit. I'll grab you a drink." I glanced at Luna. "You want something?"

"I'm good." He sat opposite Red.

I grabbed two bottles of water out of the fridge and sat next to Red as I offered her one.

"Thank you," she said quietly.

I tipped my chin and looked at Luna. "What did you find out?"

He focused on Red. "Ma'am, I had a candid conversation with your uncle this afternoon. Would you like to know what he said?"

She set her water down and barely made eye contact with Luna before dropping her gaze back to her lap. "Yes."

"All right. As you know, your mother had Huntington's Disease. I don't know if you are aware of this, but her mother also had it. She passed away when she was twenty-nine and your mother was only three. Her husband, your grandfather, remarried a couple years later. The woman had a son ten years older than your mother, who you know as your uncle. According to your uncle, your mother met your father when she was sixteen, and by then, they already knew she had Huntington's. Your mother was determined to live a normal life for as long as she could, but your grandfather didn't approve of her dating. So when your mother was seventeen, she eloped.

"Your grandfather was enraged, and according to your uncle, Burrows blamed his second wife for helping your mother elope and giving them money to live off until your father could support them. Your grandfather didn't divorce his second wife because he didn't believe in it, but he never spoke to her or your mother again. Your grandfather's wife died a few years before your mother, and Burrows never reconciled with either of them."

The color drained from Red's face. "My uncle never told me any of this."

"He told me he didn't think it was his place to tell the story unless you were to enquire about it."

Red shrunk in on herself. "Go on."

Luna nodded. "When your mother's health was deteriorating, your father attempted to contact your grandfather, but he never responded to any invitations to either see your mother or meet you. After your mother passed away, your uncle says he didn't hear from your father again until a few weeks before he died. That's when he asked your uncle to give you a job.

"Your uncle had been working in some capacity or another for the team since he was fifteen. The second his mother married your grandfather, your grandfather put him to work. By the time things fell apart between his mother and your grandfather, your uncle had already established himself as a valuable asset for the team and your grandfather never challenged that.

"Your uncle agreed to hire you, but both he and your father decided it would be best to not let anyone know who you were. When your grandfather realized who you were, he told your uncle that if anyone found out, he would fire them, your uncle, and you. When your uncle first started working for the team, your grandfather also insisted no one know who your uncle was. Some of the staff figured it out, but anyone who was ever caught gossiping about it, Burrows fired. He had a strict policy on nepotism."

"As if he were embarrassed of us," she murmured.

Luna shrugged. "Or still holding a grudge. Your mother was the apple of your grandfather's eye and his first wife was the love of his life. I think he was angry at the world, chica."

Red inhaled and let it out slow. "Thank you for telling me. I'm embarrassed that I never asked my uncle about any of this."

Luna shrugged. "Not sure what you were supposed to ask when you didn't know you had a living grandfather." He glanced at me. "I have some information about tomorrow's will reading."

Red's shoulders dropped slightly.

I tipped my chin. "Go ahead."

"Ahlstrom's been in Burrows's back pocket since he got signed. Burrows coached him on everything from press conferences to plays to apparently courting his secret granddaughter."

Rage boiled in my veins.

Luna laid out the rest of what he'd found out. "Ahlstrom's confident he'll walk away from tomorrow's reading a rich man."

I wanted to fucking hit something. "Is that legal? Can Burrows give away his team when there's a blood relative alive?"

Luna leveled me with a look. "Anything's possible."

THIRTY-SIX

Sienna

I HARDLY REMEMBERED ANDRÉ LEAVING. SITTING ON JARED'S balcony in a lounger with him at my back was a blur. I couldn't eat the dinner he'd had delivered. And I didn't say anything when he'd carried me to bed.

My mind spinning, my reality shattered, anger and sorrow and regret at so much wasted life swirled in my head, and I couldn't contain any of it. So I said nothing because I was afraid of the emotions that would come out if I did start talking.

Jared was everything he could have been and more, but I didn't even thank him. I lifted my arms when he took my shirt off and pointed my toes when he pulled my leggings off, but I didn't say a word. I quietly submitted to his care, and he'd pulled me into his arms and simply held me.

I didn't know when I'd fallen asleep, but now I was awake. With strong arms still around me, I was facing the windows overlooking the ocean as the sun inched its way up.

"You okay?"

I liked the sound of his husky and rough morning voice. "Yes."

He kissed my shoulder. "I thought I told you no lying."

"I'm not, not okay." I wasn't crying or panicking. That meant okay, right?

"Something's on my mind," he admitted.

"Okay." I sounded emotionless.

His arms tightened around me. "If you don't inherit the team, I think you need to fight for it."

"I'm not going to do that." I didn't want to. I'd thought about it all night.

"What if it goes to Ahlstrom?"

"I'm not sure I care." Wouldn't someone like him make a better owner than me? "I know I work for a defensive coordinator, but I know nothing about football. I don't even watch the games."

"This is your family's legacy, Red," he said quietly.

"The last of my family died when my father passed."

His hand ran down my arm. "You have me."

I rolled to face him. "Would you want to own a football team?"

"Fuck no." He didn't hesitate. "But that's because it's not in my family."

"It wasn't in any family I ever knew about either." Until yesterday.

"Point taken." He stroked my cheek and stared at me with his intense gaze. "You're even more beautiful in the morning."

Heat flushed my cheeks. "Thank you."

His expression turned grave. "I want to come with you today."

"You're not telling me you're coming with me?" I was only half joking.

"One-time accommodation." The corner of his mouth tipped up. "Don't get used to it."

I forced a half smile. "Can you go without hitting Dan?"

His eyes narrowed. "You know I hate when you say his name, right?"

The small smile turned genuine. "Yes." I turned serious. "Are you going to hit him?"

"No."

He said it too quickly. "I don't believe you."

"I won't hit him. I'll beat the fuck out of him. But only if he swings first or insults you."

I sighed, but I secretly loved that he would defend me. "You're going to have to get over that."

"Not gonna happen. I'll always hate him. I'd hate Vega too if I hadn't served with him."

"So you're not going to beat up Alex?" I teased him because it felt better than thinking about my day ahead.

"No promises."

"Well, if you're going to behave, then yes, I would like you to be there. And thank you."

"I'll behave in public." He winked then turned serious again. "You don't have to thank me. I want to be there for you."

"Thank you," I whispered, suddenly overcome with emotions I didn't know what to do with.

The backs of his fingers skimmed down my cheek. "Trust me?"

I closed my eyes briefly, but I didn't have to think about it. "Yes." He'd gotten me away from my house yesterday, he'd held me all night, he'd never pushed me to talk or done anything other than simply be there for me. It was more than anyone had ever done for me since before my mother passed away.

He slid an arm under my legs, rolled, and in one fluid movement, he was upright and carrying me to the balcony.

Alarm spread. "We're naked!"

"There're no reporters on the beach. Tyler gave me the all-clear twenty minutes ago." Still holding me, he managed to open the sliding glass door.

"You talked to him?" A warm ocean breeze blew across my skin and salt air filled my lungs.

"Last night after you fell asleep, I told him to make sure there were no reporters on the beach in front of the condo at sunrise." He sat down in one of the lounge chairs with me on his lap.

His hard length pressed against my thigh and desire shot through my core. "You planned this?"

He gently pulled one of my thighs and turned my hips so that I was straddling him, but with my back to his chest. His fingers found the small triangle of curls I didn't shave and he stroked lightly. "I wanted you to see the sunrise." He pulled my thighs wide.

"Jared." I nervously glanced up and down the beach, but I didn't see anyone.

One hand slid featherlight strokes across my folds as the other firmly cupped my breast. At the exact time he pinched my nipple, he sank a single finger inside me. "Right here, baby."

I gasped and my head held fell back on his shoulder.

He kissed my neck. "Watch the sunrise."

His quiet demand soaked into my consciousness, and I opened my eyes. Fire-orange and red crested the horizon, and he shoved a second finger into me. Stroking, twisting, he hit a spot deep inside me.

"*Oh my God.*" I ground my hips.

His arm snaked across my chest and he grasped my other nipple. Pulling, twisting like he twisted his fingers inside me, he worked my body into a frenzy.

"You're gonna come then I'm gonna slide inside you." His voice, all rough edges and full of promise, made my inner muscles clench around his fingers.

"I want you inside me," I begged, needing to feel him close.

"Come first," he demanded, pushing his thumb into my clit and rolling my nipple.

The sunrise exploded into a thousand points of light as my orgasm ripped from my body and shook my core. My cry of release carried over the balcony and fell to the sand. "*Jared.*" I rocked on his hand.

The sun's rays crawling up our bodies, he pushed my back forward and lifted my hips. Stroking himself through my desire once, he shoved into me. His hands curved around my hips and he thrust up as he pulled me down on his hard length.

My whole body shivered.

"That's it, gorgeous." His fingers digging into my hips, he repeated the thrust. "You feel that?"

My heart pounded as aftershocks of my first orgasm dissolved into a new burn. My nipples pulsed for attention, and my clit ached to have his rough flesh press into it. I didn't feel one thing, I felt too much. Too much need, too much want, and too much like I was falling.

"Please," I pleaded. "Don't make me answer."

Buried to the hilt, his body froze, but his huge hand grasped my jaw and tipped. My head fell back to his shoulder and his intense stare landed on me. "You got something to say?"

Yes. "No."

He stared.

My desire dripped down on him.

His nostrils flared with an inhale. "When was your last period?"

My mind struggled to catch up. "Last week."

"What day did it start?"

"Tuesday?" Monday?

"I'm coming inside you." He sank his tongue into my mouth and drove his hard length deep inside me.

Holding the front of my neck with one hand, my waist with the other, he started to move. With every thrust, he ground his hips. His pace picked up and he released my neck to grab my waist. Without his hold, our mouths separated, and I gripped the arms of the lounge chair.

Waves crashed the shore as his body crashed into mine. His hands guided me down every time he thrust up, and a second orgasm rose like the heat of the morning sun.

"*Harder,*" I cried out.

His cock swelled and he shoved me forward, changing the angle. His next thrust hit that spot deep in my body and a moan ripped from my lungs.

He did it again, but harder. "Right there, gorgeous, right there."

Oh my God. "I'm going to come."

I didn't even get the last word out before I was falling so hard over the edge, I lost all muscle control. My arms lost their purchase, my back arched, but my chest fell forward, and an orgasm so intense it was painful ruptured from my body.

With a growl I'd never heard him make, his hips jerked once and hot warmth shot deep inside me.

THIRTY-SEVEN

Jared

I'D COME INSIDE HER.

I'd fucking come inside her.

Shit fucked up in my head, and that was all I could think about. Sitting in a goddamn wood-paneled conference room like this was a fucking movie set, I couldn't focus. Her suit wasn't pink, it was gray. Clark Kent spoke quietly to her. Her useless uncle sat alone, not saying shit. And the asshole quarterback sat with two goddamn lawyers looking smug as hell, while all I could think about was if my cum was still dripping out of her.

I'd never gone bareback. And I wanted to do it again. *Right fucking now.*

Three suits walked in and sat at the opposite end of the table.

I didn't hear a goddamn word of the introductions. Clark Kent spoke for Red, and the asshole's lawyers spoke for him. Then Burrows's lawyers were opening a file and addressing DeMarco.

Estate, five million, he keeps his job, bullshit legalese, then they were done with him.

They looked at Red, and I sat up straighter. Her hand in mine under the table, I squeezed, but what I really wanted to do was pinch her perfect nipples until they darkened.

"Miss Montclair." The oldest lawyer closed the file in front of him and paused. "Your grandfather was very particular about the circumstances of your inheritance." He glanced at Ahlstrom then zeroed in on Red and dropped his bomb. "Your grandfather has left you his entire share of the ownership of the team... if you marry Mr. Ahlstrom."

Wait.

What?

I opened my mouth before I could stop myself. "She has to marry that fucking asshole if she wants her inheritance?" Pure, unadulterated rage bled from my veins and took up the whole fucking room. She wasn't fucking marrying him, no goddamn way.

Clark fucking Kent's hand landed on my shoulder. "Can you please clarify the terms of the will?"

I ground my fucking teeth. I didn't look at Red. I couldn't. If I saw even a motherfucking hint of distress on her face, I was going to lose my fucking shit.

Burrows's lawyer opened the folder. "Miss Montclair has fifteen days to wed Mr. Ahlstrom in a legally binding contract of marriage and the shares of Mr. Burrows's ownership of the team will be transferred to Miss Montclair, minus two percent, which will transfer to Mr. Ahlstrom. If the marriage is not consummated, or dissolved before one year, or if Miss Montclair refuses to marry Mr. Ahlstrom, Mr. Burrows's fifty-two percent ownership will be sold at market value in an equal split to the other four owners of the team."

"Mm-hm." Clark Kent wrote on a yellow fucking pad like

this was Law School one-oh-one. "And how much are Mr. Burrows's shares currently valued at?"

"Approximately one-point-two-five billion," the older lawyer answered.

Clark Kent looked up with his pen hovering over his pad. "And what happens to the funds received if the sale of Mr. Burrows's shares are sold to the other owners?"

"Mr. Ahlstrom, Mr. DeMarco and Miss Montclair will each receive ten million dollars. The rest of the funds will go into a trust for research for Huntington's Disease and autosomal disorders. The trust and the appropriation of those funds will be managed by this firm."

Clark Kent looked off into the distance for a moment like he was fucking lost. "And one last question. If Miss Montclair contests this will based on the fact that Mr. Ahlstrom has physically assaulted, mentally abused and illegally stalked her, what language is in place?"

Ahlstrom shoved his chair back and stood. "I never hurt her! I never even hit her!"

"Did I say hit, Mr. Ahlstrom?" Barrett calmly asked Ahlstrom.

"Sit down," one of his lawyers hissed.

I couldn't take it another second. I looked at Red.

Back straight, ankles crossed, sitting on the edge of her chair, she didn't blink. Her eyes weren't filled with tears and her lips weren't pressed together. She didn't look upset. She didn't look angry. She didn't even look agitated. Her expression was one hundred percent professional, and I fucking knew why.

I leaned to her ear and whispered so only she could hear while the lawyers all started arguing. "You are bad-fucking-ass, Red."

She looked at me, and for one split second, her expression softened and, just barely, the side of her mouth twitched, then her suit expression locked back into place. "Why thank you, Mr. Brandt."

She was gonna give up the team for her mother. I was so goddamn proud, I didn't even give a fuck about the quarterback.

"*Sie*," Ahlstrom yelled out. "Your grandfather wanted this, he wanted us together!"

With more poise than any woman I'd ever known, Red stood up. "Mr. Ahlstrom, I can assure you that what Mr. Burrows wanted is of no consequence to me."

"You're not going to keep your job if you throw away the team. You're going to need money to live on," Ahlstrom bit out angrily.

I stood and put my arm around her shoulders. "No, she won't." I couldn't give her one-point-two-five billion dollars, but I knew Red enough to know she didn't give a fuck about that.

Barrett put his pad back in his messenger bag and stood. "We'll be in touch, gentlemen. Thank you for your time."

Red reached into her purse and pulled out a small turquoise box.

I knew exactly what it was and exactly what fucking jewelry store it'd come from.

"This was never mine." Red unceremoniously dumped the box on Ahlstrom's lap. "If you're smart, you'll drop your lawsuit." She turned to go.

I took two seconds to glare at the fucker, daring him to say shit, but like the pussy he was, he didn't utter a word. Making a mental note to never buy Red a goddamn thing from that jewelry store, I ushered us the fuck out of there. We'd made it all the way to the elevator when DeMarco caught up with us.

"Montclair," he barked.

I turned and leveled him with a stare. As far as I was concerned, the fucker was just as guilty as his stepfather for not setting shit straight with Red. "Tone," I warned.

DeMarco took a breath and nodded. "I would like to have a word with you, Sienna."

"Go ahead," Red said, without a hint of distress in her voice, but her back was ramrod straight under my hand.

DeMarco's shoulders sagged. "I never married or had kids. I spend all day with linebackers. I'm the first to admit I don't know anything about women. That said, I should've approached the subject of your mother with you when you came to work for me. I apologize. I assumed you knew the circumstances."

"I did not," she said properly.

"I get that now." He shook his head. "For whatever it's worth, even if you had known, I'm not sure it would've made a hell of a difference. I knew Jed most of my life. He wasn't just stubborn, he invented the word. He never forgave me, and I had no part in your mom running away. Can't say I didn't understand it though. Football is all I know, but if I didn't have that, I would've walked away too."

"Thank you for your thoughts." She started to turn toward the elevator.

"One last thing." He stopped her.

"Yes?"

"I know we've never been family, not in any traditional sense, but just so you know, I've got no stake in what you do with the team. The will provides me with my job for as long as

I'm breathing, and that's all I ever wanted. You want to sell the team, you got my blessing. Hell, if you want to keep working for me, you still got a job. You're the best damn assistant I ever had."

"Thank you, Ken."

"You're welcome." He tipped his chin at me. "Take care of her."

"Plan on it."

DeMarco nodded and looked back at Red. "The funeral's next Saturday, in case you want to attend. The other girls in the office have the details."

"Thank you."

"No problem." DeMarco rubbed the back of his neck. "I'm going back to read through the will."

"Mr. DeMarco," Barrett interjected. "May I suggest you have representation for yourself?"

DeMarco cocked his head and studied Barrett for a moment. "Anyone ever tell you that you look like Superman?"

"Frequently," Barrett admitted.

DeMarco slapped Barrett on the shoulder. "Get some new glasses, son."

Biting back a laugh, I hit the call button for the elevator. DeMarco went back to the conference room as the three of us stepped inside the elevator.

Red waited until the doors slid shut. "Mr. Barrett, I would like to sell the team."

Barrett looked between us. "I feel like I'm missing something."

I filled him in. "Her mother and her grandmother died from Huntington's."

"Ah." He scratched his chin. "Now I see."

Red cleared her throat. "I would also like to be in an advisory role for the appropriation of the funds for research. Do you think you can make that happen?"

Barrett stared off into space like he did in the conference room. "I think I can make that happen. Are you willing to submit a statement on the details of Mr. Ahlstrom's mistreatment of you?"

"He never laid a hand on me in anger."

"I think a character assessment as to his mental state when he was threatening Mr. Brandt at the restaurant and at his house will suffice."

"What are you getting at?" I asked.

Barrett smiled. "Leverage."

"You got enough to make the lawsuit go away?" I didn't think for one second that Ahlstrom would drop the suit simply because Red told him to.

His smile went wide. "I believe I do."

The elevator stopped and the doors slid open to the garage level. Tyler stood outside the black Luna and Associates SUV he'd dropped us off in.

Barrett held his hand out. "Mr. Brandt." We shook and he held his hand out to Red. "Miss Montclair."

She looked up at him and smiled. "It's Clark Kent, not Superman."

"Yes, well." He chuckled. "I can't say I've ever represented a client who sold a professional football team to fund medical research. I'm feeling a bit like Superman right now to be honest, Miss Montclair."

"Then maybe you should keep the glasses," she said coyly.

The fucker grinned at her. "They are useful."

I stepped between them. "Do something about the press."

Barrett didn't even flinch. "I will issue a press release confirming Miss Montclair's relation to Mr. Burrows and leave everything else vague. But when the sale of the team goes through, I suspect she will receive a lot more attention."

"I'll handle that."

Barrett nodded. "As you wish. I'll be in touch."

I ushered Red into the waiting SUV.

THIRTY-EIGHT

Sienna

MY HEART POUNDING, MY PALMS SWEATING, I SILENTLY chanted it over and over. *I did the right thing. I did the right thing.*

In a dark navy suit and perfectly pressed white dress shirt that was open at the neck, Jared slid effortlessly into the back seat beside me. "Talk to me, Red."

Watching him get dressed this morning, knowing how rough around the edges he was, I'd never seen anything sexier than him putting on a suit. The fact that I could feel his release inside me had only intensified the moment. "I did the right thing."

He glanced at Tyler. "Give us a moment."

"Yes, sir." Tyler got out of the vehicle.

Jared's golden-brown gaze focused on me and his expression locked down. "Marry him. I'll wait a year."

He said it so matter-of-factly, I was taken aback. "You want me to marry him?"

"I want you to get what's yours."

"That team isn't mine. It never was." Doubt crept into the pit of my stomach.

"It's yours more than anyone else's."

An ugly feeling spread through my veins. "You want me to sleep with him?" Because that's what the terms of the will stated. Consummation.

His jaw ticked, but his expression didn't waver. "I want you to get what's yours," he repeated.

Poisonous doubt, about him, about the team, about everything in my life filtered into my mind and took hold. "You want me to sell myself, is that it? You think because you sold your body that everyone has a price?" I regretted the words the second they left my mouth, but I couldn't stop myself. "You see one-point-two-five billion dollars on the table and you're willing to sell me to get it?"

His nostrils flared and his voice went low and controlled in warning. "Red."

"No, don't *Red* me. Don't for one second think you get to dictate what I do with my body or who I do it with. And the fact that you would send me to someone who used me and cheated on me and was nothing more than a despicable opportunist just for a mess of zeroes tells me more than I ever wanted to know about you." I grabbed the door handle.

He reached across me and his hand clamped down on my wrist. "I was offering this for you, goddamn it!"

"I don't want the stupid team, I wanted my mother to live!" Traitorous tears welled. "But I don't get that, do I? I don't get a family. I don't get a football team. I don't even get a man who isn't willing to sell me in one way or another! Now, *let go*." I yanked my wrist.

He let go, but then both hands grabbed my face and his lips were on mine. His tongue swept once through my mouth and a sob broke free.

I hit his chest with both fists. "*No.*"

"Let it out, baby." He spoke against my mouth. "Let it out."

I hit him. Over and over. His chest, his arms, everywhere I could reach. I hit him and I sobbed. I sobbed because my mother was dead. I cried because my father lied to me. I was devastated because I'd never be a part of the family that'd belonged to me. Life was short and everything felt wasted.

His hands stroked my hair and my back. He held me and took the blows and never let go. He whispered over and over, "*You're okay, baby. You're okay.*"

But I wasn't okay. I may never be okay. "You threw me away," I accused. "You threw me away again!" And that hurt the most because he'd become more important to me than anything else in my life.

He pulled back just enough to look at me. "I had to offer, Sienna. You know that."

I didn't know that. "You didn't offer. *You commanded.*"

"I'm not going to be your catalyst for regret. You get one chance at this. The annual income from owning that team over the years will exceed the current price on the table. You know that."

I didn't think about it that way, but it didn't matter. "One-point-two-five billion dollars isn't even real to me. That's so much, it's like cartoon money."

"You could do a lot more than fund just one or two charities with it."

The fight left me as I realized he was right. A hundred ideas swirled into my head, but it all boiled down to two things. Life was short. You didn't get second chances. And no way was I going to give someone like Dan Ahlstrom what he wanted, no matter what it cost me. There wasn't another choice. There never was. The moment I'd heard that the money would go into a trust fund for Huntington's research, there was never any other choice. For that, I would sacrifice. Not for anything else.

Except for the man in front of me.

Because as I stared into his honest eyes and felt his strong hold on me, I finally understood what it took for him to offer me that.

"I'd never let you sleep with another woman for money." I knew that's what he'd done. I knew his past. But I didn't mean that and I was hoping he understood my form of an apology.

"I know."

"My decision was made the second I heard trust fund for Huntington's."

He stroked my face tenderly. "I had to make sure."

I inhaled. "It felt like you were throwing me away."

His nostrils flared. "I never would've let him touch you."

I pointed out the obvious. "Then it all would've been for nothing because the will stated consummation."

"I would've tortured him until he lied to the lawyers then I would've beaten the fuck out of him on principal."

Completely inappropriately, I smiled. "You're crazy."

"No." He shook his head once. "I'm in love."

THIRTY-NINE

Jared

THREE WEEKS LATER, WE STOOD IN BARRETT'S ALL-white, modern-as-shit office as he set paperwork in front of each of us.

Barrett pointed at the pile in front of Red. "This is for the sale of the shares. I've highlighted everywhere you need to sign, and this is the contract for becoming an advisor for the trust fund."

"Thank you." With a smile on her face, Red signed her rights to the team away.

I had to give Barrett credit. When he'd pointed out how much Burrows's firm stood to make being trust fund advisors versus no guarantee of retainers if Red took over the team, they agreed to create a position for her.

I'd filed charges against Ahlstrom and the piece of shit did his best to fight them, but the prosecutor's office apparently favored veterans over professional football players. When he wouldn't drop the lawsuit, Barrett told his attorneys that Red would fight the ten-million-dollar clause, and he would walk away empty-handed. He caved. I think he knew from the get-go his chances of getting a piece of the team were slim to none. Burrows was just using him to get Red to do what he'd wanted, but just like her mother, Red was her own woman.

"Mr. Brandt, these papers release Mr. Ahlstrom of any further charges should any injuries or damages appear latently."

I signed.

A few dozen signatures later, Red was done. She looked up at me with a sparkle in her eyes I'd never seen. "I did it," she whispered.

Yeah, she did. "I'm fucking proud of you, baby."

Heat hit her cheeks. "Do we get to celebrate now?"

My dick got hard. I'd told her the second she signed away the team, I was going to show her all the ways a man could take a woman. I'd fucking held out coming inside of her for three goddamn weeks. I hadn't come in her pussy, and I hadn't come in her mouth. And I'd never taken her ass. I was going to work her so fucking hard, she'd remember this day forever.

"Yes." Barrett laughed. "You two go celebrate."

The sexual tension between us was thick as hell. He probably wanted us out of his office before I took her right on his white fucking desk.

"Thanks, Barrett." I barely spared him a glance before putting my hand on Red's back.

"Yes, thank you, Mr. Barrett."

"I'll let you know if anything else comes up, but I don't foresee anything. You two enjoy your day."

Already walking Red out of his office, I guided her to the Mustang and held her hand as she got in the passenger side.

The media had died down, but we'd also laid low for three weeks in my condo. Luna kept a detail on us, and we didn't do shit but fuck and eat and walk the beach at night. I used the gym in the mornings before she got up, and she cooked food like a trained chef. I couldn't have dreamed a better fucking life.

I slid behind the wheel and had started the engine when she surprised me with a hand on my junk.

I chuckled. "You just going for it, Red?"

"Yes." She licked her lips.

Damn. "Taking advantage of the tinted windows?"

"Maybe." She pulled my zipper down and her small hands took my already hard cock out of my jeans.

I didn't get another word out. Her lips closed around my shaft and she sucked exactly how I'd taught her.

Fuck me.

I couldn't drive home fast enough. She worked me and I kept us on the road. Pulling into my garage, I reluctantly stopped her, because as much as I wanted to fill her sweet mouth, this wasn't going to happen in my fucking parking garage.

"Come on, baby." I pulled my cock out of her mouth and barely got my jeans fastened over my hard-on. "We're taking this upstairs."

"Okay." She didn't even wait for me to come get her. She opened her door when I opened mine.

I fucking smiled at her eagerness, but she had no idea what I had in store for her. I ushered her into the elevator and backed her against the wall. My hands on either side of her face, I purposely didn't touch her anywhere. "Do you know what I'm going to do to you?"

"No," she breathed.

I dragged my nose up the side of her neck without actually touching her skin. "I'm going to take every inch of your body and make it mine."

She shivered. "I'm already yours."

Not yet she wasn't. But she would be. "Almost, baby."

The elevator doors slid open, and I let us into the condo. But the second I closed the door behind me, she dropped to her knees.

Fuck.

Submissive as hell, she was the sexiest woman I'd ever laid eyes on, and my dominant side came out with a vengeance. "Unzip my jeans."

She unzipped them.

"Take my cock out."

She licked her lips and did exactly as I said.

"Stroke me then put your lips on me and suck like I taught you."

It was the last fucking coherent thing I said, because she didn't just wrap her sexy lips around me, she took me all the way down her throat. Stroking my balls, she worked me hard.

Gripping handfuls of her hair, my dick a fucking rocket, my balls drew tight. I didn't want to hold back. I wanted to come in her sweet mouth where no man had ever come before. The thought, her mouth, her sexy ass on her knees, I fucking lost it.

Growling, I shot stream after stream into her mouth.

And she swallowed every drop.

"*Goddamn.*" When I could fucking move again, I slowly rocked in and out, not wanting to leave her mouth, but at the same time, wanting to bury my dick in her tight pussy, which I knew would be wet as fuck. "That was fucking amazing, Red." I stroked her cheek and pulled out.

She fingered an escaped drop of my release on her lip and licked it. "I liked that."

Thank fuck. I held my cock and dragged the head across her lips. "I fucking loved it."

She kissed my shaft. "How long before we can do that again?"

About thirty fucking seconds, she had me so fucking turned on. "Anytime you want."

She kissed me again and started to get up. "You're insatiable."

"Only with you." I couldn't get enough of her. I helped her up and unbuttoned her blouse.

"Can I ask you something without you taking offense?" she blurted.

Christ. "Is this your second question?" Because she'd never asked me a second one. I slid her blouse off her shoulders and let it drop to the floor.

"No."

Her lace bra was so damn sexy. "Did you suck me off to set me up for this?" Only half joking, I stroked one of her nipples through the lace.

She innocently blinked. "No."

"Fine." I reached for the hook on the back of her bra.

"Did you do well in school?"

My brain scrambled and I looked at her. "Why?"

She shrugged and her bra strap fell down her shoulder. "Just curious."

She was up to something. "No."

"No, you won't tell me, or no, you didn't do well in school?"

"I was shit for paying attention." It wasn't until I was in the Marines and directions were fucking yelled at me that I excelled.

"Mm-hm." She gripped my biceps like she needed me for support. "And was there a subject that was harder than the others?"

I forgot about getting her bra off. All the subjects were fucking hard. "I was an equal opportunity slacker."

"You were slacking or were you trying and still failing?"

Inhaling, I counted to ten, but it didn't help. I was getting pissed. "I told you who I was. I haven't changed in the month you've been fucking me."

Her back stiffened and church manners surfaced. "I apologize. I wasn't trying to offend you. I was merely trying to find out if you had trouble in school before you joined the Marines."

"Why?" I crossed my arms. "I did fucking fine in the Marines. I lived to tell about it, didn't I?"

She inhaled and looked at me like she was steeling herself. "I think you have dyslexia. I think you had it before you enlisted, and I think it got worse after you got injured because you have PTSD."

Anger, explosive and misdirected and fucking consuming, detonated. "I am fucking *fine*," I ground out.

Clueless to what she'd fucking unleashed, she started talking. "I know you're fine. You're more than fine. You're a survivor. You're strong and adaptable, and you've managed to excel despite all of it. But I really think that with some targeted training or specially focused learning, you can have better tools to help you read and write. Not that you need it. I know you're fine, but it might make things easier on you. A lot of people live with dyslexia and do really well."

I zipped my fucking jeans. Gripping her upper arms, I set her a foot to my left and aimed for escape.

"Jared? Where are you—"

I yanked open the front door then slammed it shut behind me.

Seventeen flights later, I was gunning the Mustang and peeling out of my garage. Pressing the home button on my cell, I barked out a command. "Siri, call Dane."

Two rings came through the speakers in the car, and he answered but he didn't say shit.

"You home?"

No intonation in his voice, he replied. "Yes."

"I need to shoot."

"Long range or target?"

I wanted to fucking unload M16 clips into every goddamn asshole who'd ever made an IED. "I don't fucking care. I'm on my way." I hung up and floored it.

She started calling a few seconds later.

I ignored it.

Fuck her. Fuck her and her fucking PTSD and dyslexia. Who the fuck did she think I was? I was a fucking marine. I wasn't a goddamn pussy. She could go fucking fuck herself and her goddamn Google shrink diagnosis. She didn't know shit.

I was fucking irate when I turned down the dirt road that led to Dane's. A quarter mile in, the fucking forest cleared and I saw Dane standing next to an off-road Jeep parked in front of his house.

I threw the Mustang in park and got out.

He didn't even say hi, he just fucking nodded and got behind the wheel of the Jeep.

I got in the passenger seat and glanced at the small fucking armory in the back seat. Next to a shit ton of clips and boxes of ammo, there was also a bottle of Jack.

He started the engine and drove across his lawn straight toward the tree line. The sun beat down on my shoulders, reminding me of Afghanistan, and I got even more pissed. But the second he cleared his yard, the Jeep was throwing me around in my seat. I buckled in and held the fucking roll bar as Dane drove like the crazy fuck he was.

Not even bothering to bypass small limbs or palmettos, the fucker drove through the scrub like he'd done this a thousand times, which he probably had.

"Where are we going?" Branches hit the windshield and scratched the fuck out of my arm and the paint job on the Jeep.

"Out."

We usually shot behind his garage at the targets he'd set up on the tree line. He had more acres than I could fucking count, and I hated indoor ranges so I always came here when I needed to offload.

I didn't ask what *out* meant. I didn't fucking care. Fifteen minutes later, we were in the middle of nowhere and the Jeep couldn't fucking pass any deeper into the woods.

Dane cut the engine, got out and tossed me a tactical vest.

"You gonna fucking shoot at me?" I wouldn't put it past the crazy fuck.

"Holds the clips. Pick which weapons you want."

I strapped the vest on, grabbed the retrofitted AR-15 and loaded as many clips as I could hold while my boots sank into swamp mud.

Dane checked his weapon. "There're 238 targets over forty-six kilometers."

Jesus fuck. I looked around, but I couldn't see a fucking thing except trees, palmettos, vining shit and moss. "You did this?"

He gave me a clipped nod. "Approximately five targets every klick. Start east, follow the footpath." He grabbed a sniper rifle and two 9mms.

I headed east.

FORTY

Jared

THREE HOURS LATER, I WAS DRENCHED IN SWEAT. Bitten to hell by mosquitoes, I'd only managed to hit eighty-seven targets. Dane, that fucker, had hit double that.

"Where the hell are you?" I called out. "I'm almost out of ammo."

He stepped onto the path five yards behind me. "Your aim is off. You're pulling left every shot."

"Maybe it's your fucking homemade riffle." He'd illegally rigged it to shoot automatic, and I'd burned through my ammo.

"There's nothing wrong with the weapon." He passed me.

"We going back?"

"You have no more ammo," he countered.

"I said almost."

"Three rounds."

Damn. "You fucking counted?"

"Yes."

Crazy fuck. "You should've warned me about the targets."

276

Some were full-sized, wooden cutouts in human form, some were no more than two cut branches twined in the middle to form an X. There was shit high up in the trees and half forms lying on the ground. Ninety percent of the way, his footpath was no more than a fucking lack of scrub brush. Half the time I didn't know where the fuck I was going.

"Who pissed you off?" he asked.

I shot the last three rounds at a pile of logs I'd already hit, then threw the weapon strap over my shoulder. "I met someone."

"The redhead."

It wasn't a question. "How did you know?"

"Your name was all over the news."

Fuck. "I thought I could go straight."

He didn't comment.

I swatted a mosquito on my neck. "She fucking brought up PTSD."

He still didn't comment.

"I hated those fucking doctors at the VA." Telling me I needed to address my issues, telling me I had to take fucking drugs. "I didn't need the shit they pushed on me then and I don't need it now."

"Narcotics dull your reflexes."

"No fucking shit." We walked a few more kilometers, and I opened my mouth again like a fucking pussy. "She says I have dyslexia."

"You do."

I stopped and said the only thing that made sense. "Fuck you."

He turned to face me. "You went west when I said to go east, you could never read a map downrange, and every time you text me, you reverse letters in your spelling in a systematic way that never varies."

I stared at him. "It was the blast wave. It fucked my head up."

"Your head is fine. You couldn't read maps before the IED."

"You fucking asshole."

He stared me down. "She's right."

"Fuck you. Again."

He turned back and started moving.

I followed. "Well, what the fuck am I supposed to do about it?"

"Nothing."

"She said I need to learn better tools to deal." Or some shit like that. I'd stop listening after her Google diagnosis.

"You're not fucking her hard enough." He moved through the woods like a fucking panther.

"You're an expert on relationships now?" Fucking dick. "When was the last time you spent more than sixty minutes with the same woman?"

He avoided branches as if he'd choreographed that shit. "Last night."

I grunted in response and swung at a low-hanging branch. "I need a fucking machete to get through this shit. How often you come out here?"

"Enough. Go home and listen to what she has to say."

"You're a fucking pussy."

"You're a dyslexic dick."

Feeling like a dick for walking out on Red, I pulled into the underground parking at the condo. Wondering what the hell

I was going to say to her, I didn't see him until I was out of the Mustang.

In a fucking hoodie and board shorts, the asshole quarterback stepped in front of my car. "I want to talk to Sie."

"Go fuck yourself." A fucking hoodie? Seriously?

He stepped forward. "Let her answer her fucking phone," he demanded.

I calculated all the ways I could take him down. Throat, neck, head, chest, balls, the possibilities were making my hands twitch. "Want to know why you're still standing?"

His hands fisted like he was a fucking fifteen-year-old in the school yard waiting to get hit. "You won't touch me because you know it'll piss off Sie."

I laughed. "Try again."

"*I want to talk to her*," he yelled.

"You know Florida law on trespassing, Oklahoma?" I was going to fucking crucify Tyler for letting him get in the garage. "I can kill you in self-defense and walk away." Please, *please* fucking make the first move. I was itching to pound his fucking face in.

Veins popped on his neck. "You're letting her *give away* the team!"

He was so fucking stupid, he almost didn't deserve a response. *Almost.* I smiled. "Paperwork's already signed. I got hard just thinking about your one fucking shot at team ownership going down in flames."

He lunged. Zero combat training, he grabbed the front of my shirt with both hands and I let him. Strategically turning toward the security camera, I made sure the feed got a decent shot of his hands on me then I moved. My elbow slammed into the side of his head and I kneed him in the balls. He went down like a fucking pussy and my knife strike to his neck finished him off. It was so fucking easy, it wasn't even satisfying.

I fished my cell out of my pocket and told Siri to call Tyler. "Yes, sir?"

"There a reason Ahlstrom's in my fucking garage?"

An engine turned over. "Shit, sir. Sorry, sir! Do I need to call for backup? I'm across the street. I'm pulling into the garage now. What's your location?"

Motherfucking rookie. "Why the hell were you across the street?"

"Vantage point, sir." The Luna and Associates SUV barreled into the garage and pulled up next to me.

I hung up.

Tyler jumped out, his hand on his weapon. "Where is—" He saw Ahlstrom at my feet and froze. "*Shit*. Is he dead?"

Jesus Christ. "He's unconscious. Pull the security footage, call the cops and I'll give a statement tomorrow." I needed to see Red. "He was trespassing and violating a restraining order." Let him dig himself out of that hole.

"Copy that." Tyler pulled his cell out and dialed.

"Handle this," I warned. "I don't want to be disturbed the rest of the day."

Nodding once, he spoke into his cell. "I have an intruder." He rattled off my address and I headed for the elevator.

I walked into the condo a filthy fucking mess and threw my keys on the counter.

"*Oh my God*." Red rose off the couch. "What happened to you?"

"I went shooting with Dane." I stepped out of my ruined boots. "I'm going to shower. Then we'll talk, but you need a new phone number."

"What? Why?"

"Ahlstrom was in the garage, he's been trying to call you. I don't want him to have a way to contact you."

Her mouth opened then closed then she nodded. "Okay."

I saw the unasked question in her worried expression. "I didn't hurt him." Much. "But he'll be arrested for trespassing and violating a restraining order. The team will have to deal with him." She was done with that asshole, once and for all.

She didn't say anything as I strode toward the bathroom. Five minutes later, dirt was still running off my body, and I didn't know what the fuck I wanted to say to her. I soaped up one more time, rinsed and shut off the water. Hastily toweling off, I threw on fresh jeans and a T-shirt then I hesitated in front of my dresser. Inhaling, I grabbed what I needed, shoved it in my pocket and went looking for her.

She sat perched on the edge of the couch, her back straight and her expression locked. I didn't have to think what to say because she started talking.

"I'm sorry. I didn't mean to offend you. I overstepped, I know."

Fuck. I sat down next to her and pulled her into my arms. "I'm sorry I walked out."

Her voice went small and quiet. "I didn't know if you were coming back."

Goddamn it. I pushed her back and took her face. "Red, no matter how mad I get, I'll never fucking walk out on you. I love you. You know that."

Tears welled in her eyes. "I love you too."

My heart fucking soared every time she told me, but her tears gutted me. "Don't cry, baby."

She sucked in a breath. "I can't be in a relationship where

you walk out every time you get mad without saying a word. I need more than that."

I fucking got it. She was throwing down a limit. But I was who the fuck I was, and sticking around when I was pissed wouldn't do either of us any good. "I'm sorry. Next time I'll tell you where I'm going. But I need you to understand that sometimes I'll need a little time to myself to cool off."

"I understand that, as long as you tell me what's going on."

"Deal."

"What did Dan want?" she quietly asked.

Fuck, I hated her saying his name. "He was making a last-ditch attempt to get you to not sign away the team."

She frowned. "I was always going to give away the team."

I knew that, she knew that, Ahlstrom was a fucking tool. "I'm done discussing him." I kissed her once then forced myself to pull back and address the other elephant in the room. "I don't like labels, Red."

A small smile touched her lips. "I'm getting that."

"I'll think about what you said, but that's all I'm promising."

She hesitated. "Okay."

Damn it. "What?"

She inhaled then blurted the words out. "I got you something. I really want to give it to you, but I don't know if I should."

Jesus fuck. "If you got me a book or any other kind of self-help bullshit, you can fucking forget it."

"It's none of those things." Her shy smile appeared and my dick took notice.

"*Christ*. What is it?"

"Hold on." She gracefully rose. Her silk shirt fluttered around her braless tits as her leggings hugged her ass.

I didn't want whatever she had. I wanted to fuck her and I wanted to claim that sweet ass she'd been holding back from me.

Thirty seconds later, she was back with a long, thin, white box. She set it on my lap then sat down next me and tucked a leg under her. "Open it."

I didn't need to open it to see what it was. "You got me a smart watch?" A fucking pussy, computer geek, goddamn smart watch?

She rolled her eyes. "Stop being judgmental. It's manly, I promise. Open it."

I opened the box. Stainless steel, link band, it wasn't fucking hideous.

She cheerfully plucked it out of the box and turned it on. "I already set it up for you." The display lit up and it looked almost like a military watch with multiple dials.

My eyes fucking crossed. I hated watches.

Oblivious, she fitted it on my wrist. "All you have to do is press a button and it can tell you the time. It has GPS and you can even tell it to dial your phone and call me."

"I can already tell my cell to dial you." And text her. Voice command was a fucking ingenious invention.

"Yes, but this will be easier." She fastened the clasp. "There." She smiled like she was fucking happy, and I couldn't hate the goddamn watch.

I grasped her chin and kissed her. "Thank you." I meant it. As uncomfortable as the whole thing made me feel, she was fucking sweet and I loved her for it. No one had gotten me a gift since I was a kid.

"Each day, I'll show you a few things you can use it for."

"That's fucking great. Get naked." I had a promise to keep.

EPILOGUE

Jared

SHE STARED AT ME, AND THE HINT OF A SMILE TOUCHED her lips. "You get naked first."

I eyed her. "You telling me what to do, Red?"

The smile spread across her face. "Maybe."

Oh fuck yes. My shy girl was asking for it. "How fast are you?"

Her eyebrows drew together. "Why?"

"Wrong answer." She was over my shoulder in half a second flat, and I was on my feet.

Her squeal echoed through the condo. "*Jared Jacob Brandt,* put me down!"

"Not a fucking chance." I spanked her. "For future reference, you gotta be quicker than that." I walked toward our bedroom.

"I didn't know you were going to go all fireman on me!"

"Fireman, huh?" I rubbed my palm over her perfect ass. "You got a thing for firemen?" I didn't know what the fuck I'd do if she said yes. "Think before you answer that."

She gripped the back of my shirt and giggled. "No! No firemen! Only marines."

I pulled back and spanked her again. "Correction, *marine*. Singular."

"Yes, yes, marine!"

I smoothed my hand over her ass. "That's the right answer." I eyed the balcony. I loved to fuck her out there, but for what I had planned, I needed a bed. I stopped in front of ours and slid her down my body.

She shivered when she felt my hard cock. "Hi," she purred, her face flushed.

The corners of my mouth tipped up. "Hi." She was so fucking beautiful I forgot myself.

She grasped my biceps and squeezed. "I gave away a professional football team," she whispered, smiling.

I stroked her cheek. "Your mom would be proud."

She turned serious. "I know why she walked away from her family."

I did too. But I humored her. "Why?"

"Love," she said simply.

I tipped my chin in agreement. "Nothing more powerful than that."

Her eyes went wide and she laughed. "You nodded!"

I fought a smile. "It was only once. Doesn't count."

"Yes it does." Her face turned soft. "I'm wearing you down."

I sobered. "What do you need to wear me down for?"

Her smile faded. "I didn't mean it like that. I only meant, more like, I'm rubbing off on you." She averted her eyes halfway through the last sentence.

She was lying. Three weeks with her and I knew what she wanted. "You got something to say?"

Staring at my chest, she shook her head. "No."

"Look at me," I demanded.

She brought her head up. "Is it wrong to say I'm glad I don't have what my mother and grandmother had?"

"No." She'd told me her parents had tested her after she was born, but she didn't have the gene for the disease. "I'm fucking thankful you don't, Sienna, so damn thankful."

"Would you have fallen in love with me if I did?"

I didn't hesitate. "Yes."

"Would you have… stayed?" She bit her lip.

I cupped her face and gently pulled her lip from her teeth with my thumb. "One day with you is worth a lifetime."

Her eyes welled with tears. "Jared—"

I couldn't wait another second. "Trust me?" I stroked her cheek.

She smiled. "Of course."

I shoved my hand in my pocket. "You know what I knew when I first saw you?"

She shook her head.

"That you were special. But you know what I knew the first time I kissed you?" I brushed my thumb over her bottom lip then I kissed her once and spoke against her lips. "I knew you were mine." I took her left hand and slipped the ring on her finger.

Her eyes went wide with shock and my name whispered across her lips. "*Jared.*"

"You're mine and I'm yours." My heart pounded against my ribs. "Marry me, Sienna."

She rushed me. "Yes! Yes, yes, *yes!*" She threw her arms around my neck and jumped.

Her legs wrapped around my waist, and I fucking kissed her. My tongue sinking inside her sweet mouth, I kissed her like I needed her. I kissed her like I wanted her, and I kissed her like she was mine. Because I'd known the second I laid eyes on her, she was my future, and I was mission intent since.

Breaking the kiss only long enough to pull her shirt over her head, I lowered her to the bed.

Her hands frantically pushed at my T-shirt. "Off."

I chuckled and whipped my shirt off. "You gonna look at the ring?"

Her hands on my abs, she froze for half a second then dissolved into giggles. "Yes, YES." She held her hand up, but then she went completely still.

My heart skipped a beat. "Red?"

"It's...." Her eyes welled and tears spilled down her cheeks.

"A ruby." Two carats. I brushed away her tears. "With diamonds." Two rows of them, surrounding the ruby. "I wanted to buy you the biggest red stone I could find, but it would've looked ridiculous on those tiny hands of yours."

"Jared." Her voice broke as she threw her arms around my neck. "*It's perfect.*"

I grabbed her face. "I love you, Red. Always will."

Her eyebrows drew together.

"What?" I demanded.

She sucked in a breath. "What if it's too soon? What if you...?" She bit her lip then lowered her voice. "What if you change your mind?"

I knew what she wasn't asking. And I promised her I wouldn't ever hold this shit against her, but goddamn. "It's not how many women I've been with, Red. It's how many I've fallen in love with. And that's one woman. One redheaded, innocent, ballsy, fucking gorgeous woman." I held her with my gaze. "And guess what?" I didn't wait for her to answer. "I'm not letting her go."

"I love you," she whispered.

I fucking kissed her, and all the things I wanted to do to her, all the ways I wanted to claim her, they took a back seat to the single driving need to be inside her. My mouth everywhere, I yanked her pants offs and stepped out of my jeans.

Pushing her back on the bed, I didn't want to pin her arms above her head and pound into her. I didn't want to flip her over and spank her into submission. I crawled up her body like a starved man, and I fucking lost my shit when her arms wrapped around my neck, because this felt different than every other time I'd touched her.

Her nipples brushing my chest, her legs spread wide waiting for me, her lips wet from my kiss, she was perfect. So fucking perfect I didn't have any words except my name for her.

"Red." I sank my tongue into her mouth and fingered her sweet heat.

Her moan vibrated her chest and I couldn't wait another second.

Fisting myself, I dragged the head of my cock the length of her cunt, then I did something I'd never fucking done. I pushed inside her slowly.

Inch by sweet torturous inch, I sank to the hilt.

Her legs came up, her back arched and she broke the kiss. "Oh. *My God.*"

I ground my hips against her clit because I couldn't speak.

She drew in a ragged breath and grabbed my lower back. "Yes, please, just, oh my God."

I sucked on her neck then pulled one of her nipples into my mouth. I didn't thrust. I didn't pound into her. I ground my hips against hers and I fucking saw stars.

"I'm gonna come inside you," gravelly, rough, I grunted the words out.

Her fingers dug into my back as she rode my cock. "Yes, *please.*"

Fucking her without thrusting, moving inside her while sunk to the hilt, I felt the first clench of her tight cunt as it grasped at my cock, and I let go.

A guttural moan ripped from my chest and I filled her with my seed.

Her legs shook, her inner muscles pulsed and her nails dug into my flesh. Everything I knew about fucking changed in that single second. Her release, mine, the angle, her body under me, her utter trust—I was fucking overwhelmed.

Buried so damn deep in her, never wanting to pull out, I felt her walls pulse and clench, but she wasn't pushing me out. She was dragging me in. My cock seated against her cervix, my come spreading inside her womb, it was a fucking trigger.

I fisted handfuls of her hair and sank my tongue into her mouth. My hips pulled back and I was thrusting—into her sweet pussy and into her mouth. Her gasp as I got hard again only spurred me on. I wanted to claim her. I wanted to make her come. I wanted to fill her with my seed again, and I wanted to fuck her into tomorrow. The only coherent thoughts I wanted her to have were my name on her lips and my ring on her finger, because this woman was mine. She'd been mine since she'd stood on my doorstep and stolen my fucking heart.

And I wasn't going to let her regret her decision to choose me. In every goddamn way a man could take a woman, I was going to take her, and I was going to make her happy. Because she was so damn right that first time I took her in my bed...

That wasn't fucking.

That was making love.

And I wanted every second of it with her.

THANK YOU!

Thank you so much for reading ROUGH! If you were interested in leaving a review on any retail site, I would be so appreciative. Reviews mean the world to authors, and they are helpful beyond compare!

Have you read the other books in the Alpha Escort Series?
THRUST—Alex's story
GRIND—Dane's story

Have you met the Alpha heroes in the Uncompromising Series?
TALON
NEIL
ANDRÉ
BENNETT
CALLAN

SCANDALOUS – Tank's Story
MERCILESS – Collins's Story
RECKLESS – Tyler's Story
RUTHLESS – Sawyer's Story
FEARLESS – Ty's Story
CALLOUS – Preston's Story
RELENTLESS – Thomas's story

Turn the page for a preview of, GRIND
the next book in the sexy Alpha Escort Series!

Join Sybil Bartel's Mailing List to get the news first on the next books in this series and to hear about her other upcoming releases, giveaways and exclusive excerpts. You'll also get a FREE book for joining!

GRIND

THE ALPHA ESCORT SERIES

Dane

I'm silent. I'm trained. I'm lethal.

My hand skimming down your thigh, my gaze a weapon—I know more ways to kill you than please you.

But you're not paying for my aim. You're paying for my control. Bringing you a breath away from ecstasy, watching you beg as I hold back your release, I'll show you exactly what you've been missing. I only have one rule—no repeats, because I'm not for keeps. I'm for sale.

One slow grind and I'll give you exactly what you paid for.

ACKNOWLEDGMENTS

There are so many people I wish I could hug for helping me make this book what it is! I have this patient, kind, amazing beta reader who took on Jared (and Alex!) and read him last-minute and oh my God, I don't know what I would've done without her insight! Kristen, you rock! Thank you *so* much and I hope you are ready for Dane!

I have this amazing reader group, Book Boyfriend Heroes, and not only do I get to laugh every day with my BBHers, but they also help me out whenever I am in a jam. Jared didn't have a last name until Missy came to my rescue. Thank you for such an awesome suggestion, Missy! Brandt totally suits Jared!

So truth moment? I am absolutely terrible at grammar. But? I have the best editors ever and Virginia and Olivia at Hot Tree Editing take my words and polish them and make them pretty and there is no way I could do this without them! Thank you so very much, Virginia and Olivia! (Olivia even edited this part you are reading now, LOL!)

I doubt she will ever see this, but I want to thank my mom. If there is one person in my world who is always good-natured and always willing to help, it's my mom. She taught me your best asset is your smile, and she told me a long time ago, never explain and never complain. Even though she will never read my alpha heroes (oh God, I hope she doesn't!) I know I would not have had the courage to write about these sexy men if she hadn't taught me to not only go for my dreams, but make them happen. Love you tons, Mom!

And to my readers, it's as simple and as complex as this: I would *not* be here without you! From the bottom of my heart, *thank you*, so very much! XOXO –Sybil

ABOUT THE AUTHOR

Sybil Bartel grew up in northern California with her head in a book and her feet in the sand. Trading one coast for another, she now resides in Southern Florida. When Sybil isn't writing or fighting to contain the banana plantation in her backyard, you can find her spending time with her handsomely tattooed husband, her brilliantly practical son and a mischievous miniature boxer…

But Seriously?

Here are ten things you probably really want to know about Sybil.

She grew up a faculty brat. She can swear like a sailor. She loves men in uniform. She hates being told what to do. She can do your taxes (but don't ask). The Bird Market in Hong Kong scares her. Her favorite word has four letters. She has a thing for muscle cars. But never rely on her for driving directions, ever. And she has a new book boyfriend every week.

To find out more about Sybil Bartel or her books, please visit her at:

Website: www.sybilbartel.com

Facebook page: www.facebook.com/sybilbartelauthor

Book Boyfriend Heroes:
www.facebook.com/groups/1065006266850790/

Twitter: twitter.com/SybilBartel

BookBub: www.bookbub.com/authors/sybil-bartel

Newsletter: http://eepurl.com/bRSE2T

Made in United States
Troutdale, OR
12/23/2023

16385587R00169